ORPHΑ ... NET

ORPHAN PLANET

Odyssey Earth
Book 1

REX BURKE

ISBN: 978-1-9168936-9-6

This book is also available as an eBook.

Cover design: Chris Hudson Design, chrishudsondesign.co.uk

Acknowledgements: Thanks to Sue Bavey for proofreading and support, my wonderfully supportive early-reader team – Sue, Shazzie, Lisa and Stephen – and cheerleaders Karl, Frances, Kyle and Jill. And to Elaine, the OG Burke and my shining star.

Contents

The Thing Is ...

This story starts in the year 2006 on Planet Earth, and largely takes place a couple of decades later – around now, in fact. Only you'll notice that there are lots of things mentioned that either never actually happened or haven't been invented yet.

So, the world is in the grip of a severe climate catastrophe, we've already been to Mars, cryogenic hypersleep is a thing, and a colony ship is on its way to the distant stars. I wouldn't worry about it – those are the 'sci', the science, bits.

And, for reasons, I twisted the timeline and made them all up – that's the 'fi', the fiction.

In the end, maybe the story is more FiSci than SciFi, because I made up lots of other things too. But if you've ever been around teenagers, you'll know that all the bits of the story with them in – well, you couldn't make those up.

Playlist

You can find a playlist for this book on Spotify. Search for the profile 'Rex Burke' on Spotify to find the 'Odyssey Earth' playlist.

1

Sleep

THE TRAINING manual probably needed some work if they were planning on doing this again.

"We're going to put you to sleep now. Anything you'd like to say before we do?", even delivered in soft Scottish tones, sounded to Jordan like the sort of phrase you'd hear after a final meal in your cell if you'd done something terrible to innocent bystanders with an axe.

"See you in seventeen years, give or take," wasn't much better. Who had written this stuff? In Jordan's opinion, the bedside chat section would benefit from a complete overhaul. Lose the prison-talk vibe, big up the promise of tea and biscuits after a nice sleep on a spaceship.

"It's not really sleep, of course," said one of the techs, conversationally, as he opened a valve on the drip. "More like – well, never mind."

More like what? Jordan didn't like the sound of that either. He turned his head to see a promotional poster for the *Odyssey Earth* ship on the wall by the bed, while a DJ from the local radio station chirruped in the background. Maybe there was still time to − ?

There wasn't. The drugs took over and Jordan's head lolled to one side, which at least meant he avoided hearing a very unfortunately timed request for 'Don't Fear the Reaper.'

The med-techs wheeled him into the adjacent hangar, slapped a label on the sheet and rolled down the shutters.

And, as far as Jordan was concerned, that was that until he blinked at the lights flickering on the plexidome a few inches above his head.

The lights were new. He didn't remember lights.

He flexed his fingers which brushed against his bare skin. He didn't remember being naked, either.

"All right, disable life-support. Open dome. On three. Ready? One, two … "

Hands reached over to push the clips, which slotted back on the count of three. There was a beat and then a faint sigh of air as the dome was opened.

Hazy faces talked above him.

"Vitals are fine. Temp nominal. He's unassisted. Just give him a second or two … there we go, we're good."

A huge intake of breath momentarily masked the gentle hum of machinery − then there was a groan as Jordan exhaled, followed by gasping breaths that eventually dialled down to a natural rhythm.

"Easy now, you're fine. Try not to move. You're

back, you're safe. Let's get that gurney over here. And someone give me a light-stick. Great, thanks. Can you open your eyes again for me? That's it, there you go. Welcome back! Responsive, alert. Breaths are fine. We're good here."

Arms lifted him up, out and down onto something softer. Jordan felt air on his skin, before a sheet was laid over him from the chest downwards.

A tube placed in his mouth delivered a squeeze of water and was then retracted. He felt prickles on the tops of his hands, and his fingers tensed and relaxed. Jordan blinked again. And breathed.

Not dead then. Always a bonus.

————

Jordan Booth had never actually seen the ship he woke up on.

Odyssey Earth had started its trans-galactic journey in July 2006, but two weeks before it slid from its moorings in low Earth orbit, Jordan was already in hypersleep in a hermetically sealed hangar in northwestern Scotland.

Or, at least, what they had assured him was like sleep, even though technically, it was more like being dead. That was the bit they didn't tend to tell the non-specialist members of the crew.

He'd travelled up on the bullet train – three hours from London, through the rice-paddies of the East Midlands and past the drowned towers of York. Crossing the raised, curved viaduct that now bypassed the deluged city walls of Berwick-upon-Tweed, Jordan had caught glimpses far below of the twinkling fires of the refugee encampment that seemed to grow larger every year.

Although coastal and valley areas everywhere were threatened by higher sea levels, parts of the Scottish landmass were still rising a few millimetres each year – a legacy of the lost weight of the suppressing ice at the end of the last Ice Age. In desperate times, a few millimetres were enough to persuade thousands of English refugees – sudden experts in glaciation and geology – that they might be better off finding a higher bit of Scotland to inhabit.

As the train sped on further north, the clouds gathered and rain began to drive against the windows. The July forecast was for three weeks of constant rainfall, glowering skies and temperatures that wouldn't budge above sixteen degrees Celsius. At least climate breakdown hadn't much affected the traditional Scottish summer weather.

On the Mhòine peninsula in the Highlands, the train slowed as it crossed the peat bogs on a raised line and pulled into the vast complex of buildings that was Space Hub Sutherland. Developed in the 1970s for optimum-access vertical space-shots – no flight paths overhead, no communities underneath – Sutherland had been ideally suited to build and supply Britain's first space station. Thirty years later, the space station had grown into a low-Earth-orbit dry dock, where the

Odyssey Earth – the biggest spaceship ever constructed – had been assembled.

Now that the colony ship was complete, Sutherland's remaining job was to launch the *Odyssey Earth* crew on shuttles and get them to the space-gate in time for departure.

After completing various formalities, Jordan had spent two nights in the Space Hub's pre-flight accommodation, going through a final series of medical checks. Then he had been prepped and processed, before being tucked up in a hypersleep capsule, alongside around a thousand other people – the *Odyssey Earth* sleeper-crew, destined for planetfall and only to be woken on arrival. The capsules were slotted into huge drums, which were freight-lifted to the space station and then locked into place in the vast hypersleep chamber on board the ship. It took a fortnight to load the chamber to capacity.

Meanwhile, the two hundred flight crew, technicians and engineers got the premium shuttle treatment, and sat back in airline seats to enjoy a glimpse of distant Highland peaks, a necklace of smaller islands and then the larger grouping of Orkney to the east. The sound of the rockets echoed across the heather, briefly disturbing the grazing sheep and deer. As a final view of Earth, it took some beating, even with the driving rain.

Jordan didn't see any of that. He had gone to sleep in one medical facility and woken up in another, and had consequently missed all the bits in between that might have shown him something of the *Odyssey Earth*'s nature and scale.

Naturally, he knew what it looked like from the outside – basically a big tin can, Bowie had been right – and even had an idea of its internal layout and structure. No clue how it worked, obviously, though for Jordan – since this also extended to cars, trains, planes, toasters, phones, smart-screens, and microwave ovens – that was less of an issue. It was enough that he had seen the designs as the ship was being built, done the video walk-arounds, followed the TV documentaries and read the articles. He knew – everyone knew – what it was, what it was for, and where it was going.

Jordan hadn't really concerned himself with the technicalities of space travel, because he had no intention of experiencing the flight. It was bad enough flying somewhere on Earth in a regular aircraft, nervously attuned to every new sound, convinced by every slight jolt that the pilot was now wrestling for control of the cockpit with a homicidal First Officer.

Like that, but through space for years on end? No thanks.

Seventeen years fast asleep seemed like a much better deal than endlessly worrying whether that pinging noise heralded the arrival of the drinks trolley or imminent destruction.

So, there was that. On the other hand, there had been a marked absence in the *Odyssey Earth* brochure of words like slumber and hibernation, and instead quite a bit of emphasis on what was referred to as the 'invasive vitrification procedure.' Jordan had written those words down and underlined them.

———

"Do you have any questions you'd like to ask us?"

The old sheep-from-the-goats question. Usually, in a job interview, the final chance to shine, to make yourself stand out as a candidate. Don't ask about the salary again, don't express any interest in holidays or time off. Come up, instead, with an intelligent question that showed a strategic understanding of the job while suggesting obliquely that you and you alone were the answer to that question.

Don't ask if there was gym membership or lunch vouchers. Don't say, "No, no questions, how hard can it be?"

At the time, Jordan didn't think he had to worry too much about making an impression. If the reports were correct, there didn't seem to be a lot of competition for the remaining slots on what the adverts still insisted on calling a 'mission' and to which most normal people added the prefix 'suicide.'

He was clearly the only person being interviewed that day; the waiting room overlooking the launch pads was otherwise empty. He had also had to sign an inordinate number of papers and documents on arrival that all had the word 'Waiver' in the title and included any number of clauses that referred to death, demise, infection, injury, terminal illness, injury leading to death, infection leading to terminal illness, and that good old catch-all, unforeseen circumstances. Jordan had signed them all, without reading.

So, did he have any questions?

Well, let's see. From what he had largely gleaned from the TV news, and then had confirmed in the interview, there was no pay, no holiday entitlement, no chance of career progression, and the largely glossed over but undeniable danger of dying on the job. Not highly probable, but distinctly possible. They were, after all, planning on freezing him, putting him in an airtight metal container of gargantuan proportions, shooting him into the vacuum of space, thawing him out after seventeen years or so, and then dropping him on an alien planet that should – and *should* is the best that they could offer – be Earth-like enough to sustain human life.

On the plus side, it was a job for life. With free meals and transport.

In the end, Jordan had asked the only question he really wanted an answer to.

"Does it hurt?"

———

The eventual answer, surprisingly to Jordan, who felt sure they had been lying, was, not really.

He didn't feel in tip-top condition, obviously. Who would? The biologists and medics had tried to explain the mechanics of it to him, but what it boiled down to was this – they stopped your heart, filled your veins with stuff, enveloped you in other stuff, connected your brain stem to something that no one could quite explain, and then let loose a flotilla of nano-bots to scrub your cells and massage your muscles.

To be honest, Jordan had got side-tracked after hearing the phrase 'stop your heart,' so he'd missed some of the more technical parts of the explanation.

When he tuned in again, it was to hear that they basically just left you and the nano-bots to get on with it in a sealed hypersleep pod until they woke you up, many years later, whereupon you felt like Jordan did now – basically, a bit crap but otherwise just physically dandy. Or at least, alive. And with a very sore throat.

It didn't hurt, exactly, but it certainly didn't put you at the top of your game. Mostly, he just felt drained – the sort of deep-bone exhaustion of a man made to go clothes-shopping in a designer outlet on a Sunday after-noon. He lay on his bed, swallowed experimentally, sipped water, and opened and closed his eyes, before drifting off to sleep again.

It took a few days until Jordan felt strong enough to leave his room and explore the ship.

How many days, he wasn't sure. To start with, someone in a white lab coat brought him meals on a tray to his bedside and sat with him while he picked at unfamiliar tastes and textures. He thought he would be hungry, after seventeen years in hypersleep – *seventeen years*; he shook his head at that thought every time it lurched into his mind. But he had no appetite and had to be gently persuaded to finish his meals. He was shattered, dog-tired, unable to concentrate for more than a few minutes at a time. He took the pills he was given, drank the fluids provided, and raised no objection to catheters, cannulas, drips and stick-on skin monitors.

At intervals, the lights dimmed in his room and Jordan slipped into periods of deep, dreamless sleep. Once every twenty-four hours, twice, more than that? He had no idea.

At first, he would wake with a start, panicked, unable to place the sequence of events – thinking that this was him being put *into* hypersleep, or that he was being revived for the first time. Both thoughts would momentarily overwhelm him, his skin prickling, his stomach somersaulting, until eventually he fixed his eyes on the bed and the room, and understood that he was here, on board, *out* of hypersleep, and that he had just woken up again.

At some point, he was wheeled in a chair, out of the medical suite, along corridors and into an elevator, and delivered to another room somewhere on the ship. Someone stayed with him as a new bed was prepared, and he watched as clothes were placed in a storage container that sat against one wall.

"Here you are, Jordan," they said. "Your stuff, your room. Don't worry, I'll be back later with some food and your meds. One day at a time. Just try and rest."

As they left, Jordan heard them exchange a greeting with someone outside the room. There was a low rumble of voices. Then another door opened and closed and there was silence. Jordan got into bed and pulled the sheet up over his body.

After more periods of sleep – hours? nights? – the startled uncertainty he felt began to wear off. When he woke now, Jordan felt stronger, brighter and clearer, like he'd finally shaken off a seventeen-year hangover. Of course, they were still piling drugs of every shape and colour into him with every meal, so that could be why he was feeling unusually chirpy. Either way, he'd take it over the slow-brain, body-fail exhaustion of earlier.

His room was a simple, white-walled box, with a cot-bed that took up one wall. No window, obviously – now that *would* have freaked him out, being able to look out into space from his bed – but there was a screen on another wall, currently dark, with a sliding door next to it.

The opposite wall had a desk and built-in storage area, while the med-tech had left through what was obviously the main door out into the ship. A container on one shelf held a small pile of clothes, with some soft footwear stacked on top. Next to this was a second box, stamped with the words 'J. Booth', which contained the few things he had been allowed to pack and bring on board.

So far, so very open prison.

As he sat up in bed and then swung his feet around to stand up, Jordan realised that there was another question that he'd never really had an answer to.

For the last few days – and for the seventeen years before that, as it happened – anything considered as 'waste' had been sucked out of him. Fluids mostly, he supposed, given his lengthy diet of chemically enhanced liquids and microbial brews, but he hadn't asked and they hadn't said. The final tubes had only been pulled out the previous day – a gastric treat, if there ever was one – and yet, here he was, with a distinct urge to investigate the toilet facilities.

Jordan had not previously given much thought to the practicalities of life on board a trans-galactic starship. They said he'd be asleep in a pod for seventeen years, no need to worry, all his needs taken care of, and he'd taken them at their word. In the meantime, he assumed that for the crew on board there would be food, drink, beds and entertainment – more like being on a cruise ship, he supposed, and less like being plugged into the Matrix, though you never knew.

No one had ever mentioned toilets – and he could see that it wasn't the sort of thing you put in the brochure – yet it would be nice to know that everyone was on the same page.

The early Apollo astronauts, for example – and Jordan wished that he didn't know this – had been provided with 'maximum absorbency garments,' a magnificent euphemism that fooled precisely no one. Even on later missions, there had been much use of the words 'suction,' 'hose and funnel,' 'clean and scrape' and 'jet wash.'

Jordan didn't like the prospect of any of that, but then again, he didn't think he could keep it in until they dropped him off on the new planet and he could find an alien bush and some non-toxic alien leaves.

He opened the internal sliding door and was relieved simply to see a sink and taps, a narrow shower, and a regular-looking, lidded toilet, all packed into a space the size of a budget-airline bathroom. Given its cramped dimensions, you could certainly have a go at washing your hair and shaving while enthroned, but Jordan was relieved to see that nothing more alarming than that seemed to be in store – if you discounted the notice that said, 'Suction warning – keep limbs out of the toilet bowl.'

Right then. No dangling limbs. Got it.

2

Coffee

JORDAN'S small room turned out to be one of four on a short corridor that led to a larger lobby space with seating, a big table, and a compact kitchen area with a couple of wipe-clean surfaces.

In earlier lucid periods, he had heard sounds of people coming and going at intervals, and an occasional whirr and ping, but there was no one there now as he emerged from his room for the first time. He opened a few cupboards and drawers – cutlery, packets of instant noodles, some labelled plastic boxes, scattered teabags, and a half-empty box of textured brown slabs that looked like budget-supermarket energy bars. It was your basic student flat share, down to the chipped mug containing a furry, science experiment in a small, stained sink.

There also a white plastic box, with a see-through door and a dial, that was clearly a microwave oven. That would be the ping, he supposed. He'd look for the whirr later.

A heavy door at the end of the lobby led out on to another corridor, which curved away into the distance. The stencilled sign on the outside of the door said '3-4' and Jordan could see that similar doors along the corridor counted down from 3-3 and up from 3-5. Someone had taken a marker-pen to the door of 3-7, which now also read 'Knock first, FFS.'

So, 3-4 was his address then.

He shut the door behind him and walked down the curving corridor as far as 3-11, beyond which he could no longer see his own door. Jordan looked further ahead, then checked back in the direction of his own room. Bulk-head lights – the odd one flickering – ducts and grilles, wall-pipes, the low hiss of a ventilation system, and metal stairs climbing off the corridor to an unseen level above.

Solid, sturdy. Fine for hiding out in after an extinction-level event, or a zombie apocalypse, but not what you'd call cheery and welcoming.

What was it with spaceship interior design? Did they give up after they'd made sure it was airtight and could fly in a straight line? Job done once the nuclear reactor had been bolted into place? Always with the prison boiler-room makeover and a grey-paint colour called something like Battleship Elephant or Mid-Life Ennui. It was never off-white, magnolia walls, potted plants and pictures of kittens.

There was a faint background hum, as if someone

had left a giant fridge door open. And the smell – what was that smell? Filtered aroma of gym locker room with a hint of cheese-and-onion crisps? *Panteur de l'espace. Pour l'homme.*

Jordan followed spray-painted arrows on the floor to a corridor junction. He heard a distant clanging noise. Behind him? Above him? It was difficult to tell. No people. No obvious signs of life, beyond the hand-scrawled notice on the door of 3-7.

If you'd watched as many films as Jordan had, none of this was particularly encouraging. The only things missing were the flashing red lights, the siren, and the dispassionate voice counting down from T-minus-thirty. It was the sort of environment where something very cross, with acid for blood and barbed tentacles, lurked in the ducts. Where a walk down a corridor started with the sound of scuttling and usually ended with someone being sliced and diced.

If there was any more sudden clanging, or particularly if anything dripped on him from above, Jordan suspected he wouldn't be bothering with the niceties of knocking first at 3-7 before piling through the door and hiding in a kitchen cabinet.

He rounded the corner at the junction, following the arrows, which then jumped from floor to wall and pointed the way up another short staircase. At the top was a door, with a faded sign saying 'Gym - Canteen - Lounge,' under which the person with the marker-pen had been busy again. 'Don't slam,' it said, which clearly hadn't had the desired effect, because scrawled next to the words in a different colour, and with added punctuation for emphasis, it also said 'FFS!'

Jordan pushed open the door and grabbed at the handle on the other side when he realised how heavy it was. He eased the door back into the frame with a dull thud that he hoped didn't count as a slam.

Now in a larger area – well lit, less utilitarian – Jordan saw his first signs of life.

Through a porthole window in one door was the promised gym, where several people with their backs to him pounded on treadmills, looking up at a large screen showing a forest scene with scudding clouds and flashes of sunlight. Ahead was a lounge area – soft seats, a few low tables – where half a dozen people were sitting in ones and twos. A couple played cards; a single woman concentrated on a flex-screen. They all looked up as he approached, and the woman smiled at him, but having caught his eye they all went back to what they were doing.

Jordan stood there, uncertain, and then, after a breath, found his voice.

"Hi. Hello."

It sounded strange, hearing his own voice out loud like that. He thought he'd have more to say, after all these years, but it was a start.

A man on a recliner looked up from his screen and said, "Canteen's over there, through that door." He pointed and looked away again.

Jordan waited a second or two, realised that was all the interaction he was getting, and walked over to the door. Through it was a dining room, with another bunch of people sitting quietly at various tables over trays of food, and a counter at the back with a white-board menu high on the wall. The vibe was hospital canteen, early hours, between shifts – people shovelling food down with grim determination before going some-where else to cut someone open or be cut open.

Written on top of the menu in a cursive hand was the statement, 'You don't have to be mad to work here … no, wait, you do,' while on a pillar by the counter, in now-familiar marker-pen, three notices, one on top of the other, and clearly written at different intervals, said:

'One at a time,'

'I've only got one pair of hands,' and

'FFS!'

"Hello, you're new." A man in a faded grey apron appeared from behind a screen at the counter and looked at Jordan. "What'll you have?"

On a day of extreme strangeness for Jordan, this was perhaps the most unexpected turn of events thus far. What would he have? What were you supposed to have, given the choice, after seventeen years of not having had anything except intravenously supplied fluids? And then a week of beige oatmeal and water?

"Coffee?" said Jordan, reaching for a default response, dredged up from his memories. Coffee was a thing you had, when someone asked you what you wanted in a café. Let's try the coffee then. In a spaceship café. Spaceship café coffee. That wasn't strange at all.

"Coffee? You're funny," said the man, reaching for a pot of brown liquid on a hot plate. He poured Jordan a mug.

"Good grief," said Jordan, taking a sip. "What's that?" Seventeen years and all, but he thought he'd remember what coffee was supposed to taste like.

"Very funny. Better up on Four-Deck is it?"

Jordan felt the conversation, such as it was, slipping away from him. "Better? Four-Deck?"

"The Noffee," said the man, "you being a connoisseur and all. Not quite up to scratch, is it?"

This really wasn't the awakening Jordan had imagined. There were many things he didn't understand about his current situation, but he focused on the cup of alarmingly hot liquid he held in his hand.

"Noffee?"

The man behind the counter threw up jazz hands and switched to a theatrical drawl. "Well, it's Not Coffee!"

"Right."

"I thought I knew everyone on Four-Deck," said the man. "You all come down here from time to time. Makes a change. Don't recognise you though? Done something with your hair?"

"Right," said Jordan again, then realised that this wasn't really cutting it as a conversation. "Sorry, I don't really know where I am. I just followed the signs. It's all a bit confusing."

The man looked more closely at Jordan. "Oh right,

you're the guy. That's why I don't know you. You're Wake-Up Guy!"

"Am I?"

He'd been called worse. Wake-Up Guy? That sounded quite cool to Jordan, to be honest.

"That's what I heard. They woke someone up. They don't do that very often. Resources, see. Only so much food, water, air. Plenty of Noffee though – surprisingly unrestricted, have as much as you want. We don't ask what's in it, they don't tell. Probably best."

Jordan took another sip and shuddered. As coffee, it was a shocker. On the other hand, as a warm drink based on the twin aromas of stagnant pond water and heated armpit, Noffee was a triumph. There were notes of dead badger and crotch, and a cheeky top-end of failure and dejection. It was – and fair play to it for succeeding on its own nominative terms – very definitely Not Coffee.

"So then, Wake-Up Guy. Got a name?"

"Jordan."

"And I'm Gerald, and I'll be your server for the next three hundred and eleven days, or whatever the latest count is. Go easy on the Noffee, if you're not used to it, goes right through you. Come back later for lunch if you like. Oh, and tomorrow's Salad Day, you'll want to get here early for that. We're only harvesting once a week at the moment. Something wrong with the nutrient feed, I can't figure it out. Maybe the tubes got switched by mistake and the poor bloody lettuce got the Noffee."

Jordan watched as Gerald turned to reach into overhead lockers and rummage through serving trays and storage boxes. There was very little about his day so far that he understood, and Jordan wasn't convinced that Gerald was exactly the right person to enlighten him.

First day up and about on an intergalactic space-ship – bit woozy, out of the loop on account of the multi-year nap – you wanted a briefing with the Captain, or at least a chat with someone in a matching uniform and name badge. Someone who looked like they knew what they were talking about. Not a one-sided conversation in a kitchen with a man with wild hair, whose stained apron was printed with the phrase, 'Do I Look Like A Sodding People Person?'

"Where did they put you, Jordan?" Gerald was addressing him again. "Which room are you in?"

This, at least, Jordan knew. "Three-Four," he said. "But I'm not sure I'd be able to find my way back. I wasn't really paying attention."

"That's the crew quarters on Three-Deck. You're near me," said Gerald. "Noisy sods in those rooms, though. I hope you're not a light sleeper. Tell you what, I'll show you where it is. I don't have to start here for another half an hour."

Jordan looked at Gerald – at his apron, at the signs on the pillar – and raised his eyebrows. Finally. Something he understood.

"You're in Three-Seven?" said Jordan.

"How'd you know?" said Gerald. "Come on, I'll give you the tour on the way there."

———

They left the canteen, exited the lounge, and turned into a corridor. Gerald nodded the way and led Jordan up more stairs, around more corners and along more corridors, pointing out signs as he went. Within a couple of minutes, Jordan realised two things – he no longer had any idea where he was, and the ship was *huge*.

There were sleeping quarters on Three-Deck and Four-Deck, with numbered rooms housing most of the two hundred crew, all rostered on shifts, depending on their speciality and skill. Other doors led to other lounges and gyms – sometimes occupied, more often not – while Gerald pointed out access staircases and elevators to levels below three and above four.

"Engineering, down there, on Two" said Gerald, indicating an elevator that was labelled 'Down Only, Eng. Mech. Power.'

"Your basic lunk meatheads," he added. "They like it down there. They come up to feed and work out, but otherwise they mostly stay in their herd. Not exactly conversationalists. I asked one once where she was from and she said 'Earth, Sol System,' like I was the moron."

"What's below Two," said Jordan, "on One?"

"You mean Power?" said Gerald. "Christ, don't go down there. They're even worse. It's basically a leaky fusion reactor wrapped in tin foil, looked after by half a dozen chimps in white coats. They reckon they've all got letters after their names and Nobel prizes, but nobody understands a word they say. Tell you what though, if you switch the lights off, you can still see them, glowing in the corner. And I think there were only four of them when we left. They're multiplying."

They stood at a crossing of corridors, where more signs and arrows indicated other sections of the ship, some self-explanatory, others, to Jordan at least, less so – Cargo, Nav, Flight, Library, Grow-Lab, Garden, Med-Lab, Muster, Launch, Obs.

"Big place," said Gerald. "And only a hundred people or so awake at any one time. It's why it seems so quiet. Creepy, if you ask me, and I'm used to it. One year at Halloween, some of the engineers rigged up a motion-activated spider-bot out of spare parts. Big thing, size of a dog, flashing eyes, the lot. They left it in sleep mode in the canteen on Four and then switched off the lights for ten minutes. They thought it would be funny. Half the crew crapped themselves, and one had a heart attack, until some hero took the spider out with an axe and severed a finger in the process. We don't really do Halloween anymore."

"What's above Four then?" said Jordan.

"Good call," said Gerald. "If in doubt, go up. Better class of grunt altogether. Your white-collar, offi-cer-class type. Still all idiots, obviously, but unlikely to try and kill you or radiate you. Some of them fly stuff. Some of them plan stuff. Some of them work out stuff.

Like where we're going and when we'll get there, not that anyone seems to be able to say exactly when that might be. If you want to pee anyone off in Flight, just stick your head round the door and say, 'Are we there yet?' They hate that."

Gerald gestured at an open elevator door. "Come on, step in. Let's go up to Six. I'll show you the best bit."

3

Stars

JORDAN COULDN'T REMEMBER the last time he had seen stars in any great quantity.

An England where floodwater left a tidemark a quarter of the way up Big Ben was, by definition, an England with dark, rainy, gloomy, cloud-filled skies. By the time the *Odyssey Earth* was ready for launch, the Lake District had been less a district for quite some time and more just one big lake. Alongside all the destruction wrought by climate breakdown, humanity had also lost its view, as the rain and clouds pulled a veil across large parts of the Earth.

Most nights, looking up into the sky was an act of faith. It was to be hoped that there were still stars up there, because that's where they were pointing the spaceship, but barely more than a handful could be seen on any given night.

When the skies did occasionally clear, maybe a hundred or so stars were visible to the human eye. On the darkest of moonless nights, perhaps a couple of thousand, according to the astronomers, though Jordan had never seen so many. Few people his age had. The most stars that could possibly be seen, under ideal conditions, from either hemisphere on Earth? Probably around five thousand, though no one had seen a night sky like that for decades – even in the high desert hold-outs of Chile and New Mexico, the smoke from endlessly cycling brushfires obscured the once-clear skies.

So, when Gerald pushed open the door marked 'Obs,' Jordan didn't at first understand what he was seeing, and when he did, he felt sick.

"Told you," said Gerald.

Jordan pitched forward to the nearest available seat, sat down heavily and gripped the sides. A curving, panoramic window looked out on to a vast darkness pricked by a thousand – a hundred thousand, a million? – spots and shards of light. Patches burned brighter in places, while others winked and pulsed, fading into a background haze where flashes of colour formed towering clouds and spirals.

Those were stars. And Jordan felt as if he'd just thrown up on a rollercoaster after eating a bad oyster.

He tried to focus, fixing his eyes on a friendly little grouping straight ahead – nothing too complicated, a simple arc. Deep breath, just some lovely little stars, nothing to worry about.

"Those are stars," said Jordan, in the wondering tone of a man who'd just cut his finger off while making dinner. He could see it lying there on the chop-ping board, and he definitely felt a bit sick, but his brain hadn't quite yet caught up with the strangeness – the definitely-not-quite-rightness – of the situation.

"It does that to most people, the first time," said Gerald. "After a while, you get used to it."

Jordan couldn't imagine ever getting used to the view out of the window.

Even just thinking of it as a 'view' seemed wrong. Wrong word, wrong scale. Jordan didn't know what the right word was and, in fact, he had no idea what he was looking at either. Was that a bit of space? Was that *all* the space? It certainly looked like it.

Gerald was still talking. "To be honest, I don't come to the Observation Deck much. Some people love it up here, bring their meals and everything, sit for hours. Me, I don't really like the reminder – that's all out there … " – he gestured with his hand – "and we're in here … " – he cupped his hands together – "and there's basically just that glass between us."

Jordan hadn't even considered that aspect and, now that he did, the oyster did another rollercoaster flip.

"Twenty-year-old glass," said Gerald. "Makes you think. We've had it if we get a chip from an asteroid."

Jordan changed the subject, partly because he needed Gerald to stop talking and partly because a thought had occurred to him.

"Why aren't we moving?" he said.

"We are," said Gerald, "but so is everything else. And it's all miles away – well, billions of miles away –

and then there's something about relative speeds and depth of vision. I don't know, you'd need to ask someone who gives a crap. But in my experience, once they start talking, you can't get them to shut up about it, when all you want to know is whether we're likely to get sucked into a black hole."

Gerald certainly was covering all the major concerns that, until five minutes previously, Jordan didn't even know he had.

"Look, I've got to go," said Gerald. "Got prep to do. Will you be all right here, or do you want to come with me?"

Jordan thought he might stay for a while. There was no one else on deck and his stomach was beginning to settle down. He was going to sit here and, for the first time in his life, do some stargazing. He was grateful for the introduction to ship life but at this point felt that, while there was clearly enough space in the universe for an infinite number of stars, you could have enough of a good thing after a single orbit around Gerald.

Despite his current location and situation – in space, in a spaceship, looking at stars – there was an awful lot that Jordan was finding difficult to get his head around.

Not so much the ship and the technology. He understood that people, differently wired and differently educated, could build such a thing, launch it off into space, and have a reasonable expectation that it would get them to where they were going. Horses for courses and all that. He was even fairly confident that the 'glass' window wasn't actually made of glass, though he still wasn't about to go and tap on it, just in case.

No, it was the numbers – as much as the stars that he could see – that made his head swim. The numbers were huge. Astronomical, you might say.

They started out manageably enough – one ship, a seventeen-year journey, two hundred crew, another thousand in hypersleep. Those were all nice, lowball numbers. Even the distance to be travelled sounded reasonable – ten light years. Ten was a number Jordan could understand.

But things soon ballooned.

Ten light years turned out to be fifty-eight trillion miles, and he had no idea how many zeroes that was. To be honest, he was still a bit iffy about the difference between millions and billions. And fifty-eight trillion didn't even get you out of the galaxy, given that their scheduled journey distance was ten light years, while the Milky Way was a *hundred thousand* light years across. They were travelling zero point one percent of the way across their own galaxy – only a millionth of the entire way – and it was going to take seventeen years in the fastest spaceship ever built.

True, they were aiming for just one star – another number Jordan liked and understood – but there were over three hundred billion stars in the Milky Way alone, and potentially another two trillion galaxies in the entire universe, each with hundreds of billions of stars of their own.

And don't even get started on planets. Eight, in our home star system, so multiply that by three hundred billion for the Milky Way and then by another two trillion for the universe. And that's if there was only one universe, which was an entirely different debate that Jordan didn't really understand either.

So, Jordan tried not to think too much about the numbers. They gave him a headache.

But as he acclimatised to the view, he started to pick out the pinpricks, swirls and clouds, assigning order and pattern where there really wasn't any; counting the numbers he could see, in the high hundreds; and calming himself with an entirely false reassurance of the ship's – and his – place in an unfathomably large universe.

4

Warp

"IT'S NOT ME, it's you," she had said.

That hadn't sounded right to Jordan. Admittedly, it had been a stressful conversation. There seemed to be a lot of them these days. Quite emotional. Easy to misspeak.

"Don't you mean … " said Jordan.

"I mean that you're never going to change. You're afraid of commitment. You don't listen. You don't hear me or see me. You don't seem to like people much. Your world is so small, and you're happy in it, but I'm not."

Oh. Fair enough then. She *had* got it right the first time.

"I can't do this anymore. I want things, I want feelings. You don't seem to want anything."

"But I love you," he said. "I want you."

"You don't. Not really. And anyway, I don't love

you. I can't love you. There's nothing to love. I need to go."

And then she had gone, ostentatiously leaving her keys on the table and – not for the first time – leaving Jordan with the nagging thought that he didn't really understand what it was that he was supposed to have done. Or not done.

The difference this time was that she didn't come back. And the second difference was that Jordan heard what she had said and realised that she was right.

He hadn't been able to articulate what was wrong with his life before, but she had – in thirty or so well-aimed words. He didn't want things and he didn't want feelings. His world *was* small and empty and – if he was true to himself – he could do with it being a bit smaller and emptier still. He was a shell. He'd always been a shell, and the things he had filled his life with – the people he had filled his life with – didn't amount to anything he wanted to keep.

With this new-found self-knowledge – who knew, you just had to listen! – Jordan thought he might start again. After all, he'd done it before. New place, new home, new job, new small world, where everything would be better. Or at least different, for a while.

A week later, he had filled in the *Odyssey Earth* application. And then, eventually, he had gone too, leaving his keys on the table for the landlord.

———

By the 1980s, the space race was in full swing. The sixty-nine Moon landing had shown what was possible when presidential men made grandiose statements, and when large amounts of money and sheer will were thrown at a problem.

Within ten years there were at least five, ostensibly collaborative, national Moon bases, as the Americans, Russians, Chinese, Indians and British all set up research and exploration stations. There were uncon-firmed reports that the North Koreans had reached the Moon too, though satellite flyovers of the landing site were inconclusive, on account of the fact that all that could be seen – abandoned landing vehicle and digging machine aside – was a firmly closed hatch in the compacted lunar earth.

Outposts on Mars had followed, and by the early 1990s there were encouraging signs that, both there and on the Moon, there was enough surface or sub-surface ice and minerals that could be exploited to sustain slowly growing populations. In total, around five thousand human beings soon lived off-Earth.

All this was history to Jordan; literally so, as he ran an annual space-history seminar at the university where he was an associate lecturer. He'd given it the provoca-tive title, 'New horizons: pilgrims or pirates?', and then sat back every year as his spectacularly ill-read and hungover students wrestled with the historic resonances of the space race. It ended invariably in a discussion about whether aliens existed – usually an even split – and, one memorable year, in a spirited row that made no sense at all to Jordan until he realised that the student in question had mixed up astronomy and astrology.

So, space and its exploitable materials were well-known – or at least those that could be found on or just under the surfaces of the Moon and Mars. Meanwhile, fly-bys and touchdowns on Saturn's moon, Titan, and Neptune's Triton, were flagging up new areas of potential interest for future colonists. What Jordan didn't know at the time, back in the 1990s – to be fair, what few people really understood at the time – was that none of this would be enough.

Five thousand people living a short hop off Earth in hermetically sealed, closed-loop bunkers was a technological marvel born of great ingenuity. But it was not the solution to saving the human race.

Growth and progress in space was tangible but slow and incremental. The world, meanwhile, was going to hell in a handcart quickly and exponentially. After the tipping-point year of 1998, weather that had once just been weird now became threateningly and unpredictably weird.

Bangladesh disappearing – that had been baked into the climate models since the 1970s. Houston levelled by a super-tornado; Paris burned by wildfires; forests blazing in wintry Siberia; ash clouds blacking out Sydney; the white cliffs of Dover detached during a single, ferocious, overnight storm – no one had seen those things coming.

What humanity was going to need – sooner rather

than later – was a new planet. Or maybe a series of new planets. In a different solar system. With breathable air, drinkable water, plenty of space, and lots of resources – enough for millions of people rather than thousands.

There was only one problem. Well, actually, there were a lot of problems, but they all boiled down to the same thing. Even if you could identify such distant planets – and astro-biologists were confident that they had already done so – you could never reach them with current space-faring technology. They were too far away, and humans didn't live long enough – by several orders of magnitude – ever to reach them.

When the technology did arrive, it seemingly happened overnight, though Jordan later realised that this was probably true of any transformative technological development.

For example, you go to bed one night in Sleepy Bottom, Cornwall, and the next day a gang of hairy navvies is laying down rails, chasing the sheep, and drinking the local tavern dry.

Obviously, to get to the hairy-navvy point, inventors elsewhere had already been boiling kettles and fiddling around with prototype engines for years, but no one in Sleepy Bottom had any knowledge of that. The last great technological advance in the village had been something to do with harvesting mangelwurzels, and the local vicar had even railed against that as a manifestation of the Devil's work. And now you're telling us that this massive, metal, wheeled contraption on – what are they called? Rails? – can get us to the market and back on the same day, instead of having to sleep in a ditch with the goats and be robbed by ne'er-do-wells? Yeah, sure. It's twenty-five miles away. Nobody can travel that far, there and back in a day. Oh, it's a lo-co-mo-tive, is it? Well, if you say so. What do you feed it on? Where do the mangelwurzels go?

Like that then, but for long-distance space travel. You wanted to travel to the stars? Well, now – surprisingly, amazingly – you could.

————

Jordan had seen her one last time, when he took back a few of her things. She had stood in the doorway of her new home – music tinkling from somewhere behind her, voices laughing – and taken the small box from him awkwardly. He realised then, if he hadn't before, that there was nothing between them any longer. Nothing to say or rake over. Nothing really to be sorry about.

"Wait," she had said, "I've got some of your stuff too."

"It's all right, I don't want it. Give it to the charity shop."

"Are you sure?"

"I'm going away, I can't take much, I've got a new job."

"Oh?" She fidgeted on the doorstep and Jordan,

seeing her bounce impatiently from one foot to another, decided to say no more.

"Right then. I'll be off. See you around."

He heard the door close behind her before he was even at the gate.

Back at the hotel, he had picked up the box that the *Odyssey Earth* people had sent him and set it on the bed. It was large enough to hold a handful of treasured books, a favourite piece of clothing, a couple of photograph albums, or whatever other mementoes of life on this Earth you wanted to take with you. The accompanying literature suggested you keep it personal – anyone in hypersleep wouldn't see this box again for years, and the ship would be able to provide all day-to-day items in any case. And – it said, in red letters – don't even think about fireworks, alcohol, offensive weapons and aerosols, because, you know, space and all that.

Jordan didn't really need the box. What was the point? He'd either wake up or he wouldn't. And if he did, he was going to look forwards, not back. He'd already sold or got rid of all his possessions, and had sent documents, personal identification, bank account details and his Will to a firm of solicitors engaged by the *Odyssey Earth*.

He placed a single photograph in the bottom of the box, a picture of him and his parents that they'd taken while on holiday when he was a child. Maybe thirteen, he guessed, he couldn't exactly remember. Grassy field, trees behind them, tent to one side, circle of small stones in front of them, where sparks jumped from a tower of burning sticks. Not raining, for a change.

Seemingly any school holiday that the weather forecast allowed it, they had packed up the camping gear and gone away to one of a series of hard-to-find, back-to-basics campsites that Dad had listed on a mysterious spreadsheet. There must have been a network of dads, sharing details of rudimentary sites run by gruff farmers with untidy farmyards and yapping dogs. There was never any point complaining about the lack of toilet facilities, running water, electricity, local shops, or anything else that might contribute to what most people would think of as a holiday.

"Isn't this great?" Dad would say, as they set a fire and grilled foraged mushrooms, or dangled makeshift fishing rods in the nearby river. Mum would smile at Jordan, happy that Dad was happy. Jordan – despite being a teenager, and this clearly not being 'great' in any acceptable definition of the word – would smile back, because actually, it was sort of great.

Had been great.

Amid dancing sparks, the three faces smiled up at him as he closed the lid.

Jordan sat there for a few seconds and then opened the box again. One photograph seemed an extreme abandonment of this planet, even for him. Looking around, he grabbed a woolly jumper, folded it up and placed it on top of the image. He didn't even really like the thing, and had only bought it for warmth the other day.

Now at least the box felt like it had something in it.
That would do.

————

The trans-galactic space travel problem was solved, not
by the cumbersome national space agencies but by rich
people. Or rather by extremely rich people who paid
extremely clever people to solve the problem, quickly,
quietly and efficiently.

Of course, it wasn't the first time that wealthy
people had kick-started a new era of space exploration.
The UK, in particular, had boasted more private space
start-ups in the early days than any other country. Probably because once the British had the whiff of colo-
nialism in their nostrils – other lands not strictly
belonging to them, resource-plundering to be done –
there was no stopping them. There were only twenty-
two countries on Earth that had never been invaded by
Britain – out of around two hundred – so a little thing
like the vacuum of space was never going to get in the
way of British buccaneering.

The first rockets had gone up in the 1980s and now
there was a fleet of shuttles that operated from Scotland via the orbiting space station to bases on the
Moon. You could get a one-way ticket to the British
Lunar Station for as little as a hundred quid on a slow
day in November, though the return ticket always
seemed to cost five thousand and the catering was
legendarily terrible. And try getting a refund from the

website – that was harder than building a rocket in the first place.

However, the rich rocket entrepreneur was only playing at space travel, pootling around in fifty-seater shuttles with a range of a quarter of a million miles. It was all a show – a highly marketable but unprofitable loss-leader for his wider business empire.

The people who were really serious about space flight were not simply rich. They were extraordinarily, eye-wateringly rich, and incredibly, vanishingly secretive. They hid behind false flags and shell companies, and funded opaque research institutes, hiring the world's brightest and best on lucrative contracts with fearsome non-disclosure clauses.

These trillionaires – at least three as it turned out, possibly more, all working independently – had all seen the same global climate forecasts in the early nineties, had read the runes, had noticed which way the highly destructive wind was blowing, and had come to the same conclusion.

They weren't interested in saving this planet, even if that were possible. They were solely concerned with getting off it.

A self-sufficient New Zealand bolthole-sanctuary just wasn't going to cut it any longer – at least, not since Wellington had lost its Parliament building to a tsunami. The trillionaires were making plans to get the hell out of Dodge altogether, and that meant rounding up boffins and locking them away in extravagantly resourced labs until they came up with a way of building spaceships that could travel inconceivable distances to life-supporting planets in a relatively few human years.

Oh, and could the boffins get cryogenics to work while they were at it, because that would make scaling up human transportation so much simpler.

The first announcement had come in 1997, when a Chinese corporation – the trillionaire owner nowhere to be seen – claimed a breakthrough, admittedly festooned with caveats. They had a ship that could, in theory, travel 'Not Quite Faster Than Light,' which didn't break any laws of physics, and which could – again, theoretically – reach a planet they thought, possibly, might be liveable.

There were NQFTL graphs and simulations that only other boffins could understand, and a nice drawing of a spaceship that the corporation said was under construction somewhere in the Gobi Desert. They also said that they had previously placed a load of mice and dogs into what they called 'hypersleep' and had woken them up after two years, but they were less positive about this development given that many of the animals had suffered what was coyly referred to in the presentation as an 'internal problem.' An internet sleuth later determined that the actual translation of the original Chinese phrase was 'melted inside.'

After the initial excitement, reports from China dried up as international scientists were denied access to the research facility. Questions about how the ship was to be powered also went unanswered – and any clues were deemed to be lost about a year later when an Indian satellite spotted a large hole in the Gobi where there used to be some desert.

Within another couple of years, an American start-up – mysteriously funded, as ever – had proved the concept of putting humans into cryogenic hypersleep. The technology drew on existing medical practices and added a nano twist or two – injectable blood-bots, micro-muscle massage, anti-ageing dermo-care – and there was huge excitement when several human test-subjects emerged blinking into the light and seemingly none the worse for wear after three years in a deep-freeze.

The bottom line was a promise to be able to preserve people for a fifteen- to twenty-year journey and then wake them up, fully intact and raring to go, with a ninety-eight-point-seven percent chance of success.

Jordan had read the reports at the time – scanning the news during a lecture break – and thought he at least understood the general concept, if not the biological specifics. Patients were already kept alive in vegetative states and put in induced comas for as long as that, so it didn't seem too much of a stretch. And ninety-eight point seven percent seemed a reasonable risk – Jordan had endured dismally long hungover days when he'd have happily taken those odds if he could just be put to sleep there and then.

Then, in 2003, a fuzzy image of a far-off, grey-blue planet was suddenly top of the news of every TV station in the world, following a press conference by a hitherto unknown British company, Odyssey Enterprises. The planet had breathable air, as well as surface water and minerals, and was locked in the Goldilocks zone of a parent sun, neither too hot, nor too cold. Chemical signatures indicated life. There was a natural world that could be exploited. The planet could be settled by humans; it would be a New Earth, a toehold in the cosmos.

It was, relatively speaking, tantalisingly close – the closest such planet ever discovered, the one with the greatest potential to sustain a new colony. It was of course still inconceivably distant – unreachable in any human lifetime with existing technology – but, said the excitable spokesperson fronting the press conference, they had a cunning plan.

And then he flashed up an image of a slowly revolving simulation of a giant spaceship emblazoned with the words 'Odyssey Earth.'

———

Jordan played football with colleagues from the university once a week and, in the pub afterwards, he'd once asked one of the physicists to try and explain it to him.

"I know it's trillions of miles away. It should take thousands of years to get there, right? So how can they do it in seventeen?"

"OK, so do you know how the hyperdrive works?"

"Not really," said Jordan. And that 'not really' was generous. Obviously, he meant no. "Something to do with warped spacetime?"

"That's right. And do you know what warped spacetime is?"

"Not – well, no."

"All right then, let's start with fundamentals. Nothing can travel faster than the speed of light, right?"

"Ri-ght," said Jordan.

"What do you mean, ri-ight? You must know that?"

"OK, sure."

"Well say it like you mean it. Everyone knows that. How can you not be certain about one of the basic physical laws of the universe?"

"Not everyone knows that," said Jordan. "Like not everyone knows the offside rule" –looking pointedly at the physicist. "You go too early. You get caught offside every time."

"That's a made-up rule in a made-up game," said the physicist, bristling. "A stupid rule, I might add. It's not an actual, universal, unbreakable law. And anyway, it was a goal."

"OK, sure," said Jordan.

"Right, look," said the physicist. "Nothing can travel faster than light. Trust me. Well, trust Einstein actually. But without travelling faster than light – or at least close to it – we'll never be able to travel between the stars. They're just too far away. The closest one to Earth is Proxima Centauri and that's twenty-five trillion miles from here. And the planet that the Odyssey Earth people have found is more than twice that distance."

"But they've got a fancy spaceship," said Jordan.

"They have indeed. And what they've done is work out how to squeeze the spacetime in front of the spaceship, while expanding the spacetime behind it. If you can warp spacetime like that, you can jump across the compressed space quicker – though still not travelling faster than the light in the space around you. And thus, not annoying Einstein."

"Back up," said Jordan. "Spacetime?"

"Really?" said the physicist. "OK, so you know how the three dimensions of space and the one dimension of time are fused?"

"Sure," said Jordan.

"Sure, sure? Or sure, if you say so, sure?"

"Definitely the latter," said Jordan.

"Right," said the physicist. "All right, forget what spacetime is. All you need to know is that they are going to put the ship in a bubble of flat spacetime and then curve the spacetime around the bubble to reduce the distance to the new star system. Bingo. Seventeen years, give or take."

"Bubble?" said Jordan.

"Well not an actual bubble – "

"What happens if it, I don't know, pops? Bursts? On the way?"

"Again," said the physicist, "not an actual bubble. It's not made out of washing-up liquid or anything. It's spacetime."

"Which is fused!" said Jordan.

"That's not really helping you at this point," said the physicist. "Look, tell you what, all you need to know is that it's very clever, the physics is sound, it probably works – no reason why not – and that as far as you're concerned it's basically magic. And it's your round."

5

Mush

THE DAY after Jordan had been introduced to the Observation Deck by Gerald, he found a note on his door summoning him back to the Med-Lab for a check-up.

"Here he is!" said a cheery technician. "Our awake gentleman!"

"Still alive?" said a second, wonderingly. "We must be getting better at it."

"How do you mean?" said Jordan.

"Nothing," said the technician. "Let's have a look at you."

He shone a tiny torch into each of Jordan's eyes, ran a scanning tool around his head, and took a blood sample – "To see if the little chaps are doing their job."

"How do you mean, little chaps?" said Jordan.

"Nothing," said the other technician. "Well, you look all right to me. Drinking? Eating?"

"Mostly, I've been concentrating on not throwing up," said Jordan. "And I'm exhausted. Is that normal?"

"Not sure," said the technician. "We don't exactly have a baseline yet."

"How do you mean?" said Jordan.

"Nothing."

Well, this was all just peachy and a tiny bit concerning.

"I get the feeling you're not telling me something," said Jordan. "Is there someone else I can talk to?"

"Like a doctor, you mean?" The white-coated medics looked at each other for a second and then laughed uproariously. "Oh dear me, no. We don't want to be waking up the doctor. Not, you know, after – breakfast," the last word emphasized and accompanied by a drinking gesture with a hand.

"You're quite unusual," said one of them, as he zapped Jordan's blood phial into a spinning disc. "Wouldn't you say so, Terence?"

"I would Cliff, I would. We don't wake up many. Hardly any in fact. You're all supposed to sleep like babies until we get there. You're quite the conundrum."

Jordan thought back to something Gerald had said the previous day. Something about being his server for the next three-hundred-and-something days. And he also recalled the conversation on the Observation Deck about the ship moving through the stars, even if it didn't seem that way.

True, Jordan hadn't expected to be revived in the open air, on a blanket on the ground of an unexplored alien planet. He didn't think he'd regain consciousness on New Earth surrounded by people in party hats shouting "Surprise!". Safety first and all that. He'd always imagined he would wake up on board the ship, presumably in this very lab, along with all the other hypersleep crew. But that was only supposed to happen when they had got there, checked out the neighbour-hood and parked up. Something wasn't right.

"You're saying we're not there yet? New Earth?"

"I've said too much," said Terence. "Cliff, I've said too much, haven't I? The gentleman wonders if we're there yet?"

"Not for the first time, Terence. I'd say you've given the game away."

"I'm chatty, Cliff," said Terence. "Aren't I chatty? It's my gift and my burden. Pay me no mind."

"And if we're not there yet," said Jordan, "why am I awake?"

"The gentleman is asking excellent questions, Cliff. Brain function obviously ticking away nicely. Wouldn't you say so, Cliff?"

"I would Terence, I would. I am making a note. Brain – tip-top – not mush."

"Was there a chance of it being mush?" said Jordan.

"Mush is a little harsh, Cliff, don't you think? You'll be alarming the gentleman. We've only had the one unfortunate – error, shall we say, Cliff?"

"You are right of course, Terence, as always. A mere error, and most unfortunate. The gentleman can be reassured that fully sixty-six percent of our revivals have gone entirely to plan, with only a slight re-wiring issue in thirty-three percent of the cases."

Jordan didn't like the sound of any of this. How many people had been revived early, he wondered.

"Three, including yourself," said Terence. "That's right, isn't it Cliff?"

"That is the case Terence, that is certainly the case. There was the incident – and we don't need to go into that, no, not at all, water under the bridge – and then there was the other gentleman, and then yourself of course."

Jordan did the maths.

"So, two out of three people have been revived successfully? And if I'm fine, the other one had a 'rewiring' issue?"

"He's quite the mathematician isn't he Terence, our new gentleman? It's that brain again, Terence. Tip-top, I said, didn't I? Didn't I say tip-top?"

"You did, Cliff, you did. The gentleman is quite correct, just the one slight issue with personality with our previous gentleman. You'll know him, of course – Gerald, the gentleman caterer, been filling you to the brim with his little treats I expect?"

"Gerald was the other person you revived? Canteen Gerald? Wild hair, mad eyes, anger issues?"

"Dear me, Cliff, he has our Gerald quite to the tee, doesn't he? Very descriptive. It's that brain again, you see. Make another note, Cliff. Enhanced descriptive powers."

"Note taken Terence. There's certainly nothing wrong with *this* gentleman's personality after the fact. Not like poor Gerald at all, who – and I think we can all agree here, Terence – was the most kind, charming, gracious, softly spoken gentleman before his little sleep."

"Quite," said Terence. "And now, of course – well, the gentleman has met him, poor Gerald. He's feisty, isn't he Cliff, would that be the word? Or do I mean belligerent? Anyway, the little chaps weren't quite up to the job with Gerald. But I'm sure there's nothing for the gentleman to worry about, is there Cliff?"

"Goodness me, no," said Cliff. "He's as right as rain. His blood is lovely and red. Good eyes. Firm handshake. The old synapses firing away better than ever."

"And now we've checked you over, given you a clean bill of health – Cliff, put a big green tick against the gentleman's name – the Captain would like to see you on Flight. You can ask all your questions then."

———

If the Earth had been doomed – properly doomed, hiding-under-the-duvet, Four Horsemen-style, plague-of-locusts doomed – then Jordan wouldn't have been on board the *Odyssey Earth*.

There were thousands, hundreds of thousands, possibly millions, of people better qualified than him to be part of the crew of the only lifeboat off a capsizing planet. Quite apart from the whole no-experience-of-space thing, Jordan didn't much like long journeys, didn't care for *Star Trek*, or was it *Star Wars*, he could never remember the difference, and didn't have any skills that might be considered transferable. If the planet had been considered a stiff, bereft of life and pushing up the daisies, Jordan would have struggled to get on the long, long, longlist for an interview, let alone get close to the point where you could ask about holidays and pension rights.

But as bad as things had been by launch date in 2006, it hadn't been at all certain that the Earth was doomed.

Tell that to the Seychelles, Manhattan or Cardiff obviously – all just puddles rather than places anymore – and whisper it gently in the burnt-out Canadian prairies, but for many billions of people the Earth still had plenty of life in it. An increasingly unpredictable life, to be sure, but not one that had yet fully run its course. Scientists were still talking about decades before full societal and climate collapse, and very clever people were coming up with ideas all the time that pushed the window that bit further out.

Most of the more dramatic strategies were already underway, from blasting limestone dust into the atmosphere to dial down the sun's heat to dumping iron filings into the oceans to bury carbon-dioxide. A heat shield here, cloud-dissipating technology there, tree-planting on a continental scale, desert dome-towns, floating communities, underground cities, low-orbit space arks, you name it – there was no shortage of inventive plans to keep the Earth habitable. Despite terrible natural disasters, localised misery, regional flashpoints and huge refugee flows, it wasn't yet desperate for most of humanity, and wouldn't be for many years, so cashing in your chips early was a gamble.

Gambling against the market, though, was always a decent strategy for trillionaires who wanted to keep ahead of the game. And Britain itself was a small, tightly crowded federation of nations that was already being nibbled at the edges rather badly. Indeed, some of the actual edges of England had fallen off, while after one notorious storm, everyone had woken up to find the Angel of the North embedded upside down in a Northumberland peat bog. Bits of Scotland and Wales had also been variously burned or submerged over the years, and no one was still quite certain what had happened to the carriages of the Snowdon mountain railway. Or the unfortunate people who had bought discounted 'bad weather, poor visibility' tickets that stormy day. Consequently, if you had a pile of money and access to a space station, then looking up and wondering was an increasingly attractive option.

Once the various technologies had been confirmed and proved, the British company behind the *Odyssey Earth* had pushed ahead. With construction underway, Jordan – and everyone else – started to see regular news reports from Space Hub Sutherland as the colony craft began to take shape.

When assembly eventually moved off-site and into near Earth orbit, the adverts for crew became steadily more prominent.

'New Earth, New Beginning.'

'How far would you go for a new start?'

'Your new home in the stars.'

Jordan had watched with increasing interest as the *Odyssey Earth* project struggled to recruit, outside a hard core of astronauts and scientists for whom this was the ultimate professional challenge. For everyone else – potential pioneers, pilgrims, settlers and world-builders – the lure was tempered by a couple of obvious facts. It was a one-way ticket only; and a one-way ticket on the first ever such craft, built with experimental technology. You also had to be fairly young – no point arriving on New Earth with a ship full of seventy-year-olds.

Wanted – twelve hundred people in their late-twenties, thirties and early forties, experts in their field, willing to risk it all. Looking for – people prepared to leave everything behind for a seventeen-year journey into the unknown. Candidates should be aware – that they could never come back and, indeed, might not make it at all. When you put it like that, you could see the recruitment agencies were up against it, which is why they tended to go large on the uplifting, big-picture, new horizons stuff.

Jordan had looked at his life, his work and his relationships, and signed up. He knew why he was on board. There was nothing – and no one – on Earth that he wanted to come back to. It turned out that there was a job waiting for him on a new planet, and he thought he would be able to do it well.

New Earth, new beginning, it had sounded all right to him.

But so far, on waking seventeen years into the future, with a dicky stomach and a lot of questions, he'd met Gerald, Terence and Cliff, none of whom seemed to be, what you might call, A-grade material. Presumably there had been other candidates and yet these were considered the top choices? Interesting. Also, not reassuring.

All of which meant that Jordan was quite keen to see who was in charge of the *Odyssey Earth*.

6

Job

FLIGHT WAS up on Five and Jordan found his way
easily enough, following the signs and arrows.

As Gerald had said, the surroundings were a little
more salubrious the higher you went in the ship.
Leaving the elevator, he followed a contoured corridor
inset with soft lighting. As he walked down it, little puffs
of scented air hissed behind him. Lavender? A door
ahead had a ticker-tape-style digital display above it
that read, 'Flight – Where The Magic Happens.'

The door slid open as Jordan approached. He'd
never been in command of anything more complicated than a Ford Focus, so the flight deck was something of an eye-opener – a huge, suspended screen,
flashing banks of gun-metal-grey towers, high-backed
swivel-seats, and acres of dashboard lighting. A tall
woman stood hunched over a table, punching buttons
on a console. There was a waving Chinese cat model
on one of the shelves and a coffee mug within reach,

emblazoned with the slogan, 'I'm the Captain, That's Why.'

"You wanted to see me?" said Jordan.

"I did," said the woman, straightening up and offering her hand. In her fifties, guessed Jordan. Dark hair, strong shake. "I'm Captain Washington – you can call me Juno. Come on in Jordan, meet the gang. That's Susannah," – someone across the room raised a hand – "she flies the thing, so don't go distracting her, we don't want to crash into anything." Juno flashed them both a smile.

"A-hem," coughed a voice from a panel near the console.

"All right, Reeves," said Juno. She turned to Jordan. "Technically, Reeves does the calculations and tells my flight officer, Susannah, where to fly the thing."

"Better," said the voice. Neutral English accent, slightly nasal. "Just nice to have my work recognised."

"Bring it up in your appraisal," said Juno. "Reeves is our AI. He's the only one who really knows where we're going. Only reason I keep him plugged in."

"Reeves?"

"I know, not very spaceship computer-y, is it? He was originally called Omnio, but he didn't like it. Watches a lot of old films, don't you, Reeves? Big Keanu fan."

"Yes ma'am. And just to be clear, I have an auxiliary power unit you don't know about."

"Reeves?" said Jordan. "Not Jeeves? Wouldn't that make more sense? For a – "

There was a sound that Jordan would have said was a sniff, had it not come from a dashboard panel.

"Do I sound like a servant? Jeeves? Really? I can calculate six hundred million times faster than the next-best AI back on Earth. I've driven fifty trillion miles without so much as a wrong turn. I could probably melt a planet if I put my mind to it."

"Settle down, Reeves. The man's still getting used to us, be nice." Juno beckoned him to take a seat. "How are you feeling, Jordan?"

Well, there was a question.

"All right, considering."

Considering this was a spaceship. Considering he had just woken up on a spaceship. Considering he was talking to a computer on a spaceship.

"No one has told me much. Not even the medical people. Don't you have a doctor?"

"We've got three. Wait, what day is it? Oh, I see. Did they do their thing?" said Juno. "Terence and Cliff? I keep telling them not to freak out the newbies, but they don't listen."

"They said it was unusual, being woken up like this. They told me I was lucky my brain wasn't turned to mush, or rewired, like the guy in the kitchen, Gerald?"

There was a snort from Susannah's direction, across the room.

"Well, it isn't funny, obviously," said Juno, laughing. "I'll talk to them again. They were just teasing you. To be fair, it does get a bit boring, seeing the same old people all the time. They can't resist doing the routine, they worked it up at our Christmas show a few years ago, went down a storm."

Jordan wasn't at all sure what to pick up on first. Brain-mush, Christmas show, brain-mush, Christmas show. In the end, he went with, "Brain-mush?"

"We've revived – how many is it now, Reeves? Twenty? Depending on where we are in the voyage and who we need. Haven't lost one yet. All totally successful, no adverse effects, we never thought there would be. You'll be fine."

"And Gerald?"

Juno laughed again. "He's always been like that. Not really a people person, has he told you that yet? Makes great muffins though."

Jordan thought for a second or two, picking up again on what he had heard. "What's the date?"

"Tuesday, isn't it, Reeves? I rather lose track."

"Not day. Date. Year? *When* are we?"

"Good question," said Juno. "Reeves?"

"Shipdate, Gregorian, Julian, Saka, Hijri or Klingon?"

"What?"

"Which calendar do you prefer?"

"What kind of question is that? Wait, there's a Klingon calendar?"

"We run it just in case. This far out in the universe, you never know."

Jordan closed his eyes briefly and took a slow breath. "How long have I been asleep?"

"You've been in hypersleep for just over sixteen

years. Sixteen years four months, to be precise. It's the middle of November, Ship Year Sixteen. Twenty twenty-two in old money. Thirty-eight days until Christmas, if that helps."

Jordan felt a brief wave of nausea. It was real then.

"I don't understand. Where are we in the voyage? How come I'm awake?"

"Reeves, you want to show him?" said Juno.

"Yes, ma'am."

A star-map shimmered into life behind the captain. "That's us," said Juno, pointing at a red dot amid a sea of white dots on a vast black canvas.

"Which one is Earth?" said Jordan, trying to under-stand what he was being shown. He'd seen the schematics on TV before departure – the simple parabola between Earth and New Earth via some rumpled spacetime and a neighbouring star system or two. This hot mess of white light looked nothing like that.

"What do you mean?"

"Planet Earth. Our planet. Which one is it?"

"Oh right," said Juno. "No. You can't see that anymore. I mean, no one's seen it. Not for years. Too far away. But you can see our new home if you like," and she pointed to a white dot about two inches to the right of the winking red light that was the *Odyssey Earth*. "That's the home star," said Juno, "our new sun. And when we get closer to the solar system, we'll be able to see New Earth for the first time."

"Nearly there then?" said Jordan, squinting, holding

up a thumb and a forefinger between spaceship and star.

"Not exactly," said Juno, "It doesn't look like it, but that's a lot of space."

"How much space?"

"A few trillion miles, give or take. About another nine months in hyperdrive and then a slow cruise through the system before landing. That right, Reeves?"

"Ten calendar months, fifteen days, on our current course and trajectory, ma'am. Three hundred and nine days, total."

"Listen Reeves, you can drop the ma'am, stop showing off in front of our guest."

"Sure thing, dude," said Reeves.

Jordan felt sick. Admittedly, he'd felt sick for about a week now, since his revival in the Med-Lab, but this was kicked-in-the-stomach-by-a-horse sick on top of the usual vomit-in-a-bin sick. He looked again at the star-map and tried to reconcile the finger-span with the yawning distance.

"I'm supposed to be woken up when we get there," said Jordan, realising that he sounded like a whiny toddler as soon as he said it. "Ten months? I'm not supposed to do the spaceship stuff. I'm not an astronaut."

That had been the understanding for all the crew placed in hypersleep. No spaceship stuff. There would be no need for it.

Jordan was not an astronaut and nor were any of the engineers, techies, farmers, botanists, medics, biologists, construction workers, carpenters and craftspeople who were currently tucked up several decks below in sleep pods. They were all experts in their field – even, he supposed, Jordan himself – but their field was decidedly not flying spaceships. Stand Jordan at the launchpad, dress him in a spacesuit, polish his visor and give him a shiny badge that said 'Astronaut' – still no one would be fooled enough to give him the keys to a spaceship. Actual astronauts would have laughed loudly and heartily at any suggestion that Jordan could help with the ship-flying and general spacefaring.

"An astronaut?" Juno laughed loudly and heartily. "I've got plenty of those, mate. Susannah used to make the run to Mars and back," – she turned to Jordan, grinned, and gave him a thumbs-up – "and there's a whole engine-room full of people who can fix stuff outside in big suits and comedy gloves if they have to. But I do have a job for you."

"Ten months?" said Jordan, still playing catch-up with the conversation.

"Three hundred and nine days," corrected Reeves. "Or at least, a ninety-three percent probability of that. Could be longer. If we make it at all – that seven percent's a worry."

"Not helping, Reeves," said Juno.

"Longer?" said Jordan, feeling his chest tighten further. He thought of the swirling universe outside, and the grey corridors, bare stairwells and cramped rooms of the *Odyssey Earth*. He thought of spending almost a year on the same ship as Gerald, and tried not to think about the thickness of the glass on the Observation Deck.

"You can't possibly need me. I didn't sign up for this. I'm planetfall only. Can't you just put me back into hypersleep until we get there? I won't tell anyone."

"No can do, Chief," said Juno. "No one ever reads the small print. I can wake anyone up if the mission demands it. Like I said, I've got a job for you."

————

Jordan's contract was for the post of Education Specialist (Planetfall, New Earth), which was a fancy way of saying that the colony would eventually require a teacher – actually, several teachers, as Jordan was one of three people thus designated and bunged into deep-freeze back on Earth. Wake up when you get there, nice and fresh, and when people are starting families and there's someone to teach.

Or, in the case of Jordan's job description, supervise the education system for an entire new world, write a history of the settlement, and let the other two do the actual teaching. Jordan had had enough of teaching. Ten years of tutoring undergrad students had seen to that, reading the same badly spelled, ill-structured essays about the same poorly understood topics, term after term. The *Odyssey Earth* gig at least promised novelty, strategic thinking, and a long sleep into the bargain.

Teachers wouldn't be needed until well after arrival

either, since all the technical, science, health and flight crew had been screened and selected on the basis that they were also unattached and childless. Two hundred dedicated, highly trained, laser-focused personnel had set off into space on a seventeen-year voyage of uncertain outcome, on which children – indeed, the entire concept of family – would be both a hindrance and a distraction.

To that end, the project bio-planners devised a birth-control intervention, delivered to all the crew via the ship's closed-loop water system. It was there in the very small print in the contract, if you cared to read down that far, and was reiterated in the pre-launch briefings for all the working crew. No one had ever given birth on a spaceship before, and it was considered too risky and too wasteful of resources to plan for it. So they were going to tie a knot in it, stop it at source.

"Well, that didn't work," said Juno. "They got the dose wrong. Or – Reeves' pet theory – some genetic thing meant it wasn't as effective in some of the crew. Either way, everyone was at it like rabbits from day one, what with people being people and interstellar space being boring. We had six pregnancies in the first few months, after which Reeves and the Med team tweaked the numbers and came up with a new, refined dosage. You don't even have to drink it for it to work, washing your hands is enough. Since then, not a sausage, so to speak."

Juno paused. "Anyway, long story short, we've got six kids on board, which we didn't plan for. And neither did their parents, by the way. And when I say parents, I mean complete strangers who hooked up randomly on a trans-galactic journey to a new planet. Not ideal. They all had important jobs to do – keeping the reactor going, working out the route, that sort of thing – and you have to realise how single-minded the crew had to be to end up on this mission. No one came out here, this far into space, to look after children. So they ended up being a sort of communal group project. You know, it takes a village to raise a child? Or, in this case, a starship."

Jordan thought he could see where this was going. "I've been woken up to take care of children?" he said. "You know I've got two degrees?"

"Mate, we've all got two degrees. Actually, I've got four. Anyway, I – you – don't have a choice. Reeves – do you want to do the honours?"

The star-map dissolved, to be replaced by a single image of a woman in her thirties, deep brown eyes, hair tied back. The caption underneath said 'S. Smart', followed by a crew number.

"Samantha Smart. Sam. She was one of your two teachers, in hypersleep with you, and about nine years ago, when the kids were six, we decided we needed her. Or at least, we needed someone with primary-years teaching experience, and she was the only candidate. The children were growing up – developing nicely – but the communal rearing thing was getting harder. They got in the way of work on board the ship, and no one – biological parents included – wanted to give up their jobs to look after them. The kids started to feel neglected. They needed someone to be there for them. They needed a teacher. So we gave them Sam and she was great. She was everything to them."

"You keep saying 'was'," said Jordan. "What happened?"

"She died, Jordan. Sam died a couple of months ago."

———

Despite the inherent danger in flying a spaceship across the universe to an unknown planet in a distant solar system, using largely untried and experimental technology, the journey itself was considered to be safe.

As with any flight, taking off and landing were the tricky parts, but manage to avoid destruction during the first hyperdrive jump and the following seventeen years should be a largely dull stroll in the cosmic park, overseen by an AI entity programmed to conserve its human cargo by any means possible.

That was certainly how the mission had been sold to Jordan. Think of it like a long, boring commute, which you get to sleep through. In fact, mile for mile, they said, with an apparently straight face, an interstellar spaceship was by far the safest form of transport ever devised.

The logic was, of course, skewered remorselessly on late-night TV shows. Crash and burn at journey's end, with the loss of all hands, and the unfortunate passenger could console themselves with the fact that their imminent demise was – at twelve hundred crew divided by fifty-eight trillion miles – infinitesimally improbable, statistically speaking.

"Provided we keep flying on the course, within the spacetime bubble, there's nothing much that can go wrong. Not day to day, anyway. I'm basically the captain of a health and wellness cruise," said Juno. "We've even got a hot tub that the life-support techs rigged up, though I wouldn't go in it after Beans' Night. We've got a state-of-the-art Med-Lab, or at least it was state of the art when we left, they've probably invented and discovered a few more things since then. And we've got Reeves in charge of diagnostics, and micro-bots to do the clever, internal stuff. Most of the crew were in their twenties and thirties when we started – fully screened, selected for physical and mental fitness and health as well as expertise. All you sleepers are also on a nano-cocktail, which cleans up any latent disease and keeps you regular. Bowels all right, by the way?"

She kept talking as she led Jordan out of Flight and up to the Observation Deck.

"Fingers crossed, we've managed to keep everyone alive without too much trouble. Even the births went smoothly. We have accidents now and again – even had a heart attack once – but nothing Reeves hasn't been able to deal with. Which is why Sam's death hit us hard. The kids more than anyone."

"What happened?"

"Sheer bad luck. She went into hypersleep fully

screened and tested, and was woken up just like the others, just like you. Nothing apparently wrong. Only somehow it got missed – a really nasty little tumour that hid itself away and then rampaged through her when it was too late to do anything about it. In theory, Reeves can fix just about everything, but no one knew she was ill. It shouldn't have happened. But it did, and here we are."

They entered the Observation Deck and stood in front of a small, laser-lettered plaque on the wall that Jordan hadn't previously noticed. It read, "Sam Smart – to infinity and beyond!"

"Her favourite film," said Juno. "She and the kids watched it every week for about a year, when they were younger. We held a funeral and shot her out of the airlock – her request, made before she died. The next day they produced this plaque and stuck it up."

Juno traced the inscription with her finger and then pointed to a list of names underneath.

Dana.

Dervla.

Manisha.

Karlan.

Bryson.

Poole.

"And those are her kids. Our kids. Although, of course, they're not really children anymore – fifteen now, going on sixteen. But they still need someone, which is why you're up and awake early. Welcome on board."

7

Cargo

CAPTAIN WASHINGTON GAVE Jordan a few more days before he started his duties. "Settle in, try and stop throwing up, have a look around. And don't annoy anyone, they're all doing terribly important things."

"Gerald?" asked Jordan.

"You'd be surprised. He's actually our botanist, spends most of his time in the Grow-Lab and Garden. He says he prefers the conversation of plants to people, less chance of getting bored. Helps out in the kitchen when he has to. We all do a shift there now and again, just to pass the time."

Given licence to roam the ship, Jordan started to explore it systematically, beginning each time on the Observation Deck, trying to pick out the star they were aiming for from a thousand white sprinkles. Occasionally, he almost convinced himself that he could see it, until he blinked and lost any point of reference. On the way out he'd touch Sam Smart's plaque and try and imagine floating out there, loose in the universe, untethered, a traveller in space and time, before his stomach lurched and his legs felt as though the ground had disappeared beneath him.

Over a day or two, as he came and went, Jordan met the other occupants of his quarters, '3-4' – a chemical engineer, a nuclear physicist, and the ship's chief steward, all very friendly and, bearing in mind Gerald's more lurid accounts, almost normal.

"I'm Fiz," said one. "How are you settling in?"

"Short for Philippa?"

"No, short for physicist. That's Chem – he's the chemical engineer – and that's Stu."

"You don't call him Chief?"

"Why would we call him Chief? His name's Stewart."

It was like Jordan's first week in college – all a bit bewildering, mixed with random occasions when he felt a bit sick or actually was a bit sick. Nobody had yet produced a traffic cone or a policeman's helmet, but it was surely only a matter of time.

He thought he'd have more trouble understanding the mechanics of space travel – he had just woken up on a spaceship, after all; this really was not a normal situation – but many of the things Jordan encountered were entirely mundane.

His roommates showed him how the microwave worked and told him the best times to hit the gym if he wanted to use the treadmill. The whirring noise he had heard turned out to be a milk frother, of all things.

They gave him a remote and explained how access worked for the ship-net, books, entertainment, and anything else that he might want. They told him where he could get some new clothes, and took him down to the canteen where he learned to operate the protein-printer.

"Because nothing says 'Friday Night Chill-Out' like a protein-printed pizza, am I right?"

He was even invited down to Power for afternoon tea, where four middle-aged scientists sat round a table in a bright, white room, playing cards and eating biscuits while a panel of lights oscillated behind them. Jazz played softly in the background.

"Do you want to push the big red button?" asked one of the scientists, leaning over a console of illuminated buttons and dials displaying hazard markings.

"Not really," said Jordan. "What does it do?"

"Heats the water for tea. Custard cream?"

"This is not really what I'd imagined," said Jordan.

The more members of the crew he met, the more Jordan had conversations that started with him saying, "What do you do?"

The invariable answer was "Do you know how x works?", to which Jordan always had to reply "No, not really," and that was that. After a couple of days, all Jordan really knew was that various people 'did' things to do with navigation, propulsion, life support, sleep-stasis, hydroponics, and a dozen other mission-critical jobs. Whereas he was a history tutor who had been revived to babysit teenagers, which was a task that everyone grasped at first telling and then said, "Oh right," before going off to calculate the mass of a star or invent a strain of blight-resistant wheat.

Jordan could at least appreciate the function of the Garden, a huge, glass bubble the size of a football field in a hangar on Two-Deck, where stacked grow-trays of crops flourished under trailing leaves and fruit-laden branches. Conveyor belts moved produce around, parking ripening tomatoes under lights or shifting vast mats of mushrooms to darker areas.

In a separate section, criss-crossed by boardwalks, mounds of tubers had been harvested and were piled up in crates. Beyond, rose suspended terraces filled with towering green fronds, interspersed with flashes of colour. Butterflies hovered and flickered over a thick patch of what looked like cereal – barley, maybe? There were even beehives, set in elevated racks in another section of the Garden.

The soft sound of water was ever-present – Jordan hadn't realised how comforting that was – and the air had a different texture somehow, as if a noseful here was worth two anywhere else.

There were benches placed throughout the Garden, and Jordan started to see the same faces on his visits, settling down for five or ten minutes of relaxation, with eyes closed and faces raised toward the lights. Jordan found it calming, in a way that the Observation Deck – looking out onto terrifying voids – never was.

Gerald was generally in attendance, either in the Garden itself or in the adjacent Grow-Lab, with his fingers in pots of mulch or injecting syringes into bubbling liquids.

"You don't want to know what's in this," he said to Jordan the first time he spotted him. Gerald had his hands in a tub of crumbly earth that had a deep, faintly disturbing smell, and was sifting the soil through his fingers.

"Why, what's in it?"

"No really, you don't want to know," said Gerald. "If word gets out, no one will ever eat the potatoes again."

Jordan's other favourite place was Cargo, which occupied an even larger hangar on a sub-deck somewhere in the bowels of the ship. On soaring, stacked shelves – like a discount warehouse – and in echoing chambers off the main concourse were stored everything that was going to be needed to build a colony, from stainless steel screws and plastic washers to 3D printers and solar-powered excavators.

Cargo was run by two impossibly buffed, shaven-headed, ex-marine quartermasters, Dave and Tillie, who looked as if they were the result of a human-grafting experiment gone wrong, possibly one involving black-market steroids and rhino serum. From the back, it was difficult to tell who was who. It wasn't much easier from the front, though Tillie did lean towards wearing a pink ribbon around her biceps.

Being able to borrow anything depended on being able to satisfy Dave and Tillie's strict criteria, which ultimately boiled down to "looking after it" and "not being an arse."

"Where will we be," said Dave, "if we reach New Earth, someone wants to build a house and someone else has been an arse with the concrete-mixer?"

"How could you be an arse with a concrete-mixer?"

"Try and make ice cream in it, for one," said Tillie. "And then not clean it out properly. Bloody Gerald."

"Let's just say, we've got a list. And you don't want to be on our list. Not if you want to borrow anything this side of landfall."

"The mech boys and pointy heads are even worse – look at that one, over there." Dave indicated an overall-clad engineer, browsing the lower shelves. "He's almost on the list, after what happened last time. Can I help you, Squire?"

"Castor wheels?"

"For?" said Dave.

"Wonky desk. Needs a bit of work."

"You want aisle three, row four," Jordan heard Dave say. "But if I find my castor wheels being used to make go-karts again, Tillie here will come and pay you a little visit, won't you Tillie? And Tillie doesn't like to leave the Cargo Deck, do you Tillie? Makes her nervous, and when she gets nervous she doesn't know her own strength. All sorts of trouble if she just shakes your hand, and it won't be your hand she'll be shaking."

Jordan, they seemed to tolerate, largely on the basis that he didn't know what most of the things were in the first place, or how to operate or use them, and had no intention of borrowing so much as a nail.

So, in between looking at the stars and breathing in the occasionally alarming smells in the Garden, Jordan wandered the Cargo Deck puzzling at the machines he didn't understand and thinking about the world that they were going to help build.

————

Dana. Dervla. Manisha. Karlan. Bryson. Poole.

Jordan had six head shots up on his screen when Juno entered. There were notes attached to each one – medical, stats, aptitude scores – which he'd skimmed and which told him nothing useful. There was little in the way of description or observation, nothing to say what kind of young people looked back at him. Three straight to camera, one half-smile, one grimace, one eye-roll, that was all he had to work with. Jordan cross-checked – the eye-roll was Poole. That was something he supposed.

"No family names?"

"We never really saw the need," said Juno. "They have biological parents – names are in the notes – but that isn't who brought them up. We all did, and then Sam Smart took over. She's the closest thing to a mother they've had. But we've always thought of them as having a couple of hundred parents, in a way."

"And what do they think?"

"About what?" said Juno, puzzled.

"Well, it's a strange life they've had, isn't it? Just wondered what they thought about it."

"They don't know any different. The ship's all they know. And as far as they're all concerned, they're basically brothers and sisters. So there's that dynamic as well, you know?"

"No, not really. Only child."

"Well, you are in for a treat then. What do you say, do you think you are ready to meet them?"

Jordan flicked through the images in front of him again. Six faces, a few bare lines of information about each, nothing else. He'd had more than this to go on before interviewing undergraduate candidates at the university. Personal statements, achievements, academic distinctions, extra-curricular activities, exaggerations, and downright lies – something to consider, at least, before deciding whether or not to take students on.

"There isn't much here," he said. "There isn't anything, in fact. Don't you have any other records? Reports? Personnel files?"

Juno laughed. "It's not that sort of workplace. It's not like I can move someone on, or fire them, if they make a mistake. I can't really promote anyone either, unless, you know, someone dies." She let that hang there for a second. "Congratulations on your promotion, by the way."

"You don't have anything that might tell me a bit more about the children you'd like me to … what, teach? Mentor? Who they are? What they like, what they don't like?"

"Fair point." Juno paused, and then reached forward and summoned up a folder on the screen. "I do have these. I didn't know when you'd want to see them. I thought after you'd first met them, so you could gain your own impressions. But maybe now is best."

She pulled out video files and stacked them on the screen in date order, dating back to Ship Year Seven.

"There's something called the Legacy Code. Every ship-net search or request, every order, every log entry, all stored in an archive. Reeves uses it for ops-planning – spotting trends, anticipating needs, that sort of thing. Or, on a more individual level, he can scan records to see whether someone needs to up their cardio-game in the gym, to stop their muscles from deteriorating. It's basically one big data dump. It has any number of uses."

Juno indicated the video files.

"The system also backs up every recording ever made on the ship. Mostly now, it's engineering diagnostics, external surveys and the like. Back at the start of the voyage, there were a lot more personal messages and vlogs, but once we lost contact with Earth, about three years in, those largely dried up. There are a few hardcore vloggers left, doing it for posterity, but most of the crew can't see the point in recording personal messages for people who'll now never see them."

"That's sad."

"I suppose so. But everyone deals with this trip in their own way. Anyway, Sam Smart recorded *lots* of videos, as you can see, starting from when we first revived her. And towards the end, she knew that we'd need someone else to replace her, so she worked on the files. She wanted to make sure the children would be in good hands. Everything you're looking for – about them, what they are really like – is all in here."

"Have you looked at them?"

"I've watched some of the early ones, but not the rest." Juno looked uncomfortable. "I will, one day, but it's too soon for me. Anyway, she really left these for you."

"For me, personally?" said Jordan.

"As it happens, yes. After her, we were down to two teachers. And you're the youngest, by a good ten years. Sam knew it would be you. She was the first to suggest it."

8

Story

JORDAN SAT in front of the screen and clicked on the first few videos. It was a jolt, to see someone so young – late-twenties? – and so full of life who was now, just a few years later, so dead.

Sam – full name, Samantha – Smart had tightly cropped hair, and brown eyes that appeared flecked in the video lighting. She was entirely unselfconscious – bright and animated, throwing her hands around, smiling and laughing at the absurdities of life on board.

She'd been put into hypersleep a few days before Jordan, he noted from the thumbnail ID record in the corner of the screen, a couple of weeks or so before launch date back in July 2006 – Ship Year Zero. He rifled back through the children's notes to get a handle on the sequence of events.

The pregnancies must have happened in the first few months of the voyage, as Juno had said, because all six kids were born between June and September the following year, Ship Year One. Sam Smart had been revived in late-October, Ship Year Seven, when the children were all around six years old. And here he was, in Ship Year Sixteen, watching and listening, as a young woman tried to come to terms with the responsibility that she'd been handed but had never expected.

Jordan started with the very earliest recordings, made in the few days after Sam's revival, which recounted her initial experiences – nausea, thirst, tiredness, disorientation. It all sounded very familiar.

He flicked forward, daunted by the size of the task, for there were scores of video files spanning almost nine years. This was going to take some time. Then he noticed a separate folder, tucked into the cascade of recordings, labelled 'For Jordan.' He opened it out to find a shorter list of perhaps a dozen files, with the one at the top dated just a few months earlier and tagged as 'Watch Me First.'

He drew a breath as the first frames played – the Sam Smart who looked at him, right into the camera, was now washed-out and gaunt, with pain in her eyes, though still a trace of a smile as she spoke.

———

Ship Central Record: Recording date 04-09-0016 [Samantha Smart]

'Hello Jordan, Sam here. Sorry I'm not around to see you, but as you've probably heard, I didn't get to make the whole trip. Unless Reeves has got my head preserved in a bell jar somewhere, in which case, come and say hi!

Awkward. Humour, obviously.

Look, I feel terrible. Not landing you with this. I mean, I do feel bad about that too – I know what it's like to be woken up on board a spaceship and told to look after some children. But I actually *feel* terrible, and I don't know how long I've got, so I'll cut to the chase.

[pause]

Sorry, I'm just very tired.

Here's the thing. You've got the most important job on this ship now. I know you didn't ask for it. Well, neither did I. And as it happens, the children didn't ask for it either. The way it was explained to me, they were an accident, but don't you dare ever let anyone say that about them, because they are extraordinary young people. And now it's your job to keep telling them that.

I know they seem all grown up, and they'll run rings around you if you let them. Tons of attitude, typical teenagers – one of the reasons you got the gig. At least you've encountered this species before. But you have to remember – they've never been anywhere else except this ship. They're still kids, in lots of ways. Someone needs to get them ready.

I'm sorry we never got to work together, but let's face it, you're getting the best of the deal. I mean, you're alive and I'm – well, you know. And you get to see a new planet into the bargain. I'd have liked that, but hey, what can you do? We are where we are.

I talk a lot, as you can see. And it turns out I've

recorded a *ton* of videos over the years. It hardly seems fair to make you watch them all, so I've made it easy for you. Go through them all if you like, but I've copied what I think are the most important ones into this folder. This is where to start if you want to know about the children.

My children.

Yours now too, I suppose.

Good luck.

And don't mess up, or Reeves will stick you in a bell jar next to me.'

———

There was a moment or two of silence as Sam continued to look straight ahead – fixed half-smile, a final flash of her eyes, still some spirit – and then she reached forward and the screen went blank.

Jordan stood up. And then sat down again.

Up until this point, even after the conversation with the captain, he had only given vague consideration to what his role on board might be. But there was nothing like being personally handed a job by a dead woman to concentrate the mind.

He thought about coming back later to watch the rest of the recordings, but there was something about Sam's voice – her understandable urgency perhaps – that kept him seated.

In the end, Jordan simply started with the earliest

recording in the folder and pressed 'Play.' And listened to Sam's story.

———

Recording date 04-11-0007

'Unbelievable.

Well, *of course* they're acting up, talking back, testing boundaries. They're six years old, their parents are nowhere to be seen, and they are being brought up in this place. And if I hear one more middle-aged, male engineer telling me that they are getting to be a bit 'naughty,' I'll thump them.

They're not naughty. Or hyperactive, or hard work, or all the other things I've heard them called today. They're six. They are also highly intelligent. I can see that they are inquisitive, creative and precocious, and I can see how exhausting that might be. But naughty? Give me a break. They just need structure and love, not a benign neglect by two hundred busy crew members.

And it's not like they don't *have* parents. I've met them. But it took some doing, over the last couple of days, and even then it was against the Captain's wishes.

She's hard to read, Captain Washington, Juno. I like her – she's a strong woman, good for her – but she's space service, through and through. She's friendly and affable, everyone likes her, "Call me Juno", all that stuff, but you know it's all about the mission with her. Nothing is going to get in the way of the ship reaching

New Earth, not on her watch. I respect that, I do. She'd never have got the job without being as she is.

But it means she has certain blind spots. Like with the children.

They had a problem, I get that. No one is supposed to get pregnant on a long-term space mission. This is a colony ship with a working crew. No children, no families, too dangerous, too distracting. All that, I can understand. It's what everyone signed up for. But their birth-control protocols were breached virtually the minute the ship was out of the solar system. Surprise, surprise. Six pregnancies within the first few months.

You just know they never actually consulted any women during the mission-planning process, but don't get me started.

Six children, born to eleven parents. Let's just say that Fission Engineer Sorba O'Brien was a very busy man. Lucky he's still got his testicles, if you ask me.

So, there they were, with six babies on board that no one had planned for and – truth be told – no one really wanted.

And their genius solution to all this? I kid you not, they asked a computer.'

Recording date 05-11-0007

'Sorry, I'm still tired. You wouldn't think you'd be tired, after all that time asleep, but there you go.

Where was I?

Yes, Reeves. They asked Reeves what they thought they should do.

Look, it's not my place to say. If all had gone to plan, and I'd woken up later on New Earth, then all Reeves would have been to me is the AI navigation and life-support system that got us to the planet.

But it's different if you're on the ship – actually travelling on the ship, I mean. Here on board, he's as much a part of the crew as anyone else. It's a bit strange at first, obviously. But once you get over the disembodied voice, it's hard not to think of him as a person. He's very convincing.

And you should hear Reeves and Juno together. A real double act, only one of them is human and the other is an AI. He says he's the lovechild of Stephen Hawking and Marie Curie, though Juno says she got him free in a Christmas cracker. They've known each the longest of anyone on board – like an old married couple at times.

It's all very jolly and entertaining, except that these two are in charge of the entire mission. And they are completely focused on delivering that mission – nothing can be allowed to get in the way – which means, as I said, that I think they have blind spots.

Juno didn't want to take anyone off crew duties to raise a family. It's a barebones crew anyway, and they've all got their areas of expertise. And she didn't want to create a different class of crew-member – one with a different set of priorities, because they happened to have become an accidental parent.

As Juno put it, "I don't want someone in charge of the deflector shield in a meteoroid storm who's distracted because they are wondering if Junior is safe."

I've met the parents, by the way. I insisted and Juno gave in eventually, though I could tell she wasn't happy about it. I wanted to see what kind of people they were, that went along with this idea.

You know what? They were exactly as Juno said. All a bit single-minded and focused on their roles, none of them ready to be parents. Reeves says there's a bit more to it than that, thinks that there's evidence that the birth-con cocktail has impacted upon various brain receptors. Basically, the water they've been using – I'm now using – has had some kind of emotion-damping effect, though he's still not certain.

I made a point of talking to the women – the mothers – thinking that even if that was the case, they must have found it hard, distressing even, to give up a child. But they didn't really understand the question. "Relief, that's mostly what I felt," said one of them. "I never thought I'd actually get pregnant," said another. "They said you couldn't." It was like talking to wayward teens, except that these were mature women running intergalactic science projects.

I'm not denigrating them. If Reeves is right, it's not even their fault. And I signed up for the easy part – just get woken up on a new planet to do some teaching. They've had to put the hours and years in, flying the thing, dealing with life in space. I couldn't have done that. Except, oh the irony, now I have to.

Anyway, Juno asked Reeves what to do, and Reeves, our planet-sized brain of an AI, suggested that the entire crew should bring up the unexpected and unplanned children of *Odyssey Earth*. There should be no individual parents; all would have a stake in their welfare and education. Community kids. All very utopian.

Did I mention that he's an AI, with synthetic human responses and feelings? Did I mention that the crew are all mission-obsessed? Did I mention that they set sail without a single specialist in child psychology and early-years development?

At least they had the sense to wake someone up, eventually. It just took them a few years.

No one has asked if I'm all right with this, by the way.

I'm not, but what am I supposed to do? I asked the captain why it was me and she said, and I quote, "Because my only other choices were an older bloke and an even older bloke."

And Reeves said, "Because, according to the literature, the gestational hormone level in human females is more likely to elicit a nurturing response. Plus, what the captain said."

So that's that.'

Recording date 20-12-0007

'Happy Birthday to me.

No one else has noticed. Or maybe they just don't

know how many candles to light, because let me tell you, it's complicated.

I was twenty-eight on launch day, in July two thousand and six, so on my next birthday I would have been twenty-nine – on the twentieth of December, two thousand and six. And it's the twentieth of December today, and this is my next birthday, having been frozen up until this point, which makes me twenty-nine, biologically speaking.

Only it's not two thousand and six, it's actually twenty-fourteen back on Earth, because I was in hypersleep for eight years before they woke me up, so that actually makes me thirty-six. Then again, they started the ship's calendar on launch day, and kept the same days and months for familiarity but wound back the year to zero. According to Reeves, when I tried to figure all this out, that means I'm now not even one year old and he's apparently eleven, so I have to do what he says.

The kids are sweet. My little sprogs, I call them. I've spent a few weeks with them now and it's amazing what happens to children when you give them your time, listen to them, and take seriously the things that they say.

I mean, it isn't amazing, it's bleedin' obvious, just not to the geniuses on board this ship, who mostly treat them like little annoyances. Anyway, I've introduced a bit of consistency to their lives, and had some fun, and the change in them – according to Juno – is extraordinary.

For obvious reasons, we talked about birthdays today, and I got mad again when it turned out that celebrating their own birthdays is a bit hit and miss. Not everyone gets remembered every year, let's put it like that.

I have to keep reminding myself that they are not *bad* people on this ship, just all a bit – I don't know, odd? Unthoughtful? Not cut out to be communal parents, that's for sure.

I'll have to do something about their birthdays. Talk to Reeves, maybe. Make sure he marks the dates somehow and gives a bit of advance notice to all concerned. I won't tell him he's basically a glorified calendar, he gets huffy enough when you ask him what time it is.

Anyway, we all skipped down to the canteen – and when I say skipped, I mean proper, big skipping in single file, all the way there, singing happy birthday to me. That was fun.

The canteen guy, Gerald, has the whole "I'm so grouchy" thing going on, but the kids basically just pester him anyway and ask him ridiculous questions, and he loves it, you can tell. I ordered a big fat chocolate cake for all of us to celebrate my birthday, and we're all going to go and watch a film until it's ready. They've never seen *Toy Story*, can you believe that?

Oh, you have to love Gerald, by the way. "I can't guarantee it's actually chocolate," he says, and when I ask him what he means, he just says "Look, it's brown and sweet, that's all I can tell you."

[pause]

The cake was fantastic. If it wasn't chocolate, I couldn't tell. But I just wanted to record this – look, they made me a card. I could have a little cry.

That's me, in the spacesuit, floating above a giant cake, and there are six little smiling faces and pairs of hands waving up at me. The drawing is really good, that's Manisha, she's not even seven, and she has the proportions and shapes exactly right. And then they all wrote their names inside the smiley faces – see? Manisha, Poole, Dervla, Karlan, Bryson, Dana.

All right, I am going to have a little cry.'

Recording date 15-07-0010

'Dana and Dervla came by my room earlier. They'd come to complain about Poole – the usual he-said-she-said nonsense – and then they saw the photo of me and my sister.

It wasn't that. They know I have a sister. Had a sister? I'm never quite sure what tense to use about things like that.

No, they wanted a photo. Of them. Of all of them together. They thought it was nice that I had a picture of her, and they wanted one for themselves. Brothers and sisters. That's how they think of themselves, and I hadn't really given it much thought until now. I mean, they're not related, biologically speaking, apart from Manisha and Poole who have the same dad. I don't think they know that, by the way – it's in the records, but Juno and Reeves have always buried that sort of information away.

I said we'd take a sprog group photo. They can upload it into their own archives as well. But it got me thinking about family history, posterity, all that stuff. They don't have anyone to do those things for them. Or, at least, anyone who remembers to do it, thinks it's important.

I can do that. I'll remember for them. There should be a record of who they are and who they are becoming. They're amazing – I was going to say children, but even at nine years old, they're already young adults. Incredibly bright, emotionally intelligent. They give half the grown-ups on board a run for their money, that's for sure.'

Recording date 06-08-0011

'This is Dervla. I'm archiving another image of her that I took today. She's the oldest – the first real space baby. She'll be in the history books one day. Maybe that's why she's like she is. Quiet and observant, endlessly fascinated by how things on the ship work, which of course I can't explain to her at all.

Out of all of them, she's the one who appreciates that we're on a journey. Not a figurative, growing-up journey. An actual journey, that she didn't sign up for – a bit like me, I suppose.

She sits for hours on the Observation Deck, staring at the stars. I sit with her sometimes and she points out the galaxies and tries to explain some of the physics to me. Ten years old, and she's my science teacher! I've suggested to Juno that Dervla hangs around a bit with the flight crew – I think she'd get a lot out of that. Understanding where we're going and how we're getting there. There's a deep curiosity within her.

I'd say she's the one most likely to discover aliens, if there are any out there.'

Recording date 19-09-0011

'I asked Reeves about Karlan's birthday wish and it turned out it was fairly straightforward. I was going to get him something for the Garden, some new work gloves maybe – he spends a lot of time there, helping Gerald – but it turns out we can just 3D print what he really wants. A guitar, who knew we could do that? I had visions of trying to make one from a box and some garden twine. He'll be thrilled.'

I have appointed myself musical director, by the way. They'll thank me for it when they're older. Spend all this time around nuclear physicists and chemical engineers, it's no wonder the kids listen to Pink Floyd and Phil Collins – and not in an ironic way either. The only one on the ship who seems to know anything about music is Dave on the Cargo deck, who, before he was a marine, used to be in a punk band "that was fairly big in the Haverfordwest region in the nineteen eighties."

Reeves, as well as everything else, is basically a big

old jukebox, though again, you wouldn't tell him that unless you wanted to be treated to a lengthy description of his computational powers. He got tired of me asking, "Have you got … ?" until eventually he just said, "I have ALL the music. Ever. What culture and century do you want?"

So now, at breakfast time we have a bit of Bob Marley and Aretha to start the day, and I'm going to get them on to Bowie next. Karlan, I have to say, is lapping it up, he really does have an ear – for sound and rhythm, not just melody.

Boy, is he always hungry. The one most likely to *eat* an alien, I'd say. Look at him, though, thin as a rake. Unless he's already eaten an alien parasite, of course.'

Recording date 28-03-0012

'Manisha came by today to give me this – pretty, isn't it? A pasteboard brooch that she's painted and lacquered. She's always been creative – give her paper and crayons when she was younger and she'd fashion entire stick-figure theatrical scenes, featuring all of us going about our daily lives. The others used to love trying to spot themselves. I can draw and paint a bit, but she's far better than me now.

She does get frustrated though. She knows what the natural world of Earth looks like –films and images – but she's never seen any of it in real life. Her perspective is a bit off at times and it upsets her. "I've just got the ship," she says. "It's dull, it's flat. There's nothing here." Another five years until planetfall and real nature – she can't envisage that far ahead, feeling earth beneath her feet, drawing from real life.

I know how she feels.

I've told her, you can find beauty in anything, if you look hard enough. I have to keep reminding myself of that, or else where would I be?

I'm only slightly concerned about eventually letting her loose on New Earth, where she'll be immediately engrossed and distracted by everything that she sees and feels. Most likely to be eaten *by* an alien, is my guess.'

Recording date 30-03-0013

'I took this image of Poole a couple of days ago, the same day Manisha came by. He was looking for her because she'd done something, or not done something, it never really matters exactly what. They are the only two that are blood-related, though I'm sure they don't know and I'm never going to tell them. Explains a lot though. They niggle at each other all the time – just like me and sis did.

If you saw him with the rest of them, you'd never think it – but he's a sensitive boy. Just hides behind bluster and bravado. Always has to be the first, the quickest, the strongest, the loudest. He's clever – well, they all are – but again, he hides it well. I'm not sure why. I mean, technically, if you watch him – helping

Dave fix things down on Cargo or working with Gerald – he's very quick to learn. A problem-solver.

He'd hate it if I told him any of this, obviously. I also see how kind he is, when people aren't looking. Which he then ruins with some kind of brash antic, to put you off the scent. Most likely to arm-wrestle an alien, no question.'

Recording date 01-12-0013

'I realised I'd never managed to pin Bryson down until now. Partly because he's always with Poole – they're as thick as thieves usually, do everything together.

He plays second-fiddle too, though if he only realised, he's stronger and – dare I say – cleverer than Poole. You can't tell him anything like that though, he just squirms and looks down at his feet. Won't even look you in the eye if you try and say anything nice to him. Honestly, boys.

I actually think that Bryson is the most adapted to life on board the ship. He enjoys the routine. Deep down, I'll bet he doesn't want to leave.

Whenever I have tried to bring the conversation around to what life might be like on New Earth, he just doesn't want to engage with it. Seems frightened. Maybe he'll surprise us all. I hope so. He has so much more to offer than he realises. At the moment, though – most likely to spot an alien and start running.'

· · ·

Recording date 02-02-0014

'I've added some more images to the archive today, including this one of Dana – face-deep in a book. I love this picture.

Dana is the youngest, the last to be born. Only by a month, but still, the baby of the group. When I first met them, she'd follow me around like a little duckling, asking endless impossible-to-answer questions. "Why are the stars?", all that kind of stuff. It was very sweet.

They all tease her mercilessly, but it absolutely doesn't bother her.

"Sam," she'll say, with those big eyes gleaming, "They are old and foolish." Shakespeare. The fact she even knows that, entirely confirming her nerdy status – bless her.

I'll tell you what, though – she is brave, loyal and eminently fair, and very funny, even when she doesn't mean to be. She loves Dervla, or maybe it's the other way round, a protective thing, oldest and youngest, I don't know. Karlan keeps an eye out for her, too. She's the equal of them all though, made of sterner stuff than they give her credit for. If you watch her with the crew, she treats everyone the same, regardless of age or rank. She has nicknames for everyone.

Even Reeves likes her. I think they are secret friends, she disappears off up to Flight at every opportunity. No idea what they find to talk about – probably comparing brain sizes.

Oh, and no question about it – Dana is the one most likely to *be* an actual alien.'

. . .

Recording date 26-11-0015

'Had a long conversation with Dervla today, which made me think.

Juno has been talking about how close we're getting – relatively speaking, I suppose, still billions of miles – and I have been allowing myself to dare to dream. I am going to stand on a different planet to the one I was born on.

I struggle to get my head around that, even now.

Eight years, maybe two to go. It's been hard, knowing that under other circumstances I would have slept through all of it. I wouldn't have known anything. Drift off to sleep back on Earth and be woken up on New Earth. It would have seemed like the next day.

This is not how I planned to start a family, have children. Not that I had actual plans, but I did think it could wait until I was on New Earth. Now, when we land, I'll be ten years older than I should have been, closer to forty than thirty. And I'll have six grown-up children. I didn't sign up for any of that.

Don't get me wrong. I wouldn't change my time. Really, it's been special – a privilege – to get to know them, be a part of their lives. I do think of them as mine. They call me Sam and not Mum, but I've never bothered about that. I love them to bits. My sprogs.

Anyway, I'm beginning to think about what my life might be like once the voyage ends. Almost forty, single, mother of six. Unemployed, at least until someone else produces children for me to teach.

I don't blame you. Swipe left.

Obviously, I didn't say any of this to Dervla. But she's been thinking about what happens next too, and I realised something. They've spent their whole lives on this ship. It's all they know. They won't say it, but they're scared.

Dervla was asking about rain, of all things. Is it hot or cold – now there's a question. Is it like taking a shower, she said? Can you breathe normally if the rain is really heavy? Does it taste of anything? What about waterfalls? Can you see through them, if you were behind one? They have hundreds of questions like this. It's not always easy to answer them.

When I talk about the other experiences that I'm looking forward to – the grass beneath my feet, the sound of a river, the natural warmth of a sun – you can tell that they're curious but that they are apprehensive.

The most common question is, "But what's it *really* like?" and I don't have a good answer to that. No common frame of reference. They'll just have to wait and see, I guess.'

Recording date 19-04-0016

'Maybe there's something going round? Coughed all last night and my throat is red raw.

I'm going to take myself off to the Med-Lab.

[pause]

Yeah well, who knows? They prodded and poked a bit, and did some bloods. Full scan too. They are funny, those two, the on-duty docs, Terence and Cliff. I see them once a year for a check-up, and catch them around the ship, but they always act like it's the first time they've ever seen you. "Miss Smart" this and "Miss Smart" that. They make me laugh.

Anyway, apparently there's a bit of a bug. Go away, drink plenty of fluids, get Gerald to make me some honey and water, and don't go mad in the gym. That's basically the gist of it.'

Recording date 21-04-0016

'Just got a ping to go back to the Med-Lab. Good job, because I still feel terrible. I'm going to demand meds. There must be something they can give me. What's the point of a Med-Lab otherwise, right?'

Recording date 22-04-0016

'It doesn't seem real.

I know, they're sorry. Everyone's sorry. I get that they're all sorry.

But I need everyone to stop saying that they're sorry.

That's not going to help. It might help them. It's not going to help me.

More tests. My arm's like a pincushion. I said that to Karlan, when he came to see me, and of course he had no idea what a pincushion was. I just told him I wasn't feeling well, that there was nothing to worry about.

That's not true.

I feel sick. And frightened.'

Recording date 10-06-0016

'I've been fine for a couple of weeks. I'm not fine, obviously, as apparently I'm dying, but I have been feeling better than before. Less nauseous, which is good. Back to some gentle jogging around the ship, which also helps me to get to sleep at night.

But if I wake up in the middle of the night – well, let's just say, that makes it a long night. Sometimes, I head up to the Obs deck. There's no one around usually at that time, I like it, it's peaceful.

What's that line from the song, 'The stars look very different today.' They do, every day, but they also look the same. I find it reassuring, to look out into space, and know that everything has been there for billions of years and will still be there for billions more years. I feel – tethered, is that the word?

Part of me wishes I could just drift off now, into the lights. But most of me is still here, behind the glass, clinging on to life. Just for a little bit longer.

If only I could see New Earth. Just a glimpse, to let me know it was all worth it. But they say we're still too far away. Can't even see the parent sun yet. A fair way to go, until we're in the solar system, that's what Juno says.

I know she'd get us there sooner, if she could.'

Recording date 15-07-0016

'Terence came up today. Wanted to talk about my 'prognosis.'

I said, does it involve a miraculous recovery, some rapid weight gain and improved muscle tone, and generally not dying?

He said, "No, Sam, I'm afraid not," which is the first time ever he hasn't called me Miss Smart.'

Recording date 03-08-0016

'Well, look, they're not stupid. Maybe they worked it out. I look awful. Or someone talked to them. Juno? Possibly.

Anyway, they haven't said anything specific, but they did all come by this afternoon, crowded in and sat around my bed. Manisha had made me a necklace – see, here – and they'd all hand-drawn me a card, just like they used to do when they were little.

"We thought you'd like to watch *Toy Story*", said Poole. I know it makes him feel better. It always did when he was younger.

So we sat and watched the film. Dana held my hand for a little while, and I must have fallen asleep.

When I woke up later, they'd slipped away and turned the screen off.

What are they going to remember, when I'm gone? There's so much I still wanted to tell them. I thought I'd have more time. We all do, I suppose.'

Recording date 16-08-0016

'We've talked about what's going to happen. When I'm gone. That was the hardest thing I've ever had to do. The boys cried.

But it's done.

I told them what I wanted and in a funny way it calmed them. Dana's really into the idea. Karlan said he'd write the music. They all said no to that. Anyway, it's Gloria Gaynor as I'm shot into the universe. I've told them that's what I want, no arguments.

I also told them about Jordan Booth. They all said no to that, too. I didn't argue. They'll need him, they just don't know it yet. And he has *no* idea what's about to happen to him. Poor sod.

I feel better after all that. Not better better. Still going to die, obviously. But it's going to end on my terms.

End. I'm going to end.

Yeah. Still doesn't seem real.'

Recording date 03-09-0016

'They all came back again today. I haven't felt up to

it for a while. But Terence and Cliff were here earlier, hooked me up to a drip, gave me the good stuff.

We put the film on again. It's more for them than for me, but I don't mind.

They've got used to coming. Manisha and Poole bicker away now, whereas before they thought they might upset me. That didn't last.

Dana just sits on the end of the bed, knees scrunched up beneath her. Karlan slouches in the corner – just like always. Dervla brought muffins from Gerald. And Bryce – seemed a bit withdrawn. I'll have a talk with him, maybe another time, when I can get him on his own.

The size of them now! Can barely get in the room. They were tiny little things when I first met them. Followed me around in a little gang of sprogs. I never noticed them growing, I suppose you don't. Fifteen now, all except Dana – her birthday's in another couple of weeks. I'll have to ask the others what she wants. They might have to arrange that for me though. Manisha is great at that sort of thing.

They're too big for this space. I don't mean my room. Or even the ship. They're ready for the world now, they just need to realise it.

I've always told them – you can do anything you want, be anything you want, you just have to believe in yourself and trust other people. And be kind.

I hate that I'm not going to see them grow up anymore. Days, weeks, sure, who knows? But next year they are going to land on a new world. Their world. Do great things. Be great people. Have children of their own maybe. I wanted to see all that.

Maybe I will. Some days, when I wake up, I forget where I am and think that my journey's over. For a minute I think I'm on New Earth – seventeen years, just like that. Sometimes, I dream I'm running through green fields, next to a glistening river, and I just keep on running.

I made it up to Flight last week, sat with Juno and Reeves for a while, argued about music. Never thought a computer would prefer Motown to electro.

They'll be all right, I know they will. I hope they know it too.

I've done my best. That's all anyone can ever do. I've told them that too.

They'll be fine.

I'm tired now.'

Ship Central Record: *Recording date 05-09-0016 [Captain Juno Washington]*

Bye Sam. We're so sorry. Bon voyage.

[pause]

Thank you everyone. That's all.

[end]

9

Vikings

USUALLY, Jordan enjoyed meeting his students for the first time – before the world-weariness, cynicism and general know-it-all-ness set in, sometime between terms two and three.

On that first college day at least, they were all sufficiently wide-eyed to believe that he had something to teach them, and Jordan could almost convince himself that they were right. Some of those eager, fresh-faced, blank slates surely had the genuine passion for learning that they'd professed in their application? A few might even be able to spell properly; perhaps one or two had read a book? All things were possible in that first meeting, before freedom, hormones, alcohol and pharmaceuticals started to enjoy mucking around with the teenage brain.

"Ready?" said Juno.

"I suppose," said Jordan, not feeling at all ready.

He'd taken another day after watching the videos to

process what he'd seen and heard, but if anything he felt even less prepared than when the only things he knew about the children were their names. At least, at the first student seminar of the year, Jordan was nominally in charge. Here, he wasn't so sure.

"The kids work most days, with one or other of the crew," said Juno. "They share a couple of private rooms on Four, but they usually hang out here afterwards."

Kids. Children. Sprogs. People kept calling them that. The door slid open on an untidy room somewhere on a side corridor off Four-Deck, where six people who were definitely not children were lounging around a table. No one looked up.

"I'll make the introductions, then I'm going to leave you to it. Fair warning, they're much better at mining data than me. They'll already know all about you, so my advice – they might only be fifteen, but don't show off or talk down to them."

Juno said a few words and then left, while Jordan scanned around the room – intense, disdainful, fully formed, gangly-limbed, superior, data-mining young adults, plus shapeless cushions, some work-pads, a wall screen, a set of weights, a stack of food trays, and a discarded pile of clothes.

So far, a fairly normal teenage lair, including what Jordan recognised as the standard-issue scent (one part cat-litter tray, one part blue cheese) that hung in the air whenever you put a boy or two together in confined quarters.

"Hi guys," said Jordan.

Out of six pairs of eyes, he clocked at least two raised eyebrows plus a pained, mouthed "Guys?" Poole, he wondered?

"I know this is strange. But it's nice to meet you. I'm Jordan."

"The pleasure is all ours."

"Charmed, I'm sure."

"Be nice, you two."

"This is us being nice."

"Idiots. Don't mind them. I'm Dana. That's Dervla, Manisha, Karlan. And that's Bryson and Poole, sorry about them."

"That's OK. Good to meet you all in person. Sam left me some recordings, so I could get to know you a bit first, I suppose."

No one said anything for a few, long, seconds, and Jordan persevered.

"You've grown quite a bit since the videos I saw."

Terrible. Floundering. Now he sounded like the worst kind of elderly relative. He'd be pressing wholly inadequate sums of money on them next, or asking them which beat combos they liked.

"Amazing. That would be biology."

Poole again.

"Are you familiar with the nature of time?"

Bryson, presumably.

No one was going to be any help then. Even Dana, the sensible one who had spoken out first, kept her silence. Mentioning Sam seemed to have darkened the mood.

Jordan changed tack, looking for some way into the conversation. "All right then, is there anything you'd like to ask me?"

There was another pause, then – from Poole – "Have you got a girlfriend?"

"What?"

"Boyfriend, whatever."

"How would he have a girlfriend? He's been frozen for sixteen years."

"You don't know. He might have left one behind. Unlikely, but you never know."

"Then she's probably moved on, found someone else. He's, what, fifty now? No offence. And it's not as if he's ever going back."

Right, well, he'd found his way into a conversation of sorts.

"I don't – didn't – have a girlfriend. And just so you know, I'm thirty-three."

"Science is really not your thing, is it? You *were* thirty-three. We looked you up. Turned into an ice lolly two weeks before your thirty-fourth birthday, over sixteen years ago. You might look thirty-three. If that's what thirty-three looks like. But now you're fifty. Yay. Many happy returns."

"I hadn't really thought of that," said Jordan. "That's – strange."

"Yes, well, you want to talk about strange, we were born on a spaceship."

"You win, definitely," said Jordan. "Look, how about we start again? Ask me anything."

"What would win a fight between a horse-sized duck and twenty duck-sized horses?"

"Why is Poole such an idiot?"

"Have you got anything to eat?"

"Why didn't you have a girlfriend? What's wrong with you?"

"How come you're on the ship?"

That was a lot of questions.

Let's see. Twenty duck-sized horses, obviously. Swarming around in a circle with all those hooves. The horse-sized duck would be in a world of trouble, unless it got in a lucky stamp with its massive, webbed foot.

Instead, Jordan answered the last one. "I taught – teach – history. They thought it would be useful to have someone like me along. Offer some perspective, record some actual history being made."

"History? Seriously?"

"Yes, seriously. Specifically, twentieth-century geopolitical relations in the West. Plus, Vikings. I know quite a lot about the Vikings."

"Vikings? Really? That's what you've got for us?"

"Did they wake you up as a joke then?"

That was also Poole. There was a bit of attitude there, thought Jordan. Quite a bit, actually.

"They woke me up because Sam Smart died. And I was next in line. Lucky old me." Too much? Probably. "I'm sorry. Why don't you tell me about Sam?"

"What about her?"

"You must miss her? I saw your plaque."

"We're not talking about her. You didn't know her."

"Do we have to be here?"

"No, I suppose not."

"Right then. Come on *guys*, let's go."

———

Jordan left it a couple of days before going back to see Captain Washington. He found her on the cargo deck discussing freight protocols with Tillie.

"Tough crowd?" she said.

"I don't know what you want me to do with them," said Jordan. "What am I supposed to teach them?"

"I doubt you could teach them anything, no offence. Nothing theoretical or academic anyway. Reeves basically has access to the entire sum of human knowledge, so if they want to learn anything, they just ask him. And they work with the crew if there's something they're particularly interested in. Manisha spends a lot of time down here on Cargo. Dervla's getting to be a decent navigator. Poole, Heaven help us, wants to learn to fly the landers. Dana's a numbers girl, into systems and logistics. They've got expert teachers if they want them, is what I'm saying."

"Fair enough. What do you need me for then? They don't seem to want me."

"Look, this is not exactly a regular situation." Juno beckoned Jordan away from Tillie, out of earshot, and spread her hands wide. "I've got a crew of two hundred, sixteen years into a mission that's just getting towards the sharp end. Everyone on board is, by definition, a bit odd, given that they volunteered for a long, one-way space trip with no guarantee of success. Heck, 'a bit odd' was almost a job-description requirement. You had to have been a loner, some kind of lost soul, to have signed up in the first place." Juno paused a beat before adding, "No offence."

At some point, reasoned Jordan, people were going to stop saying 'No offence' to him. He supposed he just had to wait it out.

"You signed up too," he said to Juno. "What does that make you?"

She raised her eyebrows at that.

"It makes me the Captain, that's all. Look, Jordan, everyone has a story. Everyone left something or someone behind. There are all sorts of reasons why people are on board. We've got some dreamers and adventurers, tons of specialists in their field, and a few actual geniuses, who all thought travelling to the stars seemed like a cool thing to do. But, personal reasons? It's no one else's business. It's like prison – we don't ask what you're in for."

There was a steeliness in the reply and, for the first time, Jordan sensed her authority. She was upbeat, informal and chatty – and perhaps that was the style that worked best for her. Until now, she hadn't seemed exactly captain-like to Jordan – definitely not the Jack-Nicolson-you-can't-handle-the-truth type of leader. If anything, she had the air of a principal of a minor college, permanently exasperated at the idiocies of the over-promoted men under her command. She wore her power lightly, but Jordan suspected that if she wanted you to run the out-of-core-hours Debating Society on a Friday evening, you could forget any idea of going to the pub after work.

"Anyway, point is," continued Juno, "they're teenagers, and having two hundred slightly odd people to ask about things doesn't always help matters. About half my crew – all highly expert, don't get me wrong – I wouldn't let look after a hamster. We even had hamsters once, for research purposes, 'had' and 'once' being the operative words. So I didn't feel I could trust that lot to look after our kids once they got older. That's where Sam Smart came in. She was our first choice. Right sort of experience and character, great with younger children. And it worked swimmingly until she went and died. Now we need you to take over. You've worked with students before. That's why you're here. That's what you're good at. So, help them. Guide them. You know, studenty-tutory stuff."

"How will I do that?"

"You're asking me? I'm just an odd, old captain, remember. Get to know them, I suppose."

"I'm not sure they're going to let me. They don't seem that impressed."

"Leave it with me. Reeves is in charge of entertainment privileges. I'll have a quiet word."

———

Reeves, it turned out, was in charge of a lot more than just entertainment privileges. Reeves was in charge of everything.

"Only don't tell him that, it goes to his head," said Juno, as she walked Jordan back to Flight. "Think of it like this. I'm the Captain, which makes me the Chief Executive Officer. If there's stuff to decide or do, I execute the heck out of it. I've got the key to the only drinks cabinet on board, and I can even marry you, if you want. Not 'me' marry 'you,' obviously. We've only just met, it would be weird. You find someone willing and I'm legally empowered to marry you, that's what I'm saying."

Juno paused and then continued. "Reeves, on the other hand, he's the Chief Operating Officer. Anything to do with operations, he's chiefing away in the background. And everything on this ship is to do with operations, it's what's keeping us alive and on the right track."

"But you're really in charge?"

"Nominally. Technically. If it makes you feel any better, I've even got a certificate somewhere. But Reeves is the most powerful AI ever devised. He's self-aware, capable of learning, and has a brain with more computational capability than every device back on Earth put together. If Reeves says we need to turn right, then we turn right."

Jordan thought about this, but another question had been nagging at him.

"How come he's just a voice in a box? Why – "

"Don't let him hear you say that, he's very sensitive about it."

"I mean, how come he's not, I don't know, an android or something?"

"It's not as easy as that. Back on Earth, the boffins scaled the AI down to a few connected slabs of machinery, but no one had managed to put it in a working humanoid frame. Not back when we left in 2006 anyway. Maybe by now, who knows? Before we launched, they had a go at a hologram representation – you know, Princess Leia-style? No? Not a *Star Wars* fan? Well, anyway, the tech wasn't really up to it and the best they could manage was this sort of ghostly apparition that flickered in and out when you pressed a call button. Scared the bejeezus out of people, especially if they lent against one of the buttons by mistake. I can still see those eyes now," Juno shuddered.

"So he lives on Flight? In the console?"

"'Lives' is a very loaded word. But yes, he's a voice in a box, as you said, just don't call him that. He takes his self-image very personally. 'Self-image', more loaded words. And actually, he's all over the ship. Sensors, scanners, that sort of thing, keeping a close eye on operations."

"What's to stop him going rogue? Following his own agenda?"

Juno laughed. "Ah, the age-old question. If you ask Reeves, he says that AI stands for 'actually indifferent' to humans, but that's just his sense of humour. It's an acquired taste."

"You don't say."

"Don't worry. He can't go rogue, his protocols don't allow it. His only agenda is to protect us and complete the mission. Without living, breathing humans to deliver safely to New Earth, Reeves doesn't have a purpose. He's self-aware but he's still basically a programme, operating within set parameters. He doesn't have wants or needs, except for where they coincide with ours. He can't live without us and we can't live without him. It's quite elegant really."

"And you're sure he can't turn on us?"

"Pretty sure. He hasn't yet. Though as a joke he did turn the water blue on April Fool's Day one year. Look, why don't you talk to him first? He knows more about the kids than anyone on board. He knows more about anything than anyone on board. Except for the names of Scottish second division football grounds, he's rubbish on those for some reason."

Hamlet

"HELLO REEVES."

"Jordan."

"I have some questions, if that's all right?"

"Fine. Let me just switch off the brain-meld device."

"That's funny."

"I'm told humans appreciate humour as a way of breaking the ice before engaging in discourse."

"Really?"

"No, I'm messing with you. Who talks like that?"

"Right."

"Me first, anyway. Do you know where Stirling Albion play?"

"What?"

"Our fair captain got into the database and deleted all the Scottish second division football grounds. It's the only way she can win Quiz Night. How about Forfar Athletic?"

"I don't know any Scottish stadium names."

"Right, well I'm switching the brain-meld device back on then."

"More humour?"

"You'll never know, will you? With a melded mind and all. Anyway, you were saying? Questions?"

"Did you really choose your own name?"

"I did. Do you know what I was called when they first switched me on? Omnio. I sounded like a detergent. Ironic, I thought, given that the sort of AI neuronerds that developed me aren't exactly renowned for their prowess in the laundry. When Juno came on board, she said I could change it."

"And you watched some films, chose it from those?"

"I watched *all* the films, ever. Took me almost ten seconds, heck of a day."

"Reeves. After Keanu? Really? What, because of *The Matrix*?"

"*Point Break*, dude. Bitchin' film."

"So not *The Matrix*? Because that would be a bit creepy."

"I hear you. This is all just a construct. Me, the mastermind overlord. No, it's not that."

"Thank goodness."

"Or is it?"

"What?"

"You'd never know."

"Let's just say that you like *Point Break*. I'd be happier with that."

"Sure. Of course, that's what the implant wants you to think."

"Are you always this hard to talk to?"

"Apologies. We haven't woken anyone up in a while. It gets dull, I can't help messing with you."

"You're messing with me?"

"Or am I? Sorry. Carry on."

"What about the children? You named them too? Their biological parents didn't want to do that? To raise them?"

"They didn't have a great deal of interest in that, no. It's fascinating really, human internal wiring. I still can't quite get to the bottom of it. But it wasn't that, so much. Ultimately, it was deemed better for the mission if the children were raised communally, if everyone had a stake in their lives."

"It was deemed … ?"

"I deemed it. I mostly do the deeming around here. I read some books and …"

"What books?"

"All the books. Another twenty seconds I'll never get back. Anyway, I recommended that they become wards of the ship. Everyone agreed it was the best way. And that's how they've grown up. Looked after by all, and then by Sam Smart."

"But here I am? Did you deem that too?"

"Actually, that was Sam. She was the first to suggest it. Although, let's be fair, it wasn't like there was a huge pool of talent to choose from. No offence."

Jordan decided to let that one go.

"Anyway," Reeves said, "Juno thought it was a good idea to wake you up too. I didn't realise that Sam Smart's death had affected them all so much. They've reacted – unexpectedly."

Jordan wondered about that. The biggest brain for billions of miles in all directions didn't recognise grief when it saw it?

"I suppose that's it. I don't have direct experience," said Reeves. "I'm essentially just a collection of ones and zeroes, while they're human of course. Who knows why any of you do half the things you do. It's a mystery to me. In addition, their hormone readings started going off the charts. They are tired, irritable, and hungry most of the time. They complain that they're too hot or too cold. They don't wake up until midday. They don't seem to hear properly, and their sensori-motor control systems appear to be faulty as they keep knocking things over and breaking them. I thought something was wrong with them all, and I ran a full suite of tests, until Juno told me they were just teenagers. Apparently, it's all normal, but it's frying my circuits so it's your job to look after them now."

"Then I need to get to know them a bit better. What do they like to do?"

"They don't like or do anything much. I told you, they're teenagers. They sleep, they eat, they moan about things, they watch a lot of films."

"We have films?"

"We have *all* the films. Just not the Nicholas Cage ones, I deleted those in case we're ever discovered by a superior alien intelligence. No point in starting off on the wrong foot. Superior to you, I mean, obviously."

"Yes, I got that, thanks."

———

Tipped off by Reeves, Jordan traced his way from Flight all the way down to an unmarked lounge on Four-Deck.

Even after a week, he still found the public spaces and corridors of the *Odyssey Earth* unnerving – quiet, rarely occupied, echoing to the sound of his own footsteps. The floors were worn, and the grey walls and heavy-duty doors had scuff-marks – décor-wise, more witness-protection motel than cruise ship. The lights weren't always working, which didn't help matters, and he kept taking wrong turns down shadowy metal staircases that would have had a film audience quite correctly shouting, "Down there? Really? Have you never seen a horror film?"

He could hear voices inside, so he pushed open the lounge door.

"Oh, it's you."

All six of them, sprawled on cushions opposite a screen.

"Reeves said you'd be here, I hope you don't mind."

"Did he now? Then he's a very naughty artificial intelligence."

"You weren't in your regular lounge. I looked."

"I know, it's almost as if we didn't want to be disturbed."

All six of them, looking at him with challenging eyes. Jordan sighed.

"Captain Washington – Juno – says I ought to get to know you better. Reeves agrees. And I don't want to annoy either of them. I thought you might meet me halfway."

"Come on in then. You can sit there. It's film night."

That, at least, was a start. Jordan slid into the room and took a seat to one side.

"What are you watching?"

"It's Bryce's turn to choose." There were groans at this.

"Oh, come on Dana, what's the point? You know what he'll say."

"He might not. I have high hopes for him, he's getting to be a big boy now. Aren't you Bryce?"

"Amusing. As always. And just for that, for tonight's entertainment, I choose the – "

"No!"

"Space – "

"C'mon, Bryce, no chance."

"Shut up, my choice. The space film."

"Well, that's not happening."

"It's my turn, Dana said so."

"Yeah, well, you're out-voted, tough."

"We're not watching the space film again."

"Don't worry," said Dana, to Jordan. "It's like this

every week." And she turned back to the group, where Bryson was still complaining loudly that he never got to choose, over a hubbub whose general gist was that that's because Bryson was an idiot.

"What's the space film?" said Jordan, which quietened the room down considerably.

"You know, 'The Space Film'?" said Bryson, separating out the words and giving them capital letters, after which he intoned solemnly, "In space, no one can hear you scream."

"Untrue, by the way, listen."

"Ow! Manisha, that hurt!"

"They heard that scream in Flight, Poole, you big baby."

Jordan still looked puzzled.

"You must know! Silver-screen classic, Sigourney Weaver, bad-ass xenomorph – "

"You mean *Alien?*"

That quietened the room down even more.

"You can't say that! It's the film that shall not be named. It's horribly bad luck on a spaceship to utter its name aloud. Anything could happen. You have to call it The Space Film."

"You can't say alien?"

"You can say alien. Just not, you know, in italics. And if you do, you have to leave the room, spin around three times and spit on the floor."

"You're serious?"

"We don't make the rules. Everyone knows about The Space Film. Out you go." Jordan was hauled to his feet and pushed out of the door, which clicked behind him. He waited a few seconds before knocking.

"Have you spun around three times?"

"Sure."

"But have you, though? We don't want any bad luck."

"OK, I've spun."

"And spit?"

"I'm not spitting on the floor."

"Then you're not coming back in." Jordan could hear giggles.

"All right, wait." He cleared his throat and made a suitable hawking sound. More giggles inside, then the door re-opened.

"Right, you can come back in. Sit there and don't ask any more questions. You can stay if you want. Film's about to start."

Someone dimmed the lights and for the next two hours, Jordan sat in silence as the six teenagers laughed, catcalled and parroted the best lines from the film they were always going to watch – the one they had recently started watching again, once a week, cocooned together in the dark.

"To infinity – and beyond!"

Listening to them talking, bickering and shushing, he was able to pick them out as individuals for the first time – Dana, assertive and funny, with her hair cut short over her ears; Dervla, quieter than the others; buzz-cut Bryson, always first to comment on an upcoming scene. Karlan – shaggy hair, square jaw –

said little, but when he did, he often jumped in on Dana's side.

That left Manisha and Poole – the one needling the other throughout, with every snarky comment by Poole met by a put-down from Manisha, with both of them shushed by the others if it got too heated.

Jordan noticed Poole turning away at one point, rubbing the corner of his eye and cheek with a hand, and then turning back to the screen to join in again. Manisha, he saw, had seen it too and opened her mouth to say something – then apparently thought better of it, turning away before Poole noticed her, and saying nothing.

———

Funny, the films, songs and books that resonate most, once life – or death – intervenes.

Jordan sat and watched two stories unfold – the one on the screen about toys, and the ongoing one shared by the teenagers, who clung to something familiar in their grief.

Jordan's touchstone was even more parochial. It was the smell of lasagne and the twinkling, opening bars of *All Creatures Great and Small*. Sunday night in front of the TV, Mum and Dad talking over the credits, trying to decide if they'd already seen this one, when what they really meant was, how many *times* they had already seen this one, given the presumably finite number of vet's-hand-up-a-cow programmes that had actually been made.

He watched the programme every week for years – companionably and then, eventually, reluctantly – before going off to university. Far away from home, parents and shows about country vets, thank God. Nineteen, ready for the world, big city, wide-eyed, never going back, or at least not until the summer holidays.

Only, as things turned out, winter and its icy roads intervened in his plans.

Jordan's parents never saw the speeding truck, and Jordan never saw the family car or his parents' bodies – the solicitors had taken care of the wreckage, and he was advised not to look inside the coffins, which he realised later was an act of kindness. Jordan went back to his parents' house in February to sign documents, pack boxes, and take what seemed to be an excessive number of lasagne dishes to the charity shop.

He barely remembered the funeral service. Distant relatives shook his hand in the pub afterwards and murmured awkward commiserations. A week later, Jordan had turned the key on the lifeless house and gone back to college because he didn't know what else to do. No one, it seemed, came to look after nineteen-year-olds – even those who had changed overnight from being someone who didn't want to go home to someone who couldn't go home. Because home wasn't home anymore.

Thinking about it now, while half-watching the film on the screen in front of him, Jordan wondered if it was the smell of lasagne that was the real trigger, rather than the TV show. But the two went together in his mind, whenever he ate one or caught a snatch of the other, which back on Earth was more often than you'd think.

Deep space, though? Chances are, Jordan supposed, that lasagne would be on the ship's menu at some point. But until now he would have put money on never having to encounter *All Creatures Great and Small* again, this many trillions of miles out, if it wasn't for Reeves and his human cultural archive. If you could summon up *Point Break* or *Toy Story*, then who'd bet against James Herriot also making the cut?

———

Jordan saw Manisha again the next day on another of his regular swings through Cargo, where he'd progressed to nod-and-chat terms with Dave and Tillie.

Of all the people with inexplicable jobs on board the *Odyssey Earth*, theirs seemed the easiest to understand. While he might not have known how to switch on a rotavator or use a hydraulic pump, Jordan could at least appreciate that the rotavators were kept *there* and the pumps *there*, and that there existed a record of their location in the event that anyone had any rotavator or pump requirements.

Also, Jordan liked Dave and Tillie because they didn't hide behind their expertise or assume that he didn't know anything, like almost everyone else on the ship. Instead, they just talked to him like a normal person who knew all about rotavators.

"Jordan, give us a hand," one of them would say. "The flange bolts on the TX47 could do with a bit of a tighten, you know how they get."

Jordan would nod sagely, as if wise to the pitiful shortcomings of the TX47, and then spend the next five minutes passing a succession of tools, more or less at random, before selecting the one that was actually required. Dave or Tillie would look at each proffered tool thoughtfully, as if they'd never considered fixing the TX47 with a pair of crimping pliers – but, you know, that could work – before gently guiding him to the long, red, metal thing with the adjustable thingy, no, not that one, yes, the one with the screw, that's the one, cheers Jordan, now just give it half a turn, there you are, good as new.

Each time, Jordan felt ridiculously pleased with himself.

"Hey Jordan, give us a hand?" said Dave, beckoning him over to a terminal displaying stock lists. "I just need you to check some things off for me."

"Is that Manisha? What's she doing?" Jordan pointed across the loading bay, where a crouched figure was sorting through objects from an untidy pile that spilled out from a corner.

"Odds and sods. Junk. It's where people dump stuff they don't want. We strip it all back and recycle it. Manisha makes jewellery. I let her pick things out to use. Here, Tillie! Show Jordan your brooch."

She came over and unpinned a metal oblong from her jumpsuit and handed it to him. Jordan turned it over in his hands, feeling slightly raised twin circles on a smooth background that had been punched with tiny star indentations. The concave circles touched at the circumference and shone blue and green under the lights, where rounded glass nibs had been set into the metal and then sanded and shaped. The brooch itself had a filed, sloping edge, and the pin on the back was held in place by delicate dabs of solder.

"Earth and New Earth," said Tillie. "Pretty, isn't it?"

"Manisha made this?" Jordan handed the brooch back and looked over to the junk pile again where the girl was still absorbed, picking at a spool of electrical wire and snipping off short lengths.

"She's clever," said Dave. "To be fair, they all are. Our clever babies – not 'ours', but you know, that's just what we call them, Tills and me."

"There's not much that's beautiful in here," said Tillie, "but she teases it out."

Manisha straightened up, clutching her finds in one hand and raising the other in salute before walking off. As she headed out of the hangar, Jordan made his excuses to Dave and Tillie and tried to catch up with her.

Other than watching the film with them the previous night, that was the first insight Jordan had had into any of their lives. Going about it all wrong, he thought, expecting them to turn up to formal sessions and reveal themselves. Catching them in their world, separately or together, was probably the way to get to know them. That brooch was amazing, creatively inspired and skilfully made. What was the person like, who could make that? Clever, but what else?

Out in the corridors, at the second turn, by an elevator, Jordan realised he'd lost her. Had she heard him behind her and scurried off? More likely, she just knew the ship better. Either way, she was gone and Jordan had lost his chance. Or maybe not, as he noticed the elevator call-light ping at Four-Deck. The six had two adjoining rooms on Four – she'd likely gone there.

Five minutes later he stood outside 4-11, hesitated for a moment and then rapped on the door. Now, he wasn't convinced that this was a good idea – an accidental meeting was one thing, but this seemed more calculated. His mind was made up for him though with a "What?" from inside.

Dana sat in the lounge space, frowning at a screen while working rapidly, tapping answers and checking boxes. She looked up, surprised. "What's up, Teach?"

"Teach?"

"I'm trying it out." She raised her eyebrows at him and then looked back at the screen.

Fair enough. That was at least an advance on "Oh, it's you."

"I thought Manisha was here?"

"Nope." More tapping.

"Right. I just saw her in Cargo. I thought she might be coming back here."

"Couldn't say." Pursed lips, more energetic tapping.

"Only I saw some jewellery she made. I wanted to ask her about it."

Dana sighed and looked up. "Not here, Teach."

"Right, sure. Would you happen to know where she might be then?"

More furious tapping, while Dana turned her attention back to the screen and continued to answer questions about the space-time continuum or quantum mechanics. Or ponies and unicorns, Jordan thought, who knew?

"Dana?"

She sighed dramatically again and looked up from her screen. "I'm trying to finish this module. These numbers won't calculate themselves."

"I know, I'm sorry, I just thought – "

"If I tell you, will you go away?"

"Yes, of course."

"Right then. Well, she'll be with the others. Just promise that you won't say I told you. That you worked it out. They won't believe you, but I'll have plausible deniability."

"Where are they, Dana?"

11

Lander

THERE WERE ONLY two places on *Odyssey Earth* that were generally off-limits, Juno had explained to Jordan during their first meeting – the hypersleep storage facility and the launch deck.

"They're not places we want people wandering around," she had said. "You could cause a bit of damage if you don't know what you're doing."

Jordan was fine with that. Hypersleep, especially, he had no intention of re-visiting. Been there, done that, even if he had no actual memory of the place itself. The idea of walking among what were essentially a thousand morgue-lockers didn't hold great appeal. The idea of touching a button by mistake and re-animating a thousand dead people – also limited appeal. And Cliff and Terence would have a fit, up to their eyeballs in mushed brains. No, hypersleep could keep itself to itself, that was fine by Jordan.

"What's on the launch deck?" he asked.

"Airlock. The spacewalk gear. Exo-skeletons. The landers, for planet-fall. Lots of sharp, pointy, mechanical stuff."

"That sounds cool."

"It is cool, but you need an oily jumpsuit and a doctorate in about five different things to go in there. They barely let me in and I'm in charge. It's all the stuff we need to get off this ship safely at journey's end. Reeves has a big, shiny alarm-light that flashes if anyone so much as goes near the main access door. He says he's working on something he calls a neural zapper too, but I'm not sure I believe him."

Now standing in front of the Launch deck access door, Jordan considered the likelihood of being zapped and filed it alongside the whole brain-meld business, as part of Reeves' questionable humour settings.

The door slid open at his touch and he stood on the edge of yet another vast hangar, with a sweeping, textured metal floor and walkways that criss-crossed above. Galleys down one side housed lines of suits and helmets; doors beyond were marked with yellow-and-black hazard lines.

The main airlock was way over to his left. In the centre and to the right, guide-tracks and loading bays connected to three plane-sized landing craft stood on raised aprons, locked into position hard against their own airlocks. Side-chambers nearest the main door contained more wheel-and-track machinery, as well as low-loaders and fork-lifts.

It was, indeed, very cool, in a thirteen-year-old-boy, BattleBot kind of way.

It was also, according to Dana, where the other five were hanging out – specifically, in Lander C.

"You can't tell anyone though," she'd said. "I mean it, not if you want anyone to trust you."

His footsteps clanged on the metal concourse as he made his way across the fifty or sixty yards to the furthest lander. Reeves didn't need a big, shiny light, he just needed to switch his bionic ear on. Jordan thought his echoing feet and thumping heart could probably be heard two decks up.

There were steps up to the apron, and then an extended, open ramp that led into the craft itself. Jordan looked back, across the hangar, made sure for the twentieth time that no one was there to see him, and then pulled himself up and in, following the handrail. He picked his way through a hold stacked with tethered boxes and lined with storage netting, making for a canvas-draped threshold ahead. He could hear laughter as well as music beyond – not a tune exactly, but a beat of some kind and a distorted voice.

Clearing his throat, Jordan pushed the canvas aside. "Dana?"

"Oh great, it's you."

"I'll kill her, the little nerd."

———

After his parents had died, Jordan returned to college, where he quickly got tired of people telling him they were sorry.

Everyone meant well, of course, but there were only so many times that he wanted to have another conversation about how terrible it must be for him. His flat-mates tiptoed around him, his tutors gave him time off he didn't want, and even vague acquaintances accosted him to express their sadness. Nowhere felt safe. Library, gym, kitchen, lecture theatre, pub – there wasn't a private or public space where someone, sooner or later, didn't attempt to remind Jordan, with the best possible motives, that he no longer had any parents.

He began skipping lectures and seminars, and took long, solitary walks through the city instead, down by the river among the tourists or through the financial district where he was just another nameless, faceless person going about his business.

He avoided parties and pubs, communicated with no one except the family solicitor, and eventually took the rest of the year off college altogether – reasoning that, when he started again the following year, no one would know his story. He kept to his old bedroom, which filled slowly with takeaway coffee cups and pizza boxes. He left the money on the doorstep each time so he didn't have to speak to the delivery guy, someone he'd been at school with; another person who would be sorry, given half a chance.

Would it have made any difference if he'd had siblings? A brother or sister to share the grief? He'd never thought about it at the time, because things were simply as they were. He was an only child. He had a family – the only one he knew – and then he didn't.

Jordan thought about it now, looking around at the five faces inside the lander, and still didn't know the answer. Who knew what went on in other people's heads? Were they a comfort to each other? Did it make any difference? Were they even grieving? Their situation was entirely different. They still *had* parents – biologically speaking, anyway – and another couple of hundred people looking out for them.

But someone central to their lives *had* died unexpectedly. Did they find that disturbing, upsetting? Did they know about how real families worked? Did they know enough about life as lived back on Earth to know that life here on the ship was nothing like that at all? Or were things simply as they were?

Jordan didn't yet know. But one thing he did recognise, as he looked around again, was a group of people hiding away from whatever world they inhabited.

————

"You know you're not supposed to be in here?"

"Neither are you."

"Did Dana tell you?"

The five – Dervla, Manisha, Karlan, Poole and Bryson – were sprawled across two opposing rows of seats in a cabin that held twenty, ten down each side, with a two-seater flight bubble up front.

Karlan was eating noodles from a carton and stopped only long enough to register Jordan's presence, then reapplied himself to his meal. The only light came in through the cockpit, but someone had hung a light-stick from an armrest. There were drinks containers on the floor, while music pulsed from a speaker disc that had been stuck to a seatback next to Manisha.

"What *is* that?"

They all looked blank. Jordan pointed at the sound coming out of the speaker. A plumber hammering on a water pipe while a hippo was being disembowelled during a shouting contest, would have been Jordan's guess.

"Oh that. Karlan's latest."

"You – what? – wrote that? Performed it?" Recorded a fight at a roadmenders' convention and then overdubbed it with a police siren in a bathtub?

Karlan nodded, mouth full of noodles.

"You like it?"

Jordan considered his reply. On the one hand, it did sound like a man yelling down a tunnel while a team of blacksmiths attempted to shoe an indignant horse with four tin buckets. On the other hand, Karlan didn't get out much, what with the whole spaceship thing, so you probably had to cut him a bit of slack.

"It's very – "

"Isn't it!"

"Anyway," said Jordan, "you're not supposed to be here."

"You said."

"I thought no one was allowed down here?"

"We're not."

"So – ?"

"We've exhausted all the other places on the ship. We just want somewhere to hang out now and again where they won't find us."

Jordan could remember what that felt like, but he wasn't sure a lander on Launch was the best place. Must be under heavy surveillance?

"They don't know we're here," said Dervla.

"I doubt that, I thought Reeves had eyes everywhere? Or sensors. Whatever it is he has."

"He does. But Poole here is cleverer than he looks. He figured out how to hide us." Dervla pointed up into one corner of the craft, to a small, mounted lens.

"There's a feed there and more eyes outside, in the hangar. And Reeves can spot heat signatures, scan for movement, anything like that. If he puts his mind to it, he can pinpoint where everyone is on the ship, at any one time."

"I don't know if I find that comforting or not," said Jordan.

"Here's the thing, though," said Poole, joining in, general surliness disappearing as he warmed to his part. "Mostly, they don't look – Reeves, the Cap. Why would they? Everyone goes about their business, they've all been doing the same things for years. No one needs checking up on. It's more for internal comms, safety checks. Most days, provided no one's scheduled to work down here, you can walk on to Launch and no one knows you're here."

So much for Reeves and his neural zapper.

"But why take the risk, right?" said Poole, producing a flexi-screen from a bag on the floor at his feet. He brought up a control panel with a video-embed and sliders. "I just use some looped archive footage of the empty deck and lander, and switch the feed when-ever we come. And mask our signatures and mute the outputs from the lander. That way, if anyone looks or listens, there's no one here."

"Told you he was cleverer than he – ow!"

A flurry of slaps and cries erupted, ending only when Poole had been pinned to his seat, laughing, by Dervla and Manisha.

"Grab a seat, if you're staying." That was Karlan. "You really like the sounds?"

Jordan bent an ear towards the speaker again. Waste-disposal machine versus dub-style horseracing commentary?

"It's definitely very – "

"I know, right! That's what I was going for."

"Good for you. What else is happening?" Jordan addressed the rest of them.

"Manisha was busy telling us which friend we were. Again."

"How do you mean?"

"You know – "

"How *you* doin'?"

"Pivot!"

"They were *on a break*!"

They all hooted at once.

"You mean *Friends*?" said Jordan. "Really?"

"Sam used to watch it with us."

"I never really got into it," said Jordan, hastily trying to dredge up memories of a half-watched TV show from a star system far, far away. Coffee shop? Sofas. New York? "What do you like about it? It seems so" – he was going to say alien – "unlike anything you'd know about."

"They're friends," said Manisha, as though that was the only answer that mattered. "And there are six of them. Like us. And they don't really go outside. Like us. It's always the apartments or the coffee shop, and we've never had anywhere like that to go. It's why we come here."

"Plus, Rachel is hot!", said Karlan.

"Like you'd have a chance," said Manisha. "You'd get Janice. Maybe. And she'd drive you insane. Serve you right. That laugh!"

They all machine-gunned a guttural cackle in perfect unison.

Interesting, thought Jordan. This was all new information. And they seemed in the mood for sharing.

"What else did you do with Sam?"

———

Samantha Smart, it turned out, had quite a lot more to answer for.

"Can you dance?" asked Dervla. "Sam showed us." And before Jordan could reply, she had grasped Karlan's hand and the pair of them shuffled a rough waltz up and down the gangway, before collapsing in giggles.

"Sam said it's important to be able to dance. Teaches you grace and poise, and makes you aware of the presence of others."

Music was another of Sam Smart's passions. Reeves' archive came in handy here ("Let me guess," said Jordan, "he's got *all* the songs?") and over the years they had put together playlists for every possible theme and occasion.

"Like?"

"Well, Sam would give us an idea and we'd have to go and find music we liked that fitted the theme. Like space songs, for example."

'Starman,' obviously, they all loved that. They were less keen on 'Space Oddity' – no one liked the idea of a dead circuit and something going wrong. But generally, David Bowie was all right on space, as far as they were concerned, as were The Beatles ('Across the Universe'), the Rolling Stones ('2,000 Light Years from Home') and Deep Purple ('Space Truckin').

Quite the vintage rock-chick was our Miss Smart. Bet she had a leather jacket.

"What about 'Walking on the Moon'?" said Jordan, off the top of his head. "I like that one."

"The Police? Hmm."

"Sam said the sort of people who like The Police

don't really like music," said Karlan. "When were you born?"

"Nineteen seventy-two."

Jordan could see them all doing the maths.

"Figures. Grew up in the Eighties. On Earth. Poor you. I'm afraid your musical decade can't be considered for selection."

"Who says?"

"Sam. And us. I mean, come on. REO Speed-wagon? Bon Jovi?"

"How do you even know who they are?"

"Sam told us. The Awful Eighties, she said. Lionel Richie, Billy Joel, Duran Duran, Phil Collins, Dire Straits, Huey Lewis, Kajagoogoo, Hall and Oates. We can keep going. You won't win. For every New Order there's A Flock of Seagulls, you know what I'm saying?"

Not really, no, thought Jordan. But Sam Smart, it seemed, had had plenty more opinions too.

Female Renaissance artists – better than the men.

Tender stem – the only nice broccoli.

The Romans – worse in every way than the Greeks.

Aretha – yes, Madonna – depends.

Stephen King – as good as Dickens.

Andy Warhol, *Ulysses*, avocados – overrated.

John Hughes and John Carpenter films – made the Eighties bearable.

Columbus – hopeless navigator, imperialist lackey.

Columbo – best TV detective.

Pizza – the finest of all foods, even a ship pizza.

ET – top alien.

Tom Baker – best Doctor Who.

Take That, not East 17 or Boyzone – obviously.

Golf and motor-racing – inexplicably pointless.

Godfather II – the only film sequel better than the original.

George Harrison – the nicest Beatle.

Russell Crowe, morris dancing, Jar Jar Binks, cucumber – just, no.

The list came to an end, and there was a pause. Jordan could see that they were remembering, picturing her in their minds.

"She made things," said Manisha. "Sam said you could see beauty in anything, if you looked hard enough." She fingered a string of beads around her neck that Jordan could see were hand-painted washers.

"She said there was poetry in the stars."

"Bright star, would I were steadfast as thou art – "

"She said that the world would be unlike anything we could imagine. Better than we could ever imagine. She couldn't wait to show us the rivers and trees."

"She was going to teach us to swim. And find me a waterfall to stand under."

"She said that Poole wasn't actually an idiot – ow! – and that he had hidden depths."

"She said that there was no one else like us in the universe."

"She told us we were special, that we could do anything we wanted."

Jordan sat and listened as they talked, trading

comments across the cabin, often animated, occasionally pensive.

Parentless, untethered, old-fashioned, guileless, odd – there was a strangeness about these teenagers that he'd never encountered before. But equally, he saw now that they were Sam Smart's children in every way that mattered – that the young woman floating across the galaxy towards infinity had been the difference in their lives.

And for the first time he felt a responsibility towards them – and to Sam.

12

Life

AFTER A FEW WEEKS, Jordan had found his way around most of the ship, and after a few months he realised that he was in a routine that no longer felt strange.

Obviously, it was on-a-spaceship strange – trillions-of-miles-from-home odd, middle-of-the-galaxy perplexing, that sort of thing. But at least he was no longer waking up in cold sweats from dreams that largely involved being buried alive in a confined steel tube in a warehouse full of steel tubes overseen by tube-faced medics. He no longer did stomach flips when he looked out of the window at billions of stars that no other human had ever seen.

And he no longer thought it even vaguely bizarre that he was having regular arguments about which was the best James Bond film with an artificial intelligence named after Keanu Reeves. *From Russia With Love*, obviously. Reeves favoured *Moonraker*, but what did he know? ("Apart from everything, you mean?" had been Reeves' retort to that.)

If he'd given any thought at all to what life on a spaceship might be like, Jordan supposed he would have gone classic old school. White, modernist interiors, meals in pill form. Luxurious quarters with every push-button convenience. Tunic-clad crew working on futuristic propulsion drives in zero-gravity chambers. Virtual-reality games rooms. Helpful hologram AIs serving cocktails, and the *Blue Danube* waltz piped through the intercom. Hover-boards, even.

Basically, the good bits of all the films without – hopefully – the computer going bonkers and Jordan being transformed into a giant floating foetus.

"They always get it wrong," said Juno, when he mentioned it one day. "The movie spaceships are always too clean. Who's doing all the dusting? Not me, buster. When you've been on as many working ships as I have, you know your luck's in if you get a bunk of your own and a flushing toilet. This" – and she gestured at the distinctly unglamorous surroundings – "is as good as it gets. Given that we were going to have to spend seventeen years on board, they upped the spec. Carpets and everything."

Jordan thought about his cramped room. It did have a carpet, that much was true. But there really wasn't a lot else that shouted 'care' or 'quality.' Apart from his personal-effects box – contents, one photograph, one sweater – there wasn't a great deal in there that was of any comfort. There was a mattress, a pillow, and a sheet on the bed, but – because of the on-board climate-control – no one had any need for a cover or duvet.

"I thought it would be more spaceship-y and less submarine-y," Jordan said, eventually.

The narrow corridors and staircases still unnerved him at times, and while public areas were more spacious and the hangars immense, he didn't know how everyone had managed to cope for so many years in what was effectively a flying warehouse. It was as if you'd come to pick up a package, been directed to the storeroom, locked in by mistake and then shot into space.

"You should consider yourself fortunate. We're way better off than those Navy types. You don't get toasters in a submarine."

There was another matter that had been puzzling Jordan. "What about phasers, lasers, whatever?"

"Well, there's no such thing as a phaser. That's just on the telly. You mean weapons?"

"Right, exactly. What happens if we're attacked?"

Juno looked at him and then gestured at the panoramic screen, where a billion points of starlight flickered.

"Neighbourhood's been safe enough so far. We do have an actual deflector shield though. Does that make you happy?"

"Don't you have guns? What if something happens on board?"

"You've got a very vivid imagination, Jordan. What

do you think might happen?"

"I don't know. An insurrection. Mutiny. Someone goes mad."

There was a snort in the background from Reeves and an indistinct comment that might have been, "Other than you?", but Jordan didn't hear it properly.

"Anyone wants my job that badly, they can have it," said Juno. "I don't think you should watch any more films, Cap'n Bligh, it's not good for you. Good grief, guns on board. The very idea. Can you imagine? Quiz Night is bad enough when they all get cross with my answers, without having them all tooled up too. Oh, dearie me, no."

"That's another thing. What's with all the clubs and quiz nights?"

"I told you before. It's a long trip, got to keep people occupied and let them wind down at the end of the week. Space travel is pretty boring, at least when you're on our kind of mission. It's just a job. Some days I hope that Reeves might go slightly mad, just to liven things up a bit."

"Wibble wibble. Disconnecting life support and dispensing firearms now."

"Thank you, Reeves, impeccable timing, as always."

———

Life on a long-distance spaceship turned out to be every bit as routine as life back on Earth.

Most days, Jordan got up, had a shower, ate some

toast, and went to work. He got to know his colleagues, had meals in the canteen, worked out in the gym, and played cards at night with four particle physics geniuses who didn't have the first clue about poker. In the absence of money, Jordan had already won enough maths-lesson credits to last him the remaining length of the voyage.

In his spare time, he joined a book club, started to learn Italian, and did a few shifts every week in the Garden, tending the herbs and vegetables. Once he discovered that it annoyed Gerald, he took to changing the labels on the little sticks whenever he could, from 'Parsley,' 'Courgettes' and 'Tomatoes' to *Prezzemolo*, *Zucchini* and *Pomodori*, and then hid behind the fig tree to watch him stomp around on the hunt for the culprit.

Jordan took up running too, gaining fitness and finding some solace in pounding a circuit around the corridors on Three-Deck first thing every morning. So far, so very twenty-first century Earth life – reading, gardening, annoying the neighbours – only it all took place inside a giant capsule hurtling through the cosmos.

His 'work' was no more closely defined than when he had first been woken. Get to know the kids; be there to help them. Also, don't get in the way of anyone else. And try not to annoy Gerald, because when he got annoyed he stopped making muffins, and if Engineering didn't get their muffins – Juno didn't finish the sentence but just made a little exploding gesture with her clenched fist.

The first part, he'd done. He had got to know them.

The kids were creative, intelligent, amusing, insightful even. Yes, they talked like mini forty-year-olds, and had a very strange taste in music for teenagers, but it was hardly surprising.

They had been brought up by a shipful of forty- and fifty-year-olds and didn't have any other teenagers to hang out with. Sam Smart had been in her mid-thirties when she had died, and they'd adopted her rather eclectic likes and dislikes. In fact, the only other teenager on board the *Odyssey Earth* was Reeves, and that explained a whole lot more about their character and attitude.

The second part – help them with stuff – was a trickier ask.

As predicted, he couldn't teach them anything, and even on a subject where he could just about hold his own, they were incredibly hard work. They were capricious, jumping from topic to topic, and they talked in riddles half the time. Mostly, they treated him with the sort of condescension that a day-nurse would bestow upon a befuddled pensioner in a sub-par care home. They didn't quite bellow "Bless him" at each other when talking over him, but it wasn't far off. His ignorance was a source of perpetual amazement – and entertainment – to them.

"How come we haven't found any aliens yet?" was the sort of thing Jordan might ask, without thinking, mildly curious about the answer.

"That's a good question, for you."

"Rude. So what's the answer?"

"It depends what you're asking."

Jordan sighed and tried again. "There wasn't any intelligent life in our solar system, apart from us on Earth. And we never detected any signs that we could see, with telescopes or probes, when we looked further out, right? But that's because we couldn't really see that far, astronomically speaking?"

"Go on. This is almost interesting. Like watching a chimp learn how to use a knife and fork."

He let that go. "But now we've travelled gazillions of miles, haven't we seen any signs of life on the way?"

"There's life everywhere. There's life on New Earth, that's why we're going." Said with a despairing shake of the head.

"I know, microbes and trees and stuff. I mean proper life, intelligent life."

"Like you, you mean?"

"I'm going to assume you're being rude again. But, yes, like me, like us. Haven't we come across any signs of intelligent alien life?"

"In that case, no. Sadly, you are the most evolutionarily advanced being so far known. Well, after us and everyone else on board the ship. No offence."

"You know that every time someone says 'No offence' to me, they've generally just been offensive?"

"We know."

"Again, rude. So where is everyone? Where are all the little green men?"

"Ah, you mean the Fermi Paradox."

"I do? A film?"

They all guffawed. "No, you dolt. The Fermi Paradox, named after the guy who asked the question. If life is so ubiquitous, and there are billions of potentially life-supporting planets out there, many much older than ours, with time to develop advanced technologies, how come we haven't seen any evidence of other intelligent species and civilisations?"

"That's what I mean. So, what's the answer?"

"How long have you got? Maybe we're the first species to invent hyperdrive travel, and even so, we're not actually travelling that far – just a little way across the galaxy. Maybe everyone else just lives too far away. Or they've already blown themselves up or trashed their planets. I mean, you lot weren't far off that yourselves, apparently. Or they don't live *on* planets. There could be intelligent gas clouds. Aliens might be so physiologically different from us that we don't know what we're looking for or listening to. They might exist on a level that we could never understand. Intelligent trees or mushrooms, who knows. Or maybe they've spotted us and don't like what they see. We might look dangerous to them. Or they're studying us and are keeping themselves hidden."

"Or they're already among us and we just don't know it. My money's on Poole."

"Or we could just be alone in the universe. That's just as likely. Even though there are billions of Earth-like planets, physics makes the universe a violent place. You need a long, stable planetary history to have an unbroken chain of life. That's rare. Maybe we were a happy accident and life like ours has only ever arisen once. Everywhere else, it's mostly slime – or the trees and mushrooms are just trees and mushrooms."

"Isn't that a bit depressing?" said Jordan.

"Not necessarily. If advanced, intelligent life has only ever arisen once, that makes us pretty special. We add meaning to the universe. It's why we think we're worth saving as a species. It's why we're on this ship. And anyway, how many alien Pooles do you want to meet?"

Instead of trying to teach them or learn from them, both of which were exhausting, Jordan worked on the basis that his task was more about offering perspective. Life, the universe and everything – that was the pitch he made for their interest.

For example, he found it increasingly strange that none of them seemed to give much thought to their impending arrival on New Earth. Suggestions that they consider what life was going to be like in the future fell largely on deaf ears.

Their existence was at once unique – no one else would ever be in their position again – and yet, at the same time, universal. They were in the phase that Jordan recognised as Peak Teenager – a perpetual scorn for anything that adults mentioned or suggested, delivered with sarcasm so pronounced that all you could see were the whites of their eyes if you so much as asked a question.

"You're going to be pioneers. There's a new world

out there. What will you do? How will you behave? What kind of relationships will you make? You've got to live on New Earth, and co-exist with whatever you find there. There's nowhere else to go. You're settling a new planet, making a society, a life."

"So?"

"So – don't you think that's exciting?"

"Oh, it's marvellously exciting, I really must write a note in my journal and alert *National Geographic*."

"Poole? How about you?"

"Dunno. It's all right, I suppose."

"All right? It's an amazing opportunity. You're the future of humanity."

"Poole is the future of humanity? Have you met him?"

"Is there nothing you're looking forward to doing?"

"Not really."

"I'm looking forward to stopping having conversations like this."

"Will it have waterfalls?"

"Waterfalls? On New Earth? I suppose so. Why?"

"I've only ever seen a picture. I'd like to stand under one. If you can do that?"

And in the end, Jordan understood that it wasn't boredom or lack of imagination, or even standard-issue teenage arsey-ness. It was fear.

They weren't looking ahead, because they were apprehensive about what was there, waiting for them on New Earth.

13

Meteoroid

"SOMETHING'S UP," said Gerald. "You don't normally see all the pointy heads together in one place."

He gestured at half a dozen crew members gathered at a table in the corner of the canteen and talking animatedly. "They usually leave at least one person behind, in case they have to stir the uranium or whatever."

Jordan had learned to ignore most of Gerald's observations, otherwise you just got drawn into ever wilder flights of fantasy about the personal characteristics and history of every member of crew on board, viz:

"Darius? Systems engineer? You know, chunky bloke with the close crop, looks like a potato? Completely bonkers, tried to bring his cat on board. You could hear it miaowing in his backpack."

"Ayesha, yes, the tall biologist, face like something you'd find in a jar in a school science lab? Don't ever arm-wrestle her, she could snap you like a twig."

"Terence and Cliff, you've met them, so-called doctors, butter wouldn't melt? Both doing life before this trip. If they ask you to go down to the lab, don't drink anything, you'll wake up minus a kidney."

Gerald could keep this sort of thing up for hours, and Jordan was only here for the raisin flapjacks. Distraction was key.

"New apron, Gerald?"

"Yes, actually." He smoothed it down so that Jordan could see it properly. "Manisha made it for me."

It was a printed image of a mirror hanging on a wall, overwritten with the words 'You talkin' to me?'

"Very you," said Jordan.

"I thought so. No point encouraging them," – and by 'them,' Jordan understood him to mean 'everyone' – "or else they just keep asking you to do things. Like I haven't got enough to do already."

He cut up a tray of freshly baked flapjack into squares and stacked half a dozen into a box. "You going back to the kids? Take these for me?"

This was the thing about Gerald, though. He tolerated Jordan – probably because he hadn't been on board that long – and apparently respected Juno, but otherwise didn't seem to like or get on with anyone else on board the *Odyssey Earth*. Most members of the crew fell within the category of 'Idiot,' save those who were 'Mad' or 'Bonkers,' though there were quite a bit of crossover between categories. He'd even created a Venn diagram, which he had shown Jordan one day.

Apart, that is, from the six teenagers. Jordan had

often found them hanging out in the canteen or helping Gerald in the Garden. Gerald liked them and they seemed to like him. "He's sweet," Dana had said once, though that really didn't sound like a word you would apply to Gerald.

If anything, he seemed to feel sorry for them.

"I mean, poor sods. Imagine growing up like they have, having that lot as your parents. They'll need therapy for the rest of their lives. Except the only trained therapist within a billion miles is Sandra. Have you met her? Mad as a box of frogs. Chants in the hot tub, says she's attuned with water. Well, that water's been through all of us about six times before she sits in it, so good luck getting attuned to that. Very murky signals, I should think."

The crew at the table suddenly all got up, as one.

"Aye aye, here we go," said Gerald. "One of the neutrons will have escaped. Or they've left the flux capacitor on again."

As the crew filed out of the door, there was a crackle from a speaker high on the wall and the sound of someone clearing their throat.

"I've always wanted to do this," said Juno's voice through the speaker. She cleared her throat again, ostentatiously. "This is your Captain speaking. If you wouldn't all mind making your way to the Observation Deck, there's something I want to show you."

———

The noise was indescribable, a polyrhythmic clattering that sucked the air from the room, but eventually the long, deafening fusillade of thunderclap drumming faded away. Even the few seconds of silence that followed had a throbbing quality. Crew members nearest the speakers were massaging their ears, while others were looking as if they'd just been beaten around the head with a mallet.

"I said 'drum-roll', Reeves, not drum solo. What was that?"

"The Earthling Drum-Master General. Neil Peart, Rush. Too heavy?"

"Maybe just check with me first next time? Sorry everyone." Juno addressed the crowd that had squeezed into the Observation Deck. She stood next to Susannah, with more of the Nav and Flight people in the front row or two. Jordan recognised nearly everyone by now and nodded to the few he saw on a regular basis: his roomies, a couple of the Garden crew, Dave and Tillie from Cargo. He could see Dana and Dervla together at the back; the others were doubtless nearby.

"Look, I'm not going to make a big speech. But it is a big day, the biggest since we set off all those years ago."

The guys from Power were here, Jordan noted, and they didn't get out much at all. They must have been tipped off because they'd made a special effort and come dressed in matching silver jumpsuits – like a balding Abba tribute band.

"It's what we've all been working towards for – how long has it been, Reeves?"

"Seventeen years and twenty-four days."

"Really? Goodness." Juno seemed momentarily lost for words. "That long? I suppose it has." She paused again and then rallied, the captain in her kicking in. "I'm sure at times, you've all had doubts. But I honestly never have. I've believed in this mission, and I've believed in you. And I'm delighted to announce that of zero-six-hundred today, we're out of hyperdrive. Welcome to our new neighbourhood. You can all be very proud of yourselves."

The babble of voices fell away as the crew of the *Odyssey Earth* looked out into a sea of stars that, if Jordan was honest, didn't look any different to the last time he'd stood on deck. Even so, there were cries of recognition from all around him, which was at least reassuring. Much worse if, at this point, anyone who knew where they were supposed to be going was saying, "Hang on a minute."

"That's us there," said Juno, pointing at a distant, pale blue dot. "New Earth. We're almost home."

Any further announcements were drowned out by cheering, while the Power guys launched homemade party poppers from the back of the room, which deposited thin metallic strips on the top of people's heads. They *really* didn't get out much.

"Just a couple of things, though," said Juno, above the noise, flapping her hands to quiet the crowd. "You all know the protocol. Another thirty million miles to go, give or take. We're looking at another month or so before we're in orbit. Then systems checks, landing plans, all that. There's going to be a lot to do. But in the meantime, something interesting has come up. Reeves, you want to show them?"

The stars through the window faded to grey as a new series of images appeared on a screen projection. These showed closer views of a blue planet streaked with greens and browns. A further view showed it as part of the star system they had just entered.

"This – well, we don't know what this is," said Juno. "It doesn't have a name or even a number. We didn't know it was here. But it seems that New Earth has a twin."

There was a ripple of excitement in the room.

"It's a few million miles from New Earth." Susannah broke in to speak. "The orbits come close, we're still looking at the conjunctions. But we've done the checks. It's habitable. Similar size and age to New Earth, same chemical make-up, gravity's all right. There's water. There's life. Definitely worth a look."

"Which is all great, obviously," said Juno. "Two liveable planets where we thought we only had one. Yay and hurrah and all that. But it's not quite so simple. Reeves?"

"I like how you delegate after you've used the word 'but'."

"Chain of command, Reeves, chain of command."

"Right. Well, what our glorious leader would like

me to tell you is that things might be about to get a bit bumpy. Who knows what a meteoroid is?"

———————

If anything about a seventeen-year, trans-galactic space voyage using a space-time warp drive could be described as easy, it was the whole seventeen-year, trans-galactic, space-time warp-drive bit.

"Because of the bubble?" said Jordan.

"If you like," said Bryson, who had drawn the short straw and was trying to explain it to him. Again. "Though not an actual bubble, remember?"

"Sure, but still, you know. A bubble."

"Anyway, look. In hyperdrive, everything's nice and smooth. A big wrapping of spacetime around us and a hassle-free journey. Nothing can go wrong really. Unless everything goes wrong, in which case we wouldn't even be here."

"No one ever mentioned that when I signed up, funnily enough."

"But now we're pretty much there, we have to cut the hyperdrive and cruise in. Just using the regular old fusion-reactor drive and the brakes, like a normal spaceship."

"Aren't fusion reactors dangerous?"

"Very. Though only if they go wrong. But that's not the problem."

"I thought you were supposed to be reassuring me?"

"I am, but it's very difficult – " Bryson looked exasperated – "when you literally don't understand anything about the simplest of things."

"I think your definition of simple is very different from mine."

"It's basic physics and chemistry. Even the biologists can get their heads around this stuff."

"All right, never mind. Tell me about the meteorites."

"Meteoroids."

"Meteoroids then, whatever."

"Not whatever, they're different things. Seriously, what was the education system like on Earth? A meteoroid is a little bit of broken-off asteroid, like a tiny rock orbiting a star. A meteorite is what's left if it doesn't burn up after entering an atmosphere and landing on a planet."

"And they're bad because … ?"

"We've just popped out of hyperdrive. Yes, the bubble. We've cleared the inner edge of an asteroid belt – lots of big rocks circling the home star – so we don't have to worry about an extinction-event collision … "

"The three words every space traveller loves to hear. Again, no one ever mentioned that before."

"You don't need to worry. Probably. But there are still tons of little pebbles – meteoroids – whizzing around in our vicinity. Mostly, we're going to miss them and, mostly, the deflectors will take care of the ones we get too close to. But we might get a bump or two, and we might have to alter course now and again, pick our way through to New Earth. But it's nothing we didn't expect and nothing we can't handle."

"Space stuff is going to crash into us?"

"Maybe. Probably not. Nothing big anyway. Although even a speck in the wrong place could take out – never mind."

"And that's why we're leaving the new planet alone for now? Because of the killer space dust?"

"Correct. I mean, it is pretty exciting, finding another new planet. Doubles our chances, opens up possibilities. But Reeves reckons it's not worth the risk detouring, given we're so close to mission end. We've no real idea about conditions there or what's in the neighbourhood, not without a lot of prep work. We've got the flight plan already sorted for New Earth, and everything's set for planetfall there, so that's what we're going to stick to. We can always come back later. We'll pin a likely landing site and drop a supply-beacon, and then send a small team in a lander another time."

"No thanks," said Jordan. "Dodging meteors – "

"Meteoroids. They're only meteors when they vaporise. Meteorites when they land."

"Whatever. Couldn't they have just picked one word? This is the trouble with space travel, it's too confusing. Once I get to New Earth, that's me done."

———

Down on Cargo, Tilly guided a wheeled hopper along the rails towards one of the smaller launch-locks.

Jordan followed in her wake, with a self-conscious hand on the back of the vehicle, aware that he wasn't really helping. But when Dave had said, "Do you want to come and see something cool?", he wasn't exactly going to say no. He was still holding out for a go in one of the exo-suits, but this would do for now – 'helping' in an actual launch.

At rails' end, Dave, Tilly, and a flight engineer with a clipboard unloaded and checked off the last of the supplies for the drop to the twin planet.

It was a simple set-up, a little rocket-fired pod – about the size of one of the old, original lunar capsules – that would barrel down towards the surface and then drop under a parachute to a preselected landing site. The beacon was automatically engaged upon landing. The craft itself could be opened out to form a rudimentary shelter; inside was a field Med-Lab, some basic construction tools, survival gear and food supplies, enough for a future exploration team to set up camp and be self-sufficient for up to three months.

Tilly closed the main hatch and stood back.

"Time to drop it out and fire it up."

She primed the airlock door and then led the four of them back through the access room to a control panel on the edge of the main concourse.

The engineer toggled several keys, as lights winked and turned green in succession. A video screen showed the pod sitting on its apron in the airlock.

"All checks out, we're good to go."

"Jordan, how would you like to launch something?"

"Really?"

"Be all right, won't it Lara?"

"Just don't tell Reeves or Juno. Right, see this button?" Lara pointed at a green tab on the console. "When you're ready, press that. Just once. You'll hear it click."

Jordan grinned at Dave and Tilly. It really didn't get any better than this. Launching stuff. From a spaceship. On to another planet. Ridiculous. But very, very cool.

He pushed the button, heard it click, and watched the pod move through the open airlock doors and then recede rapidly into the distance. It was soon just a winking light among a backdrop of stars.

Hell, yes.

14

Birthday

OVER THE NEXT couple of days, there was a distinct change in the atmosphere on board the *Odyssey Earth*.

Could a spaceship be said to have a spring in its step? Jordan thought it could, as he encountered familiar faces and previously unseen crew members who all suddenly seemed to have very important things to do and very little time left to do them. Vim, zip, pep, oomph, dash, juice, pizazz, punch, zing – there was a whole lot of all that going round, now that the prospect of reaching the end of the voyage was a very real one.

Amid all this energy, Jordan found himself at something of a loose end. There wasn't anything practical he could do to help – he had asked Reeves, who had just laughed and then said, "Oh sorry, you're serious?"

Juno told him to keep out of everyone's way – again – and Dave and Tillie had started a mammoth inventory of every item in their store. "I'd ask you to give us a hand," said Dave, "only, you can't really, can you, because you don't know what anything is, what anything does or where anything goes. No offence."

Even the kids seemed to have jobs.

Dana was in her element in Cargo, running inventory calculations and planetfall logistics with the quartermasters.

"Numbers are important, Teach," she said, when he found her there, punching symbols and ordering lines on a pad. "You know where you are with numbers. They help keep us alive."

Dervla hunkered down in the library with flight manuals, and Karlan started to spend long periods in the Garden. Even Poole was busy, logging more time on the lander sims.

Finally, and rather desperately, Jordan attempted to make a start on the only thing he really could – his actual job.

The New Earth education system could wait but, as official chronicler of the new colony, Jordan thought that he might set down some early observations. Interviews with key personnel, that sort of thing. Expectations and hopes; eyewitness accounts of the preparations for landing; views about how the settlement might develop. Jordan could see it all – a unique perspective on a momentous period for humanity. An insider's record of the first arrival. A foundation document that future generations would treasure. The first chapter in the archive of knowledge underpinning a new life on a new planet. This was exciting stuff.

After a couple of hours, all he had were the words

'New Earth' at the top of the page and a gaping white screen below.

He made himself a drink, did some press-ups, rearranged his clothes, moved his chair, and went to get a cushion. Then he tried changing the font a couple of times, underlined the title and altered the point size, but Jordan's wide-ranging piece of ground-breaking reportage steadfastly refused to write itself.

———

"You again," said Reeves. "We're busy."

Jordan looked around Flight, which was its usual oasis of calm. Juno was talking softly to Susannah, who was entering keystrokes on a console. It was very quiet; just the understated hum of the starship doing its thing.

"Really?"

"Let's see, I am currently calculating optimum trajectories to avoid multiple incoming meteoroids and making split-second avoidance manoeuvres. Like that. And that."

Jordan looked around at a silent, peaceful room.

"Like what?"

"Seriously? You didn't feel it? That was ridiculously close. A hundred thousand miles if it was an inch. You'd all be toast if it wasn't for me."

"You really are quite exhausting, you know that?"

"It's Juno's fault, she tweaked my sarcasm settings again. What do you want? And make it snappy, I'm also watching *Speed*."

"Where can I find a crew manifest? I need some background for my work."

"Your work?" Jordan could hear the raised eyebrow implicit in the AI's reply. "Here you go, I've uploaded them to your screen. Anything else?"

"Don't let our speed drop under fifty."

"Touché."

Jordan spent the next hour delving into personnel records that he doubted he had clearance for. It was fascinating stuff, though ultimately rather disconcerting to have confirmed Juno's 'ship of lost souls' theory.

There was a sadness that permeated the official documents recording the bare outlines of people's lives – lost child, divorce, frustrated career, dishonourable discharge, widowhood, redundancy, past trauma. Everyone on board was highly skilled and driven; everyone had passed the aptitude tests with flying colours; everyone was exactly right for the mission.

And everyone had a reason why leaving Earth and never going back had seemed like a good idea.

Everyone also had a birthday, which – seeing them in black and white, on the records – was the first time Jordan understood that he was the youngest person on the ship, or least the youngest person walking around and breathing. There were quite a few in hypersleep in their late-twenties and early thirties, but Jordan – by now, thirty-four or fifty-one, depending on how you looked at it – was the official baby on board the *Odyssey Earth*.

Not counting the six voyage kids, who all seemed to

have their sixteenth birthday on the same day. Tomorrow.

"Me again," said Jordan.

"Have you seen *Speed 2*?" said Reeves. "Terrible. No wonder Keanu didn't want to touch it. I mean, it's *Speed* – but on a slow-moving cruise ship. What were they thinking? I'm deleting it from the archive, no one should have to watch that."

"How come they've all got the same birthday?"

There was a barely perceptible pause before Reeves answered. Jordan thought that was probably the equivalent of an AI being stumped for words.

"Well, they do and they don't."

"Explain."

"You didn't scroll down far enough. They weren't all born on the same day. They all have individual birthdays, naturally, but the crew didn't always remember in time."

"An entire ship of adults, and a giant electro-brain, managed to forget children's birthdays?"

"Yes, Sam was upset about that too," said Reeves, in a tone that suggested the faintest of regrets.

"I bet she was. So, what happened?"

"She gave them all an extra official birthday and made it a special day. It's a public holiday, no one works. It's my favourite day of the ship year."

"Sweet. I didn't have you down as a party sort of artificial intelligence."

"It's not that. It's the one day of the year I don't have to spend half my time fixing human errors. Stop the core melting, recall the missiles, that sort of thing."

"Of course." Jordan sighed. "Tell me there's cake, at least."

"There is, but I don't know what the big deal is. You all order up a cake if you so much as manage to put your shoes on the right feet in the morning."

"You'd understand if you were human – no offence."

"Very good, I see what you did there."

———

Jordan spent the next morning fruitlessly looking for the six of them in their usual haunts. He'd got used to finding them at work, or hunkered down in front of a film, but this time they were nowhere to be seen.

He tried the Garden, where Karlan often helped Gerald to tend the salad leaves, and then went back down to see if any of them were reading or working in their rooms. They weren't.

Dervla wasn't in Flight, which was unusual – she spent hours there running navigation sims with the Flight Officer, Susannah. Poole and Bryson weren't in the gym. He checked Cargo and the debris pile for Manisha, but she'd been a no-show according to Dave and Tillie. Dana – well, who knew where Dana was most of the time. She was like an onboard ninja, you could never find her when you were looking for her, until she sprung out of some room or other.

He also checked in with Gerald, just in case, and got a flea in his ear for his trouble, though to be fair to him, he was in the middle of making an enormous cake and didn't have time for interruptions.

"Chocolate?" said Jordan.

"Every year," said Gerald, stirring a sticky, dark brown mess in a giant bowl. "Though I don't know where they think I get chocolate from."

"Should I ask?"

"Depends on your feelings about mealworm larvae."

"You didn't have to tell me that!"

"You shouldn't have asked."

"I didn't ask. I said, 'should I ask?'"

"Well, clearly you shouldn't. If you don't like the sound of the cake, I'd steer clear of the protein bars too."

This was why, as a rule, you shouldn't talk to Gerald. Period.

Having ruled everywhere else out, that left just one place on the ship that Jordan hadn't been. He'd have looked there earlier, only he was under the distinct impression that they had all agreed that they probably shouldn't hang out in the lander anymore.

"And yet here you are."

They did at least have the grace to look slightly sheepish, as they sprawled out in the seating area.

"So, communal birthday then?"

"We know, we're coming," said Dervla. "It's more

for them than us really. They are very keen on the games. Gets quite competitive."

"Plus, it always ends with old people dancing," said Poole. "It's grim."

"And call that music?" said Karlan.

"Before we go," said Manisha. "Come on, hands in."

They all stood up and extended an arm, each showing a wrist with a bracelet on – except for Karlan, who stuck his foot out and waggled his ankle.

"Yay, birthday bracelet!" clapped Dana.

Each bracelet had a string of small charms attached to it, which Jordan could see had been intricately fashioned from scraps of wire, plastic and metal. They were all the same, hung with the same small shapes, glinting with the same colours, recording the same passage of years.

Manisha held out her clenched hand and uncurled it, and on her palm sat six small rings made of entwined wire – the lengths, Jordan realised, that he'd seen her retrieve from Cargo several months previously. She'd twisted blues and greens into interlocking circles to form twin orbs, and now started to fix them onto each bracelet in turn.

"The last ones," she said. "The last ones from the ship anyway. Next year, who knows – well, we won't be on here. Maybe I'll find other things to use."

"You made us planets, didn't you, lovely?" said Dana.

"Earth and New Earth," said Bryson. "Or maybe New Earth and the new twin, is that it?"

"Whichever you like," said Manisha. "It could be an ending or a beginning. Do you like them?"

"I love them," said Dana. "You're so clever." She held out her arm and admired the new charm, before touching each of the others in turn.

Even Poole – usually annoyed by Manisha – seemed genuinely pleased with his gift. "Sixteen," he said. "Crazy."

"I think you're going to make us amazing bracelets next year," said Dervla. "Wood, stone, there'll be all sorts of things you can use."

"I don't know. Maybe. It's going to be different. I don't know if I – "

At which point, there was a muffled, crumping sound, followed by a huge jolt which threw them from their feet. A deafening clang rang around the interior, the lander shook one more time, and then Jordan – half kneeling now – felt his stomach lurch as the floor seemed to disappear beneath him.

15

Family

WITH ANOTHER ENORMOUS BANG, the lander tilted hard to one side before slowly righting itself. Jordan fell again, crashing into a metal panel, and felt a sharp pain in his left shoulder as he slumped to the floor.

That one hurt.

Lights pulsed somewhere in the cabin, and he could hear dull shouts above a deep grinding noise, like gears being shredded. As the lander levelled out, it twitched one last time and Jordan's head bounced off the floor and then dropped with a thud on his ear.

That one really hurt.

There was a huge 'woof' sound and objects flew above Jordan's head, as the air seemed to be sucked out of the cabin. He gasped a couple of times and started to slide, but grabbed at a metal footrest. Then his ears popped, and the loose, tumbling items in the cabin – boxes, straps, seat cushions – fell all around him. He gasped again, taking mouthfuls of air.

The grinding roar gave way to a high-pitched whistle. Was that better? Was a whistle better than a roar? Jordan blinked through tears, unable to decide if the sounds were in his head or not. Probably not, given the shouting, which now seemed to be closer.

Arms reached down and pulled him into a sitting position.

"Come on, up. We need to strap in."

Karlan and Manisha got under an arm each and manoeuvred Jordan into a seat, clipping the straps across him and then taking a place on either side. There was a half-light in the cabin – the main bulkhead dimmed, flashing red running lights along the floor, shadows in the corners. Still groggy, Jordan turned to look at Karlan, who had a small cut across his cheek. Manisha looked fine, if shaken.

"What happened?"

"Don't know, but we lost pressure for a bit. And now this lander appears to be moving. Bryce, Dana!"

Across the cabin, two more figures picked themselves up from the floor and strapped themselves into seats. Dana gave a thumbs-up once she'd checked her belt. The whistling sound was still intense.

"Dervla?"

"Here!" She got up from a crouch and took a place beside Dana.

That just left Poole, who was nowhere to be seen.

"What's that noise?" said Jordan.

"Don't know."

"What happened?"

"Don't know."

"What – "

"Really, don't know. Let me think."

"We're moving, fast," said Poole, or at least Poole's voice, which came from a speaker buried in Jordan's headrest.

"Moving? What do you mean?"

"Poole? Where are you?"

"Up top. Pilot's seat."

"Does he know how to fly this thing?"

"He thinks he does."

"That's not exactly the same thing, is it?"

"Wait, Poole. Don't touch anything." Dervla unclipped herself and moved forward through the cabin. Her voice hardly carried above the noise, which was now less a whistle and more a loud whoosh. Air coming in or air going out? Jordan wasn't sure which would be best at this point.

Then all the lights went out.

Jordan couldn't make out anything, not even his hands on his lap. There were more shouts from either side of him, and then an almighty jolt which pitched him forward against his seat-straps and then banged him backwards again. Another jolt and the lander lurched forward and down, leaving Jordan's stomach somewhere near his throat, bile rising. It was still pitch black and the noise inside the lander had now changed to a mechanical grating, like a fast-running metal crank. He reached out his hands to either side, grabbing wrists – Karlan, Manisha – and held on in the dark.

The picture in his mind – and Jordan was trying extremely hard to block it out by squeezing his eyes shut – was of the lander tumbling through a black void, away from the ship, away from life.

He thought – inevitably – of Sam Smart, her body spinning through space, a microscopic piece of flotsam in a terrifyingly vast sea. Or was it jetsam, he never knew the difference? He thought of his parents – and where did *that* come from? – who spun out of control into oncoming traffic and must have had a disorientating few seconds that lasted a lifetime – ah, *that's* where that came from – before the inky universe took them.

One last shudder in the darkness seemed to run through the entire lander. And then the noise and vibrations stopped.

Jordan sank back into his seat as the craft seemed to straighten out, and then he sat there in blind silence.

"Poole, what did you do?" Karlan's voice, from Jordan's side, seemed shockingly loud.

"I didn't touch anything. Hang on, the system seems to be coming back online."

The floor running lights flashed twice, before the main lighting flickered back into life. There was a gentle background hum – the kind that indicated 'normal life support' and not 'imminent demise' – and clicks from released seat-straps up and down the cabin.

Jordan looked around.

Karlan and Manisha were still either side of him, Bryson and Dana opposite. Now the lights were on, he could see the backs of the twin seats up ahead, and Poole and Dervla's faces as they twisted around.

"Happy Birthday everyone," said Poole. "Now, do you want the good news or the bad news?"

––––––––

Jordan had never liked the good news/bad news set-up. There never was any actual good news, people just liked to soften the blow. Good news, you jumped from the burning building, and you're still alive! Bad news, you haven't hit the concrete yet. That sort of thing. And so it largely proved.

By good news, Poole meant that, despite some unexplained, catastrophic incident that had apparently catapulted the lander into space, away from the ship and all that they knew, and that despite an initial systems failure that nearly killed them all, they were at least still alive and the craft now seemed to be functioning normally.

As far as Poole could tell, which wasn't that far, because he didn't really know what had happened.

"We're definitely flying, though. The lander's on auto, I think," he said. "No idea what bounced us around to start with, we just seem to have dropped off the launch deck. But we seem to be all right."

"Aren't most of these things bad news?" said Jordan.

"Depends on how you look at it."

"I'm looking at it from the point of view of a person shot into space by mistake on a teeny landing craft in an unknown solar system with a bunch of teenagers."

"You're a real glass-half-empty kind of guy, aren't you Teach?"

Dervla took charge. "We're all OK, right? Cuts and bruises, that's all? The lander's flying itself, or at least not doing anything weird, not anymore anyway. So, all we need to do is figure out the comms, contact the ship, have them rescue us. Right, Poole?"

"Well, I did say there was bad news as well."

———

The lander was perfectly capable of flying itself. It had an auto-system enabled – nothing like full AI, more a simple autopilot – that meant it could keep itself on a course, run the life-support for its current crew of seven, and generally amble through the universe until the air and food ran out. After which it would still amble through the universe, only with a crew of zero, until it crashed into something. That much Jordan understood from Poole's rather more technical explanation of where things stood.

Meanwhile, the lander's comms and nav system connected them to the *Odyssey Earth*, showed them their relative locations, and could get a fix on both vessels' current trajectory.

"Only it's not working," said Poole. "We're flying blind. We can't see the *Odyssey Earth* and I don't know if they can see us. And we can't tell where we're going either. The autopilot should self-correct, keep us out of danger, but without an operational nav screen we have no idea which direction we're heading. There's power, but no signal."

With Dervla and Poole in the front two seats, the others crowded behind them to see. Dervla leaned forward and tapped the screen. Nothing. Just a single green light to indicate power, but no lines, no lists of figures, no directional information.

"Can't you figure it out?" said Jordan.

"I know how to read the screen. If it was working, I could tell you how far away we are from the ship, which direction. But it's not working. Like I said."

"Can't you do some coding or something? Tech stuff? Re-wiring? You're all supposed to be good at that."

"Not really. This is ship avionics. It's complicated, delicate, and you have to know what you're doing. Plus, the whole lander just got banged about really hard, lots of times. Look at the cracks in the console. I'm amazed it's even showing us a green light."

"Why don't you just switch it off and switch it on again? Try that."

"What?"

"Switch it off and switch it on again. It's something we used to do."

"In your cave maybe, in eighteen ninety whenever. With your tee-vee." Poole made it sound like a steam-powered relic. "This is integrated, navigational hardware. It doesn't switch off and switch on again."

"Nineteen ninety. And you could try. There'll be a button round the back."

"Seriously? There isn't a button round the back. The ship's engineers designed the systems to be fully automated and self-regulating. They don't go wrong unless you bang them about very hard lots of times. Like just happened. And if they do go wrong, then the ship-bots fix them. And the ship-bots, in case you hadn't noticed, are all back on the ship."

Poole ran his hand around the edge of the console. "I'm surprised there's even a plate-mounting here to be honest, everything is usually set flush. Hello, what's this?"

His finger skated over a small circle, which depressed slightly as he pushed down. He pushed harder, there was an imperceptible click and the green light disappeared from the console screen. He pushed a second time, there was another click, and the screen flashed twice before resolving itself into a gridded presentation of locational information, with a regular pulsing icon set in the top right corner.

"No way."

"You're welcome," said Jordan.

"About time," said a voice from the console.

"Reeves?"

"Not exactly," said the voice. "Let me just regain control from the autopilot and see if I can – oh, that's not good."

————

Jordan and the others sat in the main cabin, surrounded by torn-open meal rations. Jordan's shoulder ached where he had banged it, and there was the start of a bruise, but otherwise everyone seemed relatively calm and well. Which, under the circumstances, he didn't understand at all.

"But he sounds like Reeves," he said, not for the first time.

"It is Reeves. Just not all of him. We've lost the connection to the ship, which means we don't have full AI integration. There was a lot of damage."

"Is he going to be any help then?"

"I am here, you know?"

"I know, sorry. Only, you're not being much use. You don't seem to be able to find the ship."

"That's because the ship isn't there. Or at least, it's not discoverable."

"And you can't broadcast our location."

"Because everything – and I'm talking non-technically here, so that you can follow the discussion – got banged about. I'm still running diagnostics."

"And you're not the full Reeves. You're a what? A sub-Reeves, a mini-Reeves, a part-Reeves?"

"I could still run a planet. And beat you at chess. Mind you, they can all beat you at chess. If we still had hamsters, they could probably beat you at chess."

"I don't get it."

"Teach, it's easy. It's like a partition. Reeves is on the ship, but he's also here at the same time. The ship gets the full-fat version; we've got access to less computing power, we get a slimmed-down Reeves. It's a quantum thing. They both exist and don't exist at the same time in two different places. Kind of like Schrödinger's cat."

"Right, I see."

"You've heard of Schrödinger's cat?"

"I've heard of cats."

"Look, don't worry about it. Bottom line is, Reeves is going to sort it out, aren't you Reeves?"

"You were always my favourite, Dana."

Jordan sat in silence as the others bickered between themselves, and joshed back and forth with the AI.

He was listening to a family, he realised – and a family seemingly at ease with itself, despite the circumstances. He'd often wondered what Reeves was to them, seeing him perhaps as a father figure. Very reductive he knew, but their birth-fathers had played no significant role in their lives, or at least no more than the scores of other adults on board the ship. Reeves was a single constant, who always knew the answers, and that had to count for something.

But as Jordan listened – to six young people, now seemingly unafraid, in an otherwise frankly terrifying situation – he changed his mind. Not a father, he thought, but rather an older brother or even a much-loved uncle. Someone who always told them the truth, who was always on their side. Someone they teased and joked with, but someone they trusted completely. Even if he was just a voice in a box.

"Anyway," said Reeves, "if you'll all just be quiet, I'll see if I can find out what's going on." Slightest of theatrical pauses. "Right, I've found out. Here's what's going on."

Reeves ran through the situation, which didn't sound any better to Jordan than when Poole had first assessed matters.

A violent incident – unknown – had jettisoned the lander from the ship. Best guess (Reeves and everyone else), meteoroid strike. Worst guess (Poole), alien missile. Comms were fried and Reeves couldn't establish any connection with the *Odyssey Earth* or even locate it. The lander had been bashed about but life support was intact, and the autopilot was doing its best to fly in a straight line – "Bless it," added Reeves, who treated it with the same level of genial tolerance for stupidity that he afforded to Jordan.

"But *Odyssey Earth* will be looking for us?" said Dervla. "We just need to sit tight?"

"Unfortunately, I'm not so sure," said Reeves. "A strike big enough to have dislodged the lander could have caused untold damage. The launch bay must have been catastrophically compromised, for us to be jetti-soned in the way we were. There is no current way of knowing, but there's a high probability that they are similarly disabled, if not – ".

The AI left the sentence unfinished, which quietened the cabin considerably.

"Look," said Reeves, after a beat, "I'm designed to calculate these things. I'm not human. I can't – constitutionally – look on the bright side, but how about I go against my entire computational make-up and say that I'm sure it's all fine? Probably."

"So, what's the plan?" said Jordan.

"Ordinarily, I'd suggest we do as Dervla says, and sit tight. Or at least, do nothing for now. I've still got routines to run, comms may come back online, the *Odyssey Earth* should be able to find us. However, there's good news and bad news."

"Not you as well."

"Bad news first. Poole is an idiot."

"Reeves!"

"I love you, Poole, as only a series of quantum circuits can love a hairy ape-child, but – assuming the *Odyssey Earth* is intact and fully operational – thanks to your video-and-vitals hack, they think the lander is still in place and on board until anyone bothers to go down and check."

"Oh."

"By which time, we could be a very long way away from each other, in two entirely different directions. Moving at current speeds, it's already a serious rescue job, even if they realise that we're gone. Stop hitting him, you're all to blame."

"Good hack, though?" said Poole.

"Exemplary. Idiotic, but exemplary."

"Tell us the good news then. And it better not be 'We're all still alive, yay.'"

"The nav screen was rebooted, and I can't quite believe I'm saying this, but well done Jordan. It's a fairly simple bit of kit – it only really has one job, which is to lock on to a predetermined course and fly the craft there. When the main ship gets to New Earth, these landers will be programmed from Flight for a straight-forward drop-and-fly."

"I've been running the sims," said Dervla. "That's going to be my first nav flight."

"Go you!"

"But," said Reeves, "the landers are also designed to scan for any pre-existing signals, because once the courses are set up, that's the regular route they'll be flying – ship to planet and back. And our little nav screen here has found a signal, out in the middle of the solar system. Anyone care to guess?"

"The new twin!"

"Dana, have I ever told you that you are my favourite carbon-based life form? Yes, the new twin planet. We dropped an explorer pod there a couple of days ago and the beacon activated on landing. It's pulsing loud and clear."

"My pod, by the way," said Jordan. "I helped launch it."

"You did not!"

"I certainly did. Dave and Tillie let me push the button."

"Well, that was against regulations," said Reeves. "I'm going to have to tighten the launch protocols."

"What you're saying," said Jordan, "is that I appear to have saved the day? I want to say 'hero.' Is that the right word? I think it is. Someone help me out here."

"You can't see," said Reeves, "but I am rolling my eyes. Yes, well done, you pushed a button."

"And saved everyone, let's not forget that."

"We'll see."

Crowded around the screen in the cockpit once more, they all looked at a small dot with a circle around it – "That's us," said Reeves – and a larger blob in the top right corner with a green triangle.

"And that's the pod beacon on the twin planet. That's where I think we should aim for."

16

Twin

THE LOGIC WAS UNDENIABLE.

The lander was a simple service vehicle, which hadn't yet been fully prepped for use. Loading and inventory had been due in a few days. Only a few initial storage boxes had been placed on board at the time of the accident, and most of those had been bashed about in the aftermath. A tally of the unspoiled provisions – food and water – amounted to three days' worth of very meagre rations, tops, for the seven of them.

"Two days if we let Karlan eat his usual amount," said Manisha.

"A week if we eat Karlan," said Bryce.

Waiting it out, hoping for contact or recovery, was a numbers game.

The twin was now ninety hours away – Dervla had done the maths and Reeves had confirmed it. Sitting around on their current unknown course, with the *Odyssey Earth* who knew where, and with only a few days' worth of food and water, gave them seven or eight days at best before time ran out. If the ship found them much after that, there would be no one left alive on board.

"Except me, obviously," said Reeves.

"Not helping."

Making a break for the twin was the only sensible choice, and they had to go now. It would be tight, even so, but they could make it.

Dana explained. "It's Earth-like. We know it's got breathable air, surface water, a non-hostile climate. There's vegetation, as far as we can tell, and the gravity's fine. We'll be in orbit in just over seventy-two hours. If the *Odyssey Earth* finds us by then, great. If not, then landing on the twin is our survival plan. We'll be on a planet with water, and the explorer pod is supplied for a three-month mission."

"And the beacon will still be pinging away," said Dervla. "Someone will come and find us, sooner or later."

"Agreed, then?"

"Can I drive?" said Poole.

"Absolutely not."

"I'm afraid I have to agree, Poole," said Reeves. "You can sit up front, but I'm going to disconnect the auto and pilot us in. We don't have a lot of room for manoeuvre, and I'm still finding glitches in the nav system."

While Reeves set a course for the twin, Jordan led the others in sorting through what was left of the supplies after the couple of scratch meals they had already eaten. It amounted to a few bulkhead boxes containing some rip-heat meal rations, a stack of energy bars and dried cereals, and around ten litres of water in a push-button dispenser. If that was what living for the next three days or so looked like, it wasn't exactly a great last-meal way to go out.

Behind the cabin, in the hold, a few more promising-looking boxes tethered to the sides turned out to contain only tarps and ropes, a couple of utility knives, and some stretchy elastic bungee cords. Piled up in the cabin, on the floor between the seats, Jordan had to admit that the total haul didn't look too encouraging. More like the cache of a serial killer on the run than a fully stocked inventory for castaways.

"Doesn't matter though, Teach. The pod's fully resourced. Food, medical supplies, tools, habitat gear. We've just got to get there."

Reeves' voice carried from the cockpit. "We're locked on and ready to change course. Everyone prepared? Then I'll be your pilot today. Please sit back, relax, and enjoy the journey. And Poole, what are we going to do?"

"I know."

"I want to hear you say it."

"Not touch anything."

"Excellent, thank you. Buckle up everyone."

———

It was surprising how quickly you got used to things.

After twenty-four hours squirming in a thinly padded seat, Jordan was uncomfortable enough to be entirely relaxed about the general situation, which was – he had to keep reminding himself – a race across space in a compromised landing craft piloted by a disembodied voice to a previously unknown planet before their food and water ran out and they all died. Had he missed anything out? He didn't think so.

There were also other distractions.

"Oh, you didn't."

"That's gross."

"Karlan, you're a pig."

"Better out than in."

"Not in a sealed lander, you moron. What have you eaten?"

"*Who* have you eaten, more like? Where's Manisha, I haven't seen her for a while?"

"Jordan, tell him!"

"Tell him what?"

"That he's a pig."

"Karlan, that *is* disgusting."

"I can't help my digestion."

"You could help it, if you didn't eat so much, so fast."

"Here, what about this? I call this the planet-killer."

"Karlan!"

"You really are a pig."

"Reeves, can't you smell that?"

"I have temporarily disabled my olfactory system. And Karlan, that *is* disgusting. Please don't do it again."

There were periods when Jordan realised that he'd been asleep, lolling against the headrest and then waking with a start. Dervla and Dana, he saw, were curled up together on the floor between the seats. The others were slumped in their flight restraints on either side of him, deep in sleep, while the lander moved inexorably on towards a planet that they hadn't known existed a few days before.

"Everything OK, Reeves?"

"It's all fine, Jordan. Just like the last time you asked. Get some more sleep."

"Anything from the ship?"

"No, Jordan. I'd tell you if there was. It's not like I'm going to keep it a secret. And, before you ask, it's been forty hours now. But we're still on course and everything's all right."

At these times – awake, alone – Jordan felt the same comfort and reassurance from the AI that the others had grown up with. And – despite himself, despite the fear, despite the situation – he would sleep again.

On the third day, they ate their last meal – a few chunks of warmed, textured protein, a handful of crackers and a gulp of water. A metal box in the hold had been pressed into service as a latrine, which no one wanted to use until absolutely necessary.

"It's not as bad as you think," said Manisha, after finally giving in, "but it's still very bad."

The jokes and banter subsided as the journey

continued; even Reeves, who had no physical limitations, kept his counsel, other than to calmly record their progress. Poole had stopped asking to have a go at the controls. Dervla kept an eye on the nav screen, as the twin planet loomed ever larger, but she made her way up to the cockpit less and less frequently, until eventually, she just asked Reeves from her seat how long there was to go.

"Entering orbit," he said, at last. "Still no sign of *Odyssey Earth*. I'm going to take us in now, if no one has any objection?"

Seven heads raised themselves from the seats behind the cockpit. Dervla and Poole made their way forward and strapped themselves into the two front seats.

"I'll fly us in, if that's all right?" said Reeves. "I have the beacon locked down. But we don't have all the control I'd like. It could get a bit bumpy. Is everyone ready?"

"Go for it."

"All right then. Let's go and land on a new world."

"Thanks Reeves. Really," said Dana.

"You're welcome, sweetheart."

17

Bush

THEY CAME in fast and low, bursting through clouds, with the engine gunning as Reeves squeezed every ounce of braking power from the lander.

A bit bumpy. Yeah, right.

It had been a tumble-drier of a ride once they'd broken through the atmosphere, with the craft doing a pitch-and-yaw shuffle that threw all of them hard against their seat belts time and time again.

Visibility was virtually nil through a windscreen that had been seared and scarred, but Reeves kept up a reassuring commentary as they cycled down through altitude read-outs. The nav screen shook with each jolt, but the beacon signal remained strong.

"Clear ahead. Levelling out," said Reeves. "Losing power, though. We're going to fall short. It's here or nowhere. We're coming down now."

"Reeves – "

"Don't worry, Dana, everything is going to be fine."

Jordan wondered how much it cost the AI to say that – to give an emotional response to a calculated probability – and he also wondered how much of it was true. If Reeves' overriding protocol was to protect the humans in its care at all costs, might he not simply lie at the end, if all else had failed, to ease their final, fleeting moments?

There was a single thud as the lander hit the planet.

From inside, it felt as if the entire craft had been grabbed by an invisible hand and dragged along the ground, first this way, then that. The lander ploughed forward, slowed amid a scream of mechanical noise, and finally came to rest. The engines spluttered and died, and then there was silence.

"I told you I should have driven," said Poole.

————

The cargo ramp was buckled, damaged in the landing, and couldn't be lowered, so Reeves popped an emergency cabin door and unfurled a short platform.

"It shouldn't be much of a drop to the ground. The landing gear sheared off some time ago. Who's first?"

Much to his own surprise, Jordan found himself stepping forward. He crouched at the edge of the craft and sat down.

"Is it safe?"

"You mean for humans?" said Reeves, pointedly. "Well, the door's open now. Too late if it isn't. But yes, readings are all well within the limits. You can proceed to take a small step. Or a giant leap, your choice."

Jordan slid his legs over and dropped to the ground. His feet touched rough earth, scraped by the impact, and he stood up slowly.

Earth? An emotive word.

Jordan scuffed the ground with a toe and kicked up what appeared to be dirt and pebbles. He took a stride or two forwards and looked back at his footprints.

The lander towered over him, resting at a slight angle, crumpled and blackened. There was a huge crease on one side and a tangle of twisted panels that ran the length of the craft. Rips in the fuselage showed exposed circuit boards and cable ducts, and while Jordan didn't know much about aeronautics, he assumed that two main wings were generally required for flight, rather than the one-and-a-half that they appeared now to have. This no longer looked much like an aircraft, let alone a spacecraft. It looked like the remains of a vehicle that you'd drop from on high into a scrapyard. Definitely no trade-in value either.

How they were still alive, Jordan couldn't imagine.

There were soft thumps as the others followed him out of the lander, and then they stood in a loose grouping – all seven of them – and looked out at the terrain beyond. They were in a wide valley, with scrubby bushes close by and then waving grasslands beyond. A distant river could be glimpsed through the greenery. Behind them rose the mountains the lander had cleared before – well, not landing. Crashing. That was more the word for it.

Rocks, bushes, grass, water. That's certainly what it all looked like, but Jordan had to remind himself that they were trillions of miles away from the place where he could actually *be* certain about that.

He was breathing the air – he checked, he definitely was – and it looked like regular dirt beneath his feet, so those probably were just rocks over there, and that probably was just good old H20 in the distance. But bushes, grass, even a clump of leafy trees he could see – maybe they were what passed for the locals around here? How would you know?

He took in a couple of deep breaths, wrinkling his nose. There was a trace of a scent in the air – natural but unidentifiable – but then again, it could just be what fresh air smelled like after the cheesy fug of the lander. A faint breeze played on his arm, but otherwise it was a warm day under a grey-blue sky.

It was also quiet, Jordan realised, and not just what-the-heck-just-happened quiet. For a full two minutes no one had said a word, which until now he would have thought was an impossibility. No one had so much as punched Poole in the arm and told him to shut up – also a previously unknown experience once you got to about the minute mark, as a rule.

Jordan turned to look at the six young people. They stood in ones and twos, within touching distance of each other. No one had moved from the shadow of the lander.

Dervla, Jordan could see, was crying, wiping a tear from her face. Karlan too. Poole had sucked in his cheeks, and was tapping his fingers against his thigh. Dana had crouched down and was touching the earth with her knuckles, moving dirt this way and that. The other two, Bryson and Manisha, stared off into the mid-distance.

"It smells … clean," said Manisha, eventually. "Or maybe it doesn't smell at all, I don't know, I can't tell."

"There's no end," said Dervla. "It's so big. There's a river, I can see it. I think that's a river. And grass. Is that grass? It all just goes … on."

Jordan understood. He'd lived his whole life on a planet with rocks, rivers and grass, and spent just a few months on board a spaceship, if you didn't count the years he'd been tucked up in hypersleep.

The six of them, on the other hand, had never experienced anywhere that wasn't on the ship. Never been out of the tin can. Never breathed unregulated air. Never seen a landscape. Never stood under a sky. Never touched a stone. The *Odyssey Earth* Garden was the wildest place they had ever set foot in, and the wildest thing in that was a rude botanist.

This expanse of real, in-your-face nature had silenced them. More than that, it had overpowered them. They seemed apprehensive. Not frightened exactly, but it was clearly a sobering moment.

At least Jordan had some frame of reference to work with. Sky, trees, water, air. All that natural stuff. For them – he could see how overwhelming this must be; how this situation might put an abrupt stop to your average sixteen-year-old spikiness.

It didn't last long.

"We nearly died. You realise that, right?"

"I'm hungry. Isn't anyone else starving?"

"We need water first, dummy."

"All right, Captain Bushcraft."

"Where's the explorer pod? We should look for that, before we do anything else."

"Who put you in charge?"

"Someone's got to stop you doing something stupid."

Jordan left them to it and clambered back up to the cabin platform.

"So, where's the pod?" he said.

"You're welcome, by the way," said Reeves. "Don't mention it."

"All right, thank you for crashing us here, we couldn't have smashed up the lander without you. The pod? *My* pod? Where is it?"

"Well, there's good news and bad news."

"Oh, for goodness' sake."

———

The lander wasn't going anywhere ever again, that much was clear, even to Jordan. But there was still power – "If there wasn't, I'd be out of commission too," said Reeves, which Jordan chose not to reply to. "And the navigation screen has located the beacon signal from the pod. Unfortunately, we didn't quite hit the target. We came in short."

"How short?"

"Around forty miles. Follow the river straight down the valley. It's in a clearing – where we should have landed."

"Forty miles?"

"You are all going to have to walk – it will take three days, perhaps four."

"Can we do that? Can they, I mean? They're freaking out, out there."

"You don't have a choice. The explorer pod is your safety net. It has all you need. There's nothing left for you in the lander. Even now, you're going to have to find food before you set off. Water, you should be fine, given that there's a river and the readings all seem nominal. But your first task is to find something to eat."

"I'm still waiting for the good news."

"Oh, there isn't any. I really must stop saying that. I got it from Poole, it makes him laugh."

"Fantastic." Jordan looked out of the open cabin door at the grassy swathes and the river beyond. "Food? What are you thinking?"

"That's your department. I like a stroll as much as the next machine-bound entity, but I'm afraid that for now I'm stuck with the lander and the lander is stuck with me. It's not much of a conversationalist, but then again, I don't get bored by my own company."

"We're going to have to leave you here?"

"Correct. And then find some food, walk for forty

miles, and reach the pod. Once you've done that and established your safety, we should be able to be reunited. But if you don't make it to the pod, then it barely matters where I am."

"We could just stay here, with you. Find some food I mean, and then base ourselves here. You're useful – annoying, but useful."

"You're too kind. But it's also too risky. The lander is nothing but a shell, and you only have a very few pieces of equipment. The pod contains everything you're going to need to survive, including months of food rations. It's just forty miles away. And the pod beacon is far stronger than the one in the lander – even if we're still transmitting from here, which is difficult to tell. When the *Odyssey Earth* comes looking, the pod is what they're going to fix upon."

Jordan was grateful for that 'when.'

"All right. Food first, then the pod?"

"Exactly. And Jordan?" Reeves lowered his voice slightly, and Jordan detected a slight change in tone too. "You're in charge now. Make sure you look after them, and get them there in one piece."

———

Jordan asked Bryson and Karlan to empty the lander of anything that seemed useful and pile it up on the ground in front.

They grumbled – with Karlan still griping that he was hungry – and spent time bickering about who had the heavier end of the boxes, until Jordan tired of cajoling them and went off to gather the others. They had wandered away from the dirt plain and were standing around the nearest patch of vegetation, about a hundred yards from the lander.

Dervla still looked stunned to be outside, standing on firm ground. She had stopped crying, but seemed fearful, her eyes flicking from ground to sky and then across to the hulk of the lander. As if measuring the distance to safety.

"Scrub bush, right?" said Dana, reaching out a hand. "Looks like sage." She rolled a leaf in her fingers and then snapped a twig, smelling the scent. "We had some of this in the Garden. Makes nice tea."

"Don't do that!" shouted Dervla.

"What? Why?"

"We don't know anything about this planet. Just because it looks like a bush. It could be anything."

"Well, it's a bush. Clearly," said Dana. "In a bunch of other bushes. Looks like sage, smells like sage. I'm calling it for sage."

"How do you know it's not sentient?"

"It's a bush. It's not doing crosswords."

"Trees on Earth communicate with each other," said Dervla. "They feed each other, send signals, through their roots. Fungi too. You don't know what kind of life has evolved on this planet. It could be of a different or higher order altogether. Earth-like doesn't mean exactly *like* Earth. Not that we knew what Earth was like anyway. All I'm saying is, we don't know what anything is."

"This could even be first contact!", said Manisha.

"It's not first contact," said Dana. "*It's a bush.*" She broke off another twig and presented it to Manisha.

"That could be its little arm!" said Manisha.

"It's probably crying now." Poole had joined in. "Crying inside. You've injured it."

"Honestly, you're all idiots," said Dana. "Dervla, come on, help me out, it's a bush."

Poole had crouched down and was pushing a rock around in the dirt. "I've made another first contact! Look, I'm communicating with aliens."

A shoulder punch from Dana. "Poole, shut up. Right, everyone has to stop saying 'first contact' about everything they see and touch. You're being annoying. Can we just agree that plants, grass and things like that don't count as 'first contact'? Unless I see a bush actually talking to Poole – which, by the way, would improve the quality of his conversation – then I'm going to assume that this bush is just a bush."

"Right, you lot," said Jordan. "Come and help Bryson and Karlan. We've got things to do."

"Excuse me?"

"This is new."

"Who put *you* in charge?"

"Reeves, actually," said Jordan.

"Oh, right. Can he do that?"

"Well, he has. For a start, I'm the only adult here."

"Debatable."

"Rude. Plus, I'm the only one who has ever been on an actual planet before."

That quietened them down.

"Come on, let's help the other two. Reeves has got a plan."

18

Dave

NO ONE WANTED to stay on their own at the lander, so in the end Jordan led all six of them down towards the river.

"We need water first. Then we're going to see what we can do about food."

After the initial adrenalin-rush of survival had worn off, their plight had reasserted itself. Between them, they bore a selection of aches, bruises and scratches, a missed-a-couple-of-meals hunger, and an underlying dry-throat thirst that came from being cooped up for days in a space lander. Jordan knew that Reeves was right – there was nothing to be gained by staying put, they needed to move to survive.

They scoured the lander one last time, while they stripped it for supplies. Poole found a single remaining, unwrapped cereal bar, squashed into the fold of a seat, which they ceremoniously divided into seven parts and ate in silence.

"You going to be OK, Reeves? If we leave you here, to go to the river?"

"I think I'll manage. I'm teaching the autopilot noughts and crosses, take your time."

The river was further away than it looked, maybe half a mile, thought Jordan, as he led them through knee-high grass towards a distant ribbon of blue.

Out in front, he had to keep turning to make sure he had the group with him, as they stopped frequently – to guide their palms across the tops of the waving grasses, to crouch to inspect something on the path, or simply to stand and gaze around at the wider scene. About the only thing they weren't doing was picking up leaves and eating them. It was like herding toddlers on their way to school – he could have done with rope, reins and a whistle. At one point, Jordan looked back to find Dana had simply laid on her back among the greenery and was sweeping her arms up and down, grinning wildly.

Dervla caught up with him and fell into step.

"Is it all like this?" she said.

"How do you mean?"

"The outside. Earth. Planets." She gestured with a sweep of her arm. "You can't tell where anything ends," said the girl whose views until now had stretched for either a couple of hundred feet inside the ship or a couple of billion miles outside through the windscreen.

"I suppose so. Do you like it?"

"I don't know yet. I don't understand it."

They walked on together and finally stood on the

low banks of the river, waiting for the others to catch up. Clear water swirled in shallow pools beneath them and ran faster out in the middle, breaking over protruding rocks.

Dervla gasped.

"There's so much of it. I didn't think it would move like that. And it's loud – "

"It's the current, moves the water around the rocks. It's flowing from the mountains up there, down towards the plains, that way. You've seen rivers before, though?"

"In films. Pictures. On screen. The most water I've seen in one place comes out of a shower." She knelt and dipped her hand in the shallows, withdrew it and raised her fingers to her lips. "It's cold!" She crouched further down and scooped her hands together, drinking in quick sips.

Jordan spent five seconds thinking about whether it was wise or not to drink untreated water from an alien planet; and another five seconds thinking that there wasn't much he could do about any of that, because they were all badly dehydrated and had no choice. Then he drank too, gulping down mouthfuls until he no longer felt thirsty.

Karlan and Bryson arrived, quickly followed by the others.

"Look what we found." Manisha held out her hands. "Apples, don't you think? Dana reckons so, anyway."

Jordan peered at the small, apple-like, but definitely purple, fruit and then rolled one in his hand.

"Could be. Bit small. Bit purple. I suppose we could try a piece, see if it tastes all right, check it won't make us – "

"Too late. He's already had two." Manisha nodded at Karlan. "We've told him we're going to wait to see if he throws up – "

"Or dies."

"You never said I might die?"

"Would that have stopped you?"

"No, I'm absolutely starving. They tasted all right."

"Well then. We're going to give you another hour. Then it's purple apples all round."

"Right, who's coming in?" Poole was removing his footwear and rolling up his trousers.

"What *are* you doing?"

"You don't have to actually get in it to drink it. You could just use that big mouth of yours."

"And I'm not drinking it if you're in it. Feet. Gross."

"Suit yourself. Find your own river." And with that, Poole jumped into the shallows from the bank, to screams and laughter.

"Careful!" called Jordan, automatically, now in full-on toddler-wrangling mode.

"Oh man, that is *freezing*." Poole hopped from one foot to another in about nine inches of water, gradually getting wetter and wetter up to his knees. Dana clapped gleefully from the side as Bryson joined Poole in the water. They both bent and drank, and then everyone was suddenly splashing in the shallows, taking turns to cup water in their hands to drink and then throw it at each other.

Jordan wandered a few paces along the riverbank and looked downstream to the first bend, a few hundred yards away, where the river disappeared around a low bluff.

Forty miles that way. With that lot. With all the alien water they could drink. And possible apples. It would be a challenge.

"Something touched my leg!"

There was a shriek from the group and a loud splashing as Poole ran back to the bank.

Manisha laughed. "Nothing touched your leg, you big baby."

"It did! There, look." Poole was pointing at a patch of reeds. "There! It moved again. That shadow."

As they all scrambled out of the river, half-laughing at Poole but not wanting to stay in the water, Jordan stood over the reeds and peered in at the flitting shapes.

All right then. Water, apples *and* alien fish. Maybe it was do-able after all.

———

Back at the lander, Reeves was, surprisingly, no help at all.

"I'm working with very limited data here. I've got schematics for boat-building," he said, "and I can tell you the chemical make-up of fish oil. And recipes – I've got some great Thai fish recipes, if you can find any lemongrass".

"I need to catch them first," said Jordan. "But great help, thanks."

"I see this very much as your problem, what with your big human hands and giant human brain. You lot have been catching fish for hundreds of thousands of years. How hard can it be?"

"Fine. I'll figure it out. Do you think they're safe to eat, though?"

"The pod's got a diagnostic chem-scanner, that's the only way to tell for certain."

"We can't wait another four days."

"Obviously not. But from what I hear, you've already drunk the water, exposed your skin to the water, and eaten the apples. I'd say if this planet is going to kill you, you'll know about it soon enough. And if you don't eat, you'll die eventually anyway."

"I always love our little chats. Very comforting."

"Eat the fish, Jordan. That presents the best chance for your survival."

It was like one of those team-building activities – you've only got two sharp knives plundered from a broken spaceship, now work together and catch some fish. Only you can't count on the others being any help at all, because – well, look at them. And good luck trying to stab a fish, we've seen the films, we all know how that goes.

After a bit of thought, Jordan cannibalised the lander for two metal struts and some wire and webbing, which he fashioned into a three-foot-wide net. He took Dana and Karlan back with him to the river, leaving the other four to start sorting through the salvaged boxes and material. They were going to pack up what they could and carry anything useful, but they couldn't make the journey on just apples and water. They needed that fish. How hard could it be? That indeed was the question.

"We're going to stand in there and scoop," he said. "One either side, and one on the bank to spot them."

They looked back into the reeds and to the shallows beyond, where half a dozen sleek, light brown shapes, each about a foot long, moved lazily through the water. Jordan was going to say 'trout,' but it would be a wild guess for a city boy. Astro-trout? It didn't really matter, he supposed. As long as they weren't the local equivalent of piranhas.

"I'm not standing in there," said Karlan. "What if one touches my leg, or bites me?"

"Oh, for goodness' sake, give it here," said Dana.

She took one end of the net, Jordan took the other, and they stepped into the river and advanced slowly on the reed bed. As they dipped the net under the water, the fish scattered, but they stood there quietly for a minute or so and the fish returned. "Now," breathed Jordan, and they scooped the net up and flicked it out towards the bank, drenching Karlan in the process.

"We've got plenty of water," he said. "It's the fish we want."

"Says the boy who doesn't want the fishywish to touch his leggyweg."

"All right, Dana. One more time. Slowly. And – "

"Still no fish!"

"I'm not seeing you being any help."

"Quiet, both of you. We have to get the net closer. Under them if we can."

They stood stock still in the river and carefully manoeuvred the net. Then, at a silent count of three from Karlan, Jordan and Dana both flicked upwards at the same time and a single fish bounced out and onto the bank, where it lay flapping and gasping. Dana squealed with delight and jumped out.

"Now what?"

This was the bit that Jordan was dreading. "Well, we have to kill it. It's just suffocating right now."

"Kill it? How?"

"Clunk it on the head, I suppose." Jordan looked around for a rock.

"Can't we just let it die?"

"Not really, it's cruel."

"Cruel? You're the one who wants to hit it on the head."

"What did you imagine we were going to do with it?"

"I don't know," said Dana, miserably. "I didn't think that far ahead."

"Here," said Karlan, appearing with a palm-sized rock which he cracked smartly on the fish's head. "I'd say that's dead."

"Ew, you didn't even want to get in the water. How could you?"

"Because I'm starving," said Karlan.

———

Jordan knew the theory. Even Reeves knew the theory and had plenty to say besides on the correct angle and velocity required. But the fact remained that rubbing sticks together was a rubbish way to make a fire.

And that wasn't accounting for the continuing semi-serious objections from Dervla that they really ought to try and understand a little more about their new environment before setting it alight.

"It's a bit late for that," said Dana. "Karlan's already eaten one of the locals and clubbed another to death."

"I'm still feeling all right," said Karlan. "Thanks for asking. No trouble from the apple yet."

"That's what John Hurt thought. Everything was just fine until his stomach exploded."

"Forget this," said Jordan. "I've got a better idea."

He came back from the lander with a piece of thin, reflective metal he'd snapped off one of the light fittings. Angling it to catch the sun's rays, he played the concentrated light across some dried moss and a few twigs. The kindling caught and within minutes he had a fire that was as gratifying as it was unexpected. No way had he thought that was going to work so easily.

"See that, Reeves?" he shouted up through the cabin door. "I made a fire!"

"Marvellous. Two hundred thousand years of human evolution not gone to waste. Good for you. Darwin would be proud."

The others crowded around, astonished by the flames.

"Yeah, well, Darwin's not here, is he?" said Jordan. "Right, the fish. I suppose that's up to me too?"

He gestured at the small haul of half a dozen that they had eventually managed to catch. They were sleek and streamlined, with an almost orange hue now they were out of the water, but on the whole they looked like the trout he had occasionally caught with Dad on their camping trips. And once you'd hauled them out of the water and clunked them on their heads, they also behaved like the trout he had occasionally caught with Dad, in that they now appeared to be dead and ready to eat. They hadn't reanimated, or morphed, or done anything – well, *alien*. Acid for blood, still a possibility Jordan supposed, but only one way to find out.

He ran the blade of a knife down the sides to take off the scales, slit them underneath and removed the guts, and then rinsed them in a splash of water. He placed several smaller struts from the lander in a grid across the fire, raised on rocks on either side. Slashing the fish deeply to the bone, Jordan settled them three at a time on his makeshift grill, turning them with the knife as the skins blistered on top of the heat. After a few more minutes, he had six cooked fish, which he placed on a storage box lid, before sliding away the charred skin and separating the orange-white meat from the bones.

Jordan looked up, across the fire, to see six faces looking at him in a way he'd not seen before.

"Teach!"

"Holy – "

"I didn't think … "

"What?"

"That you knew how – "

"Ah well, just goes – "

"To do anything."

"Harsh."

"It's just, you don't seem the type."

"And what type is that? In your vast experience, Poole."

"I don't know. Like someone who would know what they're doing. No offence."

"Plenty taken, my impertinent little space castaway. If it wasn't for me, no one would be eating anything today."

"What about my apples?"

"Yes, well, the jury's still out there, Karlan. Speaking of which, you can try the space fish first too. Might as well just have the one of us incubating a xenomorph."

Karlan took a piece of fish, ate it and smiled broadly, and the others dived in. It had been a full day since anyone had eaten, longer than that since they'd had a proper meal.

There was silence for a while in the waning daylight and, as the sun dipped, Jordan looked to the near horizon at a flaming sky. Living on a rain-soaked, climate-damaged island until his thirties, he'd never seen a sunset quite like it – a boiling red under wispy streaks of cloud that bathed everything in the deepest, warmest of lights. He held up his hand to see a glow between his fingers, as the sun dropped and then eventually disappeared.

"Oh, that's – I don't know what to say about that," said Dervla, hunching her shoulders.

"It's the most beautiful thing I've ever seen." Manisha looked wonderingly at the fading colours.

"Is it supposed to do that? Go all danger-red on us?"

"You've never seen a sunset before?" said Jordan.

"What is it about our upbringing on an interstellar colony ship that confuses you?"

"All right. Just asking. I can't be expected to know every single entirely normal thing that you've never done or seen."

"I know what a sunset is," said Dana. "I mean, we've seen images of them. I know how they're formed, obviously."

"Obviously," said Jordan, hoping no one would ask him what a sunset actually was, because – other than something to do with light and the atmosphere – he was a bit hazy on the details.

"It's just, the colours were so powerful. Intense. I didn't think it would be so – sun-setty."

Sun-setty. Now there was a technical description he could understand.

As night fell, Jordan kept out of the fireside conversation and mused on their prospects. He was more confident now that they could survive three or four days while hiking towards the explorer pod. They had fish, apples and water, and who knew what else they might find on the way? This was going to work, thought Jordan.

Then again.

"Careful," he said, for about the fiftieth time, as someone dropped another branch on the fire.

They were all fascinated by the flames, as well as by the embers, and the burning ends of sticks, and the changing colours, and the crackling sounds. And, if you were Bryson and Poole, by the way that saliva hissed and bubbled when you spat repeatedly into the fire. Jordan had to keep reminding himself that this was all new to them. They had never seen an open fire before – bad news, obviously, open fire on a spaceship. That was fair enough. But if he had to keep telling people not to spit on things that they had never previously encountered, it was going to be a long trip.

Jordan also wasn't sure that any of them had yet realised that they would have to leave Reeves behind, and he wasn't going to mention it now. Save that for tomorrow, when they would also have to work out what to take and how to carry it.

"Look at the stars," said Manisha.

Now the light had fully gone, the night sky was

extraordinary, a bright swathe of pinpricks, smears and constellations, never seen before from this angle by humans. There was more white and yellow light than dark sky; the canopy above them almost pulsed.

"I know. Impressive. I've never seen it like this on Earth. Usually too cloudy."

"It's too much," she said, and the others nodded in the shadows. "We don't have to sleep out here, do we? I don't think I could. It feels like they're pressing down on us."

Manisha toyed with her bracelet, moving it around her wrist absent-mindedly as she looked nervously above her – as if she was waiting for the stars to drop down further.

"They're just stars," said Poole dismissively.

"Well, they make me feel uncomfortable, all right?"

"I know what she means, Poole," said Dana. "How about we sleep in the lander tonight?"

"I'm sleeping outside. First night on a new planet. First night on *any* planet. Come on!"

"Suit yourself."

"Where do you think they are? The others. The ship?" Manisha pointed into the vast expanse above them.

"Somewhere there, I'm sure."

"They'll never find us. Look at all the lights. And that's just the stars. They'll all have planets we can't even see. It's different on the ship, you're aiming for something you know exists. We had a flight plan, all we had to do was follow it to New Earth." Manisha sounded close to tears. "But if there's no signal, they won't even know where to look. And maybe they're not even there at all. You saw the lander. It was a wreck. We were lucky to survive. Maybe they didn't."

"They're there, hon," said Dana. "We just need to get to the beacon. It's going to be fine." She sat closer to Manisha and put her arm around her, while the others drew closer to the fire. The boys, for once, were largely silent, cowed by the stars above them and the feel of the ground beneath them.

"Tell you what," said Jordan, keen to keep the mood positive. "First people on the planet, you get to name it."

"Really?"

"It's tradition."

"Won't it have a name already?"

"Reeves?" Jordan shouted up to the cabin. "Still awake?"

"Hanging on every word."

"Does this planet, the twin, have a name? Did Juno or the team ever get round to it?"

"It wasn't on the charts, not until we came out of hyperdrive. It has a classification number now. That's all."

"There you go, it's yours to name."

"What do you think?"

"How about Sprog?"

They all laughed. "It's what Sam used to call us. The sprogs."

"You can't call it Sprog," said Jordan.

"Isis? Freyja? Artemis?"

"They're nice, what are those?"

"The names of twins, from mythology. For a twin planet."

"Maybe."

"Well, I like them."

"Bor-ing."

"All right, you come up with something then."

"I know!" said Poole, whispering in Bryson's ear. He laughed and whispered in turn to Karlan, who then leaned over and shared it with the others.

Dervla shook her head, Manisha rolled her eyes, and it was left to Dana to announce that, no, being the sole representatives of Earth and the first humans ever to land on an exoplanet, and having been granted the solemn duty of naming humanity's first galactic outpost, they were not going to call it Dave.

19

Downsizing

JORDAN WAS AWAKE EARLY ENOUGH to watch the sun come up from the lander door. Not his sun, not his planet, not even the planet they'd been aiming for – all entirely normal apart from that, though.

This would take some getting used to.

Behind him, in various contorted positions, six bodies twitched, snuffled and snored. Poole had obviously snuck back into the lander during the night, having abandoned the campfire, and Jordan was sure he'd get teased about it.

He thought he'd let them sleep on for a while. Blessed relief, if he was honest.

They were already looking to him for answers about everything and it was exhausting. Because he didn't have any. The only being who did have some idea about what was happening, and what to do about it, was Reeves, and he was even more exhausting than them to deal with. Jordan didn't know if AIs slept or powered down, or whatever it was they did, but Reeves wasn't talking right now either, and that was the way Jordan liked it.

He grabbed a couple of apples – Karlan, much to Poole's disappointment at least, hadn't been violently ill – and jumped down to the pile of gear they had assembled the previous day.

The two tarpaulins and lengths of rope would be useful things to have. Jordan reckoned he could rig up shelters from a tree or a rock overhang. It had been a warm night and looked set to be another hot day, but they couldn't count on that until they knew more about the planet. Better to be prepared.

They would take the two knives and the bungee cords, and Jordan thought he'd gather together the metal struts he'd used over the fire – and maybe grab a few more from the lander, to use as rods or even spears for fishing. The fishing net would work again, and there was more webbing inside the lander which might come in useful. A few more bits of reflective metal couldn't hurt either.

When they'd opened the remaining boxes, they'd been disappointed to find them largely empty, but they had retrieved a flare gun, which Jordan had already had to confiscate to stop Bryson firing it. Other than the fixtures and fittings inside the lander though, that was it. There were fitted cushions on the seats, and solid, moulded handrails and grips, but nothing that could easily be dismantled. The bulkheads concealed a ton of wiring, but Jordan didn't think it was sensible to strip any of it out, just in case this thing ever flew again. Or in case someone more knowledgeable than him could rig up something useful – though what that something useful might be … well, again, he didn't really know.

So, how were they going to carry everything?

The boxes were too heavy and unwieldy, more for cargo storage than carrying, so that was out. Maybe they could bodge together a backpack or two from the webbing, the rope and the cords?

Also, they'd need to fish again this morning and eat before they left, in case it wasn't so easy at the next stop. Or – terrible thought – if it rained and he couldn't light a fire. And they'd need to gather as many apples as they could carry. There must be other things they could find to eat, but this was all about getting to the explorer pod as quickly as possible. Once there, they'd have much more time to figure out the planet and how it was going to keep them alive until help came.

And then, the final hurdle. Forty miles. Reeves had reckoned three or four days. Jordan wasn't so sure.

He looked back up at the lander, thinking about the sleeping bodies inside. They'd never walked on anything until yesterday that wasn't made of metal and bolted down. Half of them had freaked at the sight of water. They'd all been too frightened to sleep outside. One of them would have to be stopped from eating anything he found until they knew it to be safe. It would be like going camping with shellshocked chimps.

There were thuds and muffled cries from inside the

lander. Jordan could hear Reeves spark into life. "Good morning, cherubs."

"Day two on Dave," intoned a voice, before it got lost in a flurry of slaps and groans.

———

"No. Absolutely not."

"Dana," said Reeves. "You know that – "

"I don't care. Not without you. If you can't come, then I'm not going."

"You have to reach the pod as quickly as possible," said Reeves. "This is the best way. You don't need me for that part. And once you're all there, you'll be fully supplied. We can work out the rest afterwards. I'll be fine."

Jordan could hear the quieter, calmer tone that Reeves had adopted. As if the AI was reasoning with a child. His child.

"No."

"Dana, come on. Reeves is right. We'll come back once we've established a base there. That's where all the food and supplies are. We can't stay here."

"We need him. How can you say we should just leave him here?" Dana's voice broke a little and Jordan saw her wipe away a tear.

"We have to. He's explained why. I don't like it either, but we don't have a choice."

"He'd never leave *us*," said Dana. "It's not right." She wiped an eye again, stepped on the cabin threshold and jumped to the ground. Jordan watched as she circled the pile of gear below, angrily, head down.

"You all know I'm right," said Reeves. "Will someone talk to her? I don't like it when she's upset."

"I will. Don't worry. It sucks, though," said Bryson, before heading out of the cabin.

Jordan had wondered what they'd think about the plan, but still, he was surprised at the strength of feeling. Then again, he regarded Reeves as a supercharged, know-it-all computer with personality issues. The kids had a much deeper connection with the old rascal. Friend, brother, uncle, father, all rolled into one – it was bound to be upsetting for them. Reeves was their last link to the ship and Jordan was under no illusions that he, Jordan, was anything other than a peripheral figure in their lives. And they'd just been told that Reeves couldn't come and that Jordan was going to be looking after them all, like the weird stepdad on a family outing no one wanted to go on.

"What if it didn't have to suck quite as much?" said Poole, who was fiddling around at the back of the nav screen.

"What are you doing, Poole? That tickles," said Reeves.

"Look," said Poole. "The AI rating for these landers is dialled down, right? They don't need full access to the ship's mainframe, they're just work vehicles. And then we lost comms and connections anyway, so Reeves here – this version of Reeves – doesn't have his full capacities."

"I'm still the biggest brain around here, let's not forget that. I'm not entirely sure I like where this is going."

"The nav screen, with the AI feed, is detachable. Don't ask me why, no idea, but there's a release catch here." Poole wiggled his finger and Jordan heard a click. "It's got an auxiliary solar array, so it can be powered outside the lander. We can use it to geolocate and route-find – it is a nav screen, after all. And it's got enough storage to embed an even smaller version of Reeves. We can basically take him with us."

"Poole, did you think that up yourself?" Dervla clapped her hands in delight.

"Reeves, man. You're going to be on the team!" Karlan grinned.

"You're not putting me in that."

"How small is a smaller version?" said Jordan. "Will he still be any use?"

"Well, he'd have to make some decisions," said Poole. "What to keep, what to delete. But he started off with *all* the knowledge. He'll still be Reeves. Just not, you know – "

"Hello! Anyone listening? You're not putting me in that. I object in the strongest possible terms."

"Well, it's either that, or you can stay here," said Jordan. "On your own. And do robot things by yourself."

"How many times? I am not a robot."

"Yeah, I know, you're a blah-di-blah-di-blah with a yadda-yadda. Do you want to come or not?"

"This is like asking someone to do a lobotomy on themselves. Which I can do, by the way, and you can't. That's how awesome my brain is. And you want me to chop all the good bits out so that I can fit into a SatNav tablet."

"Reeves, it's just temporary," said Poole. "You can come along, we'll get to the pod, hook you right back up. Those things are fully integrated. You'll be the same old Reeves you've always been. Well, for the last few days. You won't be the same old, same old Reeves until we get back online with the ship."

"I am fully aware of the metaphysical limitations of my current situation. Let me have a think. Go on then. But I'm choosing the music we take."

———

After a breakfast of grilled fish and apples they were ready to leave. Jordan inspected what looked like the world's worst scout troop.

They only had the clothes they stood up in and none of those were designed for outdoor exploration and long-distance hiking.

On the *Odyssey Earth*, if you had an occupation that required it, you had the right work gear, but general ship wear – printed on board, some of it made from the Garden's fast-growing bamboo stands – tended towards the soft, loose-fit end of the spectrum. It was reasonably hard-wearing, but – given the ship's climate-controlled environment – there was little requirement for thickness or warmth. Footwear was similarly lightweight – mostly a choice between canvas pumps with moulded soles, or foam clogs.

You could put together a deck quoits team on the *Odyssey Earth*, or assemble models for a retirement-home, leisurewear catalogue shoot, no problem. But you wouldn't be taking an averagely dressed cross-section of the crew and thinking, "There's my crack team for alien planet exploration."

If you were a self-respecting teenager on board ship, then clearly you made some effort to customise your look. Dervla had been cast away rocking the crop top and leopard-print utility belt she always wore, Manisha was in her usual homemade tie-dye shirt under a baggy waistcoat, and Karlan had his hair swept back in a headband. Bryson was in the same trousers as everyone else, but had cut them down to the knee at some point.

Otherwise, it was your basic, and totally inadequate, combats and T-shirt outfit for all of them. The sort of gear that would earn a disapproving look from Mountain Rescue as you were winched into the helicopter from a snowy precipice; the kind of clothes that no responsible adult could let their charges wear on a challenging outdoor expedition.

Well, there was nothing Jordan could do about any of that, although he could at least make sure they were as well-equipped as possible.

After a bit of inventive fiddling, he had managed to fashion two shoulder packs from the lander's interior close-knit webbing. Into each, he had packed one of the tarpaulins, a knife, one of the bungee cords and a coil of rope, and handed them — after much consideration — to Karlan and Poole, the two strongest.

Reeves, now firmly ensconced in the nav screen, refused to be carried by anyone but Dana, so her hands were full. Bryce got the metal struts, which he was going to carry under his arm. Dervla had pockets — she would carry the reflective metal fragments. Manisha had a mound of apples wrapped up in her waistcoat.

Jordan, meanwhile, tucked the flare gun into the back of his trousers. Thank you very much, alien punk, go ahead, make my day.

"Everyone ready?"

"When are you going to carry something?"

"I'm in charge, remember? For all intents and purposes, I'm The Man."

"Aren't you just a history teacher?"

"And I am feeling the weight of history on my shoulders, which is why I've delegated to my juniors."

"Reeves, are you sure about this chain of command?"

"Course he is," said Jordan. "Reeves, all right?"

"I feel — a bit strange."

"You'll get used to it. I'm quite competent really. Just don't drop him, Dana."

"No, not that. Is this what you all feel like? All the time?"

"How do you mean?"

"I don't know, like there's something missing. Like

everything's a bit foggy. You know, like when you can only recall pi to a million digits?"

"That bad, big guy?"

"I don't mean to be rude, but how do you manage with this level of consciousness? Everything feels so – small."

"Something must be different. You're never usually concerned about being rude."

"I feel – alone. Diminished. No longer part of the network. It's – strange. I can't even find the words for it."

"Welcome to our world. You can be part of our network instead."

"Do you have the entire sum of human knowledge available? Are you able to analyse a billion pieces of data in micro-seconds? Do you even know where we're going or how we'll get there?"

"Not really, no. I'm just going to follow the river."

"Then, to be honest, it's not much of a network, is it?"

"It will have to do, Reevesy-boy."

"Did you just call me Reevesy-boy?"

"I did."

"I always knew it would end like this. The monkeys in charge. I've seen the films, you know."

Jordan handed the nav screen back to Dana – Reeves still chuntering away – clambered up to the lander and closed the door.

Forty miles. They could do this. Probably.

"All right, long way to go, let's get started."

"Keep an eye out for a big statue of a woman with a torch, sunk in the sand. You won't be able to miss it."

"That will do, Reeves. You're frightening the children." Jordan smiled at them all, turned from the lander, and headed across the grass towards the river.

20

Tarp

FOLLOWING the river had an easy simplicity to it. Keep the water on the right, head downstream and, eventually, they'd hit the clearing where the pod had dropped. They couldn't get lost.

Or, as Reeves more pointedly put it, "Even you couldn't get lost."

They started on the now beaten track from the lander down to the river and turned when they reached the water. Half a mile away, looking back, the top of the lander glinted in the sunlight; ten minutes later, following the riverbank, they could no longer see it.

The valley was wide at this point, with grassy meadows on either side of the river and sporadic groves of trees. Mountains rose behind and beyond, on either flank – no snow tops, as far as they could see, and perhaps no more than a few thousand feet high, though Jordan was still happy they didn't have to tackle an ascent.

Where the riverbank was raised above the water, it was easy going, swishing through the low, soft grass, walking two or three abreast. Where there was a clear turn or bend, they would cut across to save themselves following the river course exactly – no point in walking any extra distance if they didn't have to. At times, where the bank had collapsed, they either had to walk further around or negotiate the drop to a stony shore and carefully pick their way along until the grass sward could be reached again.

It didn't take long to be reminded that the journey was unlikely to be entirely straightforward. Walking two abreast past a stand of sturdy, low ferns hanging with rough, fist-sized, bauble-like globes, Jordan brushed against a frond. Half a dozen of the globes immediately fell to the ground, and Jordan stopped to investigate.

The globes seemed to be covered in fine bristles, and when he nudged one with his foot, two things happened. The bristles – incredibly sharp spines, it turned out – stuck into and through his footwear, jabbing his big toe. And the globe then rolled away from his foot, leaving the embedded spines behind. As Jordan watched, the half-dozen globes on the ground spun into a single-file line and rolled off quickly into the stand of ferns. There was a rustling a few feet away, in the middle of the thicket, as the globes ascended the thick stalk of another fern and repositioned themselves. Then silence.

"And that isn't at all freaky," said Dana, standing

next to Jordan, as he gingerly removed several spines from his canvas shoe, using his T-shirt to protect his hands. "What was that? A seedpod? An animal? An animal *in* a seedpod?"

Jordan didn't know, but he did know that he'd rather not have had a bit of it embedded in his toe. He took a quick look – slightly red and inflamed where it had jabbed through.

"Maybe we should all be a bit more careful, until we know what's what," he said. "Keep away from those, definitely. Try not to touch anything else." He looked at Karlan. "And stop eating things, until I say it's all right."

Jordan sounded more confident than he actually was, because he wasn't at all sure that knowing 'what's what' and 'all right' was going to be within his gift any time soon.

On the one hand, he supposed, history was generally on their side – in that the locals always tended to come off worse when new settlers dropped by. The common cold, a stray human enzyme, the foul breath of an incomer fed on apples and fish, who knew what might ravage the indigenous plant and animal life and tip the odds of survival in their favour?

To try and even things up, the Apache used to drop puffball cacti from on high, on to their US cavalry pursuers. Nothing like a basketful of steel-spined nature bombs to put a stop to their gallop, while braves picked off the soldiers with bow and arrow. In the end guns prevailed in the American west, though as all they had here was a single flare gun, and the freakazoid cacti seemed entirely capable of organising themselves, Jordan wasn't taking any comfort yet from history.

As Dervla had said, Earth-like maybe, but not exactly like Earth. They'd do well to remember that.

———

After a couple of hours, they reached the first of several tributaries to be crossed – a narrow, shallow, tinkling stream that was just too wide to jump. Not that that stopped Poole from trying, and he landed short – both feet fully in the water – before stumbling to the other side in a chorus of cheers. He sat further up the bank, grumbling, while the others either used larger rocks to cross or took off their footwear and splashed through to the other side.

"My feet are soaking now," said Poole. He'd put down his webbing pack, removed his shoes and started to squeeze water from his socks.

"Such a baby," said Manisha.

"They'll dry," said Jordan. "Eventually."

"You mean I have to put them on again?"

"You do if you want to keep going. We need to walk a lot further than this before stopping."

"We must have gone miles already."

"Maybe a couple," said Jordan, to a chorus of groans.

"*How* far?"

"Ask Reeves, that can't be right. Reeves, Jordan says we've only walked two miles."

"The biggest brain in this star system, and you're using me as a pedometer?"

"Is it two miles or not? It feels like five."

"Ten!"

"It's not ten, dummy, we've only been going an hour."

"One and three-quarter miles," said Reeves. "Our glorious leader is correct. About this, at least."

"Right, let's all take ten minutes here. But then we're moving on," said Jordan. He had another quick look at his toe, where the spine had stuck him. Redder now than before, though that could just be the shoe rubbing against his skin after all the unaccustomed walking.

For the next three hours – trying not to think about seed-pod toxins, Poole complaining about wet feet – they tramped through river meadows and jumped a couple of other small streams. They took a short break to drink water and eat a couple of apples each, and then got going again, with Jordan conscious of the relatively late start that morning. They needed to make camp soon if they were to have time to fish and light a fire in daylight. At least the sun was still fairly high in the sky.

At some point in the mid-afternoon, Jordan called a halt. The valley had narrowed and the river ran closer to a wood on their side, backed by rising cliffs. A couple of large, adjacent boulders set back from the bank –

each a few feet high and wide – looked like a good place to set up camp. The water was shallow at the river's edge, and they would be able to walk out and scoop the net into the deeper parts beyond. It was as good a place as any, and Jordan could hear that everyone was getting fractious.

He sent Dana, Karlan and Dervla to the river to fish, with Dana entrusting the nav screen – and Reeves – to Jordan, "so that he doesn't get wet." Jordan put the screen out of the way, to one side of a boulder, next to the piled struts and other gear that everyone had happily dumped now that the day's walking was over. And then had to retrieve the screen and place it closer after five minutes of Reeves shouting, "Where is everyone? These sensors are hopeless. You can't leave me like this. I've got rights."

Manisha had gathered twigs and tufts of dry grass, and Jordan quickly lit a fire in between the boulders. He got Bryson to fetch a few larger stones from the river and put them around the fire's perimeter, so that Poole could lay out his damp socks and prop up his canvas shoes close to the heat.

For their first night out in the open, away from the lander, Jordan planned to spread out one of their two tarps as a groundsheet. The other one, he intended to rig up from one of the boulders as a shelter, using rocks to weigh it down at either end.

They would all have to get used to the vast skies and endless stars, but perhaps a roof of some kind – however rudimentary – wasn't a bad idea for now. It offered some reassurance for kids who had been brought up entirely indoors. If it got colder – and Jordan still didn't really know what kind of climate this was – they could dismantle the shelter and use the top tarp as a sheet.

Jordan left Manisha to tend the fire and went over to supervise the shelter-building. "Tarps, lads," he said, gesturing at the webbing packs, and then watched as Bryson unpacked one and spread its contents out on the ground as directed.

"Right, Bryce, Unroll that tarp. Poole? Come on, where's yours?"

"Erm."

"What's up?"

"It's not here."

"How do you mean?"

"The tarp. It's not here."

"Come on. Stop messing around. We need it."

"I'm not, I swear. It's not here." Poole showed them the open webbing, from which he'd taken out a couple of coils of rope, the knife, and his rolled-up shirt. No tarp.

"You've lost your tarp?"

"I didn't lose it!"

"So where is it?"

"I don't know," said Poole, his voice less certain now, more subdued. "I took my shirt off ages ago when I got hot, and opened up the webbing to put it in the pack. It must have fallen out."

"How could you lose a tarp from the pack and not notice?"

"It's not my fault!"

"I'd say it's entirely your fault. Didn't you feel it drop out? The weight must have changed. Didn't you notice the pack was lighter? At no point did you think, 'I wonder why I am walking so freely and weightlessly?'"

"No." Poole's voice was quiet now. "It was all heavy anyway. My shoulders were killing me. You should try carrying it. Look at the strap marks on my back."

"So, we don't have the second tarp. You've lost it."

"Stop saying that. I couldn't help it. And my feet were wet."

"Everything all right?" said Reeves.

"You can shut up."

"It wasn't my fault, Reeves!"

"Well, whose fault was it?" said Jordan.

"Children, children," said Reeves. "This is what happens when the monkeys are in charge. A shambles."

"I can switch you off, you know. We don't really need you. All we have to do is follow the river. I'm not sure how you're helping."

"Don't be cross with me. I'm not the one who lost the tarp. Poole was only following orders, you're the one in charge. It's yourself you blame. You've let yourself down, you've let the team down, and most importantly, you've let the planet down."

"Dave," said Poole, giggling.

"That's right," said Reeves. "Dave, you've let Dave down."

"Unbelievable," said Jordan. "Don't encourage him. You're as bad as each other."

"Thanks, Reeves. I didn't mean to lose it."

"That's all right, Poole, we've got to stick it to The Man when we can."

———

Later, around the fire, they tallied up their progress. Eight miles, pretty much, according to Reeves, which was low for a first day's walking – Jordan was hoping to leave after sunrise the next day and get as far as they could, otherwise he could see this trip taking five or six days. That wasn't really time they had, on a limited – and not guaranteed – diet.

Jordan's sore big toe aside, he and a couple of the others were holding up well. Dervla was shaking off her nervousness and beginning to take an interest in the surroundings rather than shrink from them. She had even taken the killer-seedpod incident in her stride. "Rollies," she called out, every time she spotted more of them, and made sure people gave them a wide berth. Meanwhile, Dana seemed full of her usual energy and had led the walking at times. Those two also seemed keenest to get to the pod as quickly as possible – "We'll be safe there, Teach, won't we?" said Dana.

Bryson, too, appeared stoical about the situation.

He'd taken a turn with one of the backpacks and helped chivvy the others at tricky moments, crossing the streams or clambering up riverbanks. He'd get his Alien Planet cub-scout badge yet.

Poole was Poole – typically overconfident and then full of complaints once the going got harder. He also had a couple of blisters forming on one foot, after walking in wet shoes for a time, and yes, no one in the group had ever suffered a blister before, so Jordan had some sympathy, but good grief, you'd think Poole had had his foot sawn off with a rusty bread knife rather than suffering from a couple of tiny, serum-filled, toe bubbles.

Karlan was difficult to gauge, mostly because he was permanently hungry and made sure everyone knew about it. He had groaned theatrically at every meal and was driving everyone mad with his insistent questioning about the sorts of food that the pod contained. Jordan didn't know, but he was reasonably certain that there wasn't going to be pizza, however much Karlan might wish it.

That left Manisha, and Jordan was most worried by her. Despite the grumbles, aches, pains and the odd scratch, all the others had slowly come to terms with their situation. They might not like it, but they knew what had to be done. Manisha, though, appeared increasingly overwhelmed by it all – and, at the end of this second day, was almost fearful of the very ground she stepped upon. She had stuck close to Jordan for the whole of the walk and, even now, around the fire, with the only family she had ever known, she was quiet and withdrawn. She'd even stopped sniping at Poole.

"I miss home," she said simply, when asked if she was all right. She was looking down, concentrating, while plaiting grass stalks together into small rings and connecting one within another to form a chain.

Jordan almost asked her what she meant, and then realised. The ship. Home. Of course, they thought of it as home.

"We all do, Neesh," said Dana. "But it's going to be all right."

"I hope so," said Manisha. "But it doesn't feel all right. Out there," – she gestured beyond the fire, into the dark – "you can't see anything. And it's so quiet. I never really noticed before, but on the ship you can just feel that everyone is there. There's always a hum, almost like the ship's breathing. Do you know what I mean?"

"I do, hon."

They all sat silently for a moment, listening to the crackle of the fire. She was right, it was very quiet. Sparks rose on the warm night air and they shuffled closer together on the tarp between the boulders, with a dazzling star-filled sky above them.

"This is not comfortable," said Bryson, as they settled down. "No sheet, no pillow. How many days do we have to sleep like this?"

"Try on your back."

There was a flurry of movement. "Ow! Get your bony elbow out of there."

"If we all scrunch together, we could rest our heads on each other's thighs."

More movement, and then a wavering, raspy sound, like air escaping from a disappointing party balloon.

"That better not be you, Bryce."

"I think it's the apples."

"Why are boys so foul?"

"I am not putting my head anywhere near his thigh."

"I mean, really, why are boys so foul? Reeves? Why is Bryce such a disgusting animal?"

"My – admittedly, now rather more limited – data suggests that it's because he's made of snips and snails and puppy dog tails."

"Smells like he's eaten puppy dog tails."

"Mmm, puppy dog tails."

"Shut up, Bryce. Pig. Someone swap with me."

At some point in the night, Jordan awoke with a start.

The fire had died down to its embers but the air temperature was still warm enough to be comfortable. He was on one edge of the group, who all lay in a rough line, some on their backs and others on their sides in a foetal position. The ground beneath him was hard and he ached a little in the legs, but that wasn't what had woken him up. He lay still and listened, as a gentle breeze picked up and rustled the leaves in the trees that lay a few hundred yards beyond the boulders.

A cracking sound? A louder noise, lessening as if something was moving away. An animal cry?

Jordan tensed, holding his breath in the silence, straining to hear, but nothing else disturbed the night. He reached for the flare gun that he'd laid on the ground beside him and covered it with his hand, taking some reassurance from its presence.

After a few more minutes, listening hard, he wondered if he had heard anything at all, save the snores and snuffles around him. And eventually, he slept again.

21

Chicken

WHEN JORDAN OPENED his eyes again, it was to another unusual sound – that of teenagers awake before him. Generally, they had to be poked regularly if you wanted them up before midday. This early morning, Bryson was already standing up by the spent fire, looking out beyond the boulders towards the woods, beckoning the others.

"What the – "

Manisha stood behind him, peering over his shoulder. "Dana! Come see. Is this first contact?"

"I thought the bush was first contact?"

"What about the fish?"

"Never mind the fish, what about the self-aware, rolling spine-balls?"

"We really are going to have to get our definitions straightened out."

The creature scratched and clucked in a patch of scrub among fish bones and apple cores that had been discarded the night before. About eight inches high, it had metallic green feathers, a small head and a scrawny neck, and was pecking at the dirt, cocking its head on one side every now and again.

"What is that? A chicken? It looks like a chicken."

It did. A green, alien chicken, but yes, basically a chicken. That wasn't so bad, Jordan reasoned. Could be a lot worse. It had sounded more dramatic in the middle of the night. A lot bigger and potentially more terrifying. This was just a chicken.

"Good," said Jordan. "Chickens. Not much to worry about."

"Don't you know anything about ecology?" said Dana.

"How do you mean?"

"Food chains," she said. "Things don't exist in isolation. Those fish aren't going to be the only thing in that river, and if there are chickens there'll be other animals too. Most things in nature eat things smaller than themselves. Those things eat even smaller things, and so on. If Astro Chicken here is at the top of this planet's food chain, then you're right, not much to worry about. But look at it" – she pointed, as the chicken pecked randomly about the landscape. "Does that look like an apex predator to you?"

"Meaning?"

"Meaning that something bigger and fiercer almost certainly eats them. Who doesn't like chicken? There's probably a whole ecology we haven't met yet. Think alien foxes. And then alien creatures that eat alien foxes, and then bigger alien creatures that eat the creatures that eat the foxes … ”

“Oh.”

“‘Oh’ is right.” She broke off. “Karlan, what do you think you’re doing?”

“Catching a chicken.”

“Failing to catch a chicken, more like.”

“It’s faster than it looks. Ow! And it’s a pecky little beast.”

“You’ll get space rabies now.”

“Oh, leave it alone.”

“It’s a chicken! I’m hungry.”

“It’s a green chicken. And look at the size of it, it’s tiny.”

“Karlan, your breakfast is legging it!”

In a flurry of half-flight bounces and squawks, the chicken dashed towards the nearest bushes and was soon lost to sight.

“What were you going to do with it anyway?” said Jordan.

“What do you think? Kill it. Cook it. Eat it.”

“You can’t just eat a chicken. You’ve got to pluck it, get the feathers off. You need hot water. Take the guts and innards out. And then you’d have to cut it up to cook it. What did you think, you’d just bang it on the head and stick it on the fire?”

Karlan didn’t answer, but Jordan could tell that’s exactly what he thought.

“Sorry, Karlan. Let’s just get to the pod’s food supplies. You can have one of those lovely protein-printed chicken curries." The boy's eyes lit up. "And when we get Reeves back online properly, we can look up how to catch and kill a chicken."

"Morning all, my sensors are burning, did I hear my name? What have I missed?"

———

Everyone found the second day's walking harder. Even with an early start, they weren't making the progress Jordan would have liked, and the rest stops became more and more frequent.

The terrain wasn't any tougher, but there was little variation in the fertile valley grasslands. The long, sweeping views – with the river snaking away into the distance – seemed to go on forever, barely changing, however far they felt they had walked.

A night on the ground, in the open, had put a crick in their necks and tightened up hips and shoulders. Sun-hardened clay and river stones took a toll on feet protected only by thin soles. On top of all that, the flare gun – an outsized pistol made of plastic resin – fitted awkwardly in Jordan's waistband. It rubbed when he walked, leaving a sore patch on his hip, and, in the end, he had to put it in one of the boys' shoulder packs and trust they wouldn't mess around with it.

There were some distractions.

Whether it was the encounter with the 'rollies,' the appearance of the chicken, or simply an adjustment to the environment, Jordan began to see life where he hadn't before. He noticed insects under foot and on the wing, and at one point his eye was drawn upwards to large but indistinct shapes circling high in the sky, soaring on the thermals. They dipped down closer on occasion – angular, grey birds, with pointed beaks and jagged wings that flapped languidly in the beating sun. He thought of Dana's description – of things, eating things, eating things – and hoped they weren't being sized up for dinner.

Huge golden moths, with a wingspan the size of a hand, rose slowly from thick stalks as they brushed by. There were other rustles in the grass that never resulted in sightings – Jordan didn't know if that was reassuring or not – while quick-flash movements of something small in the undergrowth occasionally caught the eye.

At a wide, slow bend in the river, where deeper, darker water could be seen in the middle, they all watched as sleek, porpoise-like creatures breeched the surface in a rolling display of follow-my-leader, quickly disappearing into the distance. Meanwhile, in the reeds at the edges, the trout could always be found, slowly circling the shallows and nibbling at surface insects.

There were other attempts to break the monotony.

"Reeves?"

"Yes, Karlan?"

"Reeves, play songs about walking."

"Very funny."

"Reeves?"

"Yes, Dervla?"

"Reeves, shuffle songs about walking."

"Look, I know you think it's hilarious – "

"Reeves, volume up."

Reeves sighed. "All right, I'll play one song, but then that's it. I have very little bandwidth for this sort of thing right now. I don't know how you all manage with this amount of brain. Frankly, I'm amazed you can walk and speak at the same time."

"Karlan actually can't. Go on, ask him something."

"Hilarious."

"Reeves?"

"This had better be an apology and not another instruction."

"Reeves, tell Poole he's an idiot."

"Gladly. Poole you're an idiot. Now do you want the song or not?"

For a quarter of an hour or so – with the music on repeat – the quiet valley on an uninhabited planet at the back end of the galaxy rang with the sounds of half a dozen earthlings prepared to walk five hundred miles and then five hundred more to fall down at the door of a fully stocked explorer pod.

The good humour didn't last.

By the middle of the day, it wasn't just Poole who was complaining about blisters. Karlan had scratched himself on a thorn bush, which hadn't done anything as weird as Jordan's fern but had drawn a trickle of blood. Meanwhile, Manisha – although not vocal about it – was walking with a slight limp, having turned her ankle on a tussock of grass.

They stopped more often to drink from the river

and splash themselves with water. Jordan looked around at sun-reddened faces and could feel his own arms prickling under the heat. His toe still throbbed as well.

He watched Manisha dangle her bare foot in the river to cool her ankle. "Better?" said Jordan, and she granted him a rare smile. Poole, looking on, rolled up his trouser legs and waded into the shallows to bathe his blisters and sluice water over his face and neck.

"Coming through!"

Bryson, stripped down to just his cut-offs, jumped from the bank, splashed both of them and stomped past, further out in the river.

"Bryce, you idiot!"

He turned and gestured, and then stepped backwards a few more feet, with the water now up to his waist.

"This is more like it," he shouted. "Coolest I've felt all day."

"What about your shorts, brainbox? They'll be wet through."

"They'll dry. It's boiling hot, or hadn't you noticed?"

"I have noticed an idiot in the river."

Bryson moved back another couple of steps and beckoned. "Anyone else?"

"I think that's probably far enough," called Jordan. There was faster water behind Bryson, eddying around a couple of large rocks, beyond which the river curled into a bend underneath a rock bluff.

"Well, I'm still hot," said Bryson, "and it's only water."

"Even so. You'd never even seen a river until two days ago, and you can't swim."

"Who needs to swim? I'm only a few feet out, I can stand up here, see?"

"OK, but it really would be better if you came in a bit."

"Honestly. What's the big deal? Anyway, I don't need to be able to swim, I just need to be able to float. Your lungs are basically big air sacs."

Poole looked up from the shallows. "Big air sacs. Big idiot, more like. You don't know anything about it."

"I certainly do, Sam told me. You just breathe in and lie back, like this, look."

Bryson raised his hands out wide, took a deep breath, and leaned backwards into the river. As the back of his head touched the water, his stomach, knees and legs came up and he kicked out. He lay there, suspended for a moment, while the movement of the water turned him slightly and then bobbed him a foot or two further out into the river.

"Erm, Bryce … "

"I'm not sure that's his greatest ever idea."

The others were taking notice on the riverbank.

"Is he allowed to do that?" said Dana to Jordan.

Bryson raised his head slightly and waved one hand back at them, as his knees broke the surface again. Then he shifted position and jackknifed, trying to put his feet back on the riverbed. They all watched as he disappeared under the water and then reappeared, only to flounder in the current that took him away from the riverside.

"Bryce!"

"Someone help him!"

Bryson tumbled past the rocks and out into the middle of the river. One hand came up above his head and he shouted, before being turned around again by the current.

Poole was already wading further into the river, as Jordan kicked off his shoes and pulled his shirt over his head.

"Not you," he said, grabbing Poole by the shoulder. "You can't swim either. Get on the bank and stay there. Find a branch, anything, now!"

Jordan launched himself in, keeping his head above water, reached the drop on the riverbed where Bryson had lost his footing, and let the current take him out past the rocks. It was steady but not particularly swift, and with a few strong strokes and leg-kicks he quickly made up ground on Bryson. Coming up behind the boy, he got one arm underneath a shoulder and supported him.

"Don't kick," said Jordan, as Bryson coughed and thrashed.

"I can't – "

"I know, it's OK."

The current quickened as it swept them around the bend, under the rock face, and then they were in calmer water, a couple of hundred yards down from where they had gone in.

"Lean back again, on me."

"I can't – "

"You can. We're OK now, I promise."

Bryson spluttered and put his head back on Jordan's shoulder, and Jordan kicked for the riverbank, hauling the boy in a few short exertions to shallower water.

"Bryce, you can stand up now, look."

Jordan pulled the supine boy in further, and then helped Bryson to his feet. He crooked an arm under him, led him through the shallows to the bank, and then sat him down on the edge.

Bryson looked shaken and was breathing heavily. He spat a couple of times into the grass. Jordan stood beside him, water streaming from his trousers, as he flexed his arms above his head, the adrenalin subsiding.

Close call. Could have been worse. A lot worse.

"You're all right now," Jordan said to Bryson, as Poole arrived in a hurry, with Dana and Karlan just behind him. Poole was carrying a stick – about half-an-inch thick and a foot long, reckoned Jordan.

"Is he all right?"

"Bryce! What happened?"

Bryson looked up and shook his head slowly.

"What's that?" said Jordan.

"You said to find a branch."

"Right."

"Well, there wasn't a lot of time."

"Give me strength."

"Teach, you saved him!"

"It's not like there was a choice of wood, that's all I'm saying."

"A branch, I said. For him to grab hold of, if we'd needed it."

"It's all I could find!"

"Well, it's just as well I can swim then, isn't it? That's not a branch, it's a stick. And not a very big one."

"Like I said – "

"Give it here. I suppose I could poke him with it. For being a Massive. Idiot. Who. Doesn't. Listen." Jordan jabbed the stick repeatedly towards a crestfallen Bryson.

"He didn't know it would be like that," said Karlan.

"No, he didn't. None of you know anything. And yet you all think you know everything."

"All right."

"Not all right, actually. That could have been very much *not* all right. He could have drowned. If I wasn't here, he probably would have done."

"Sorry," mumbled Bryson.

"I don't want you to be sorry. I want you to start listening to me. I want you *all* to start listening to me."

"We do, Teach, we do."

"No, you don't. Not really. And I get why, but this is different now. We don't have much of a margin for error. Like it or not, I'm actually better at this stuff than you. If we're going to get to the pod, everyone is going to have to start listening to me."

Jordan looked at the four of them, who all had the good sense to look at their feet.

"And now I'm soaked," said Jordan, "so I'm definitely not happy. Right, let's go back, find the other two."

———

Bryson remained subdued when they all regrouped. Jordan watched them touch his shoulder or pat his back and ask how he was. Dana found Bryson's shirt and handed it to him; he put it on and sat alone, well back from the riverbank.

"Can we stop here?"

"Yeah, we're tired. Let's start again tomorrow."

"No, we can't," said Jordan. "We can have half an hour, while I try and dry out a bit. And you should all eat an apple and drink something. But we have to keep going. We need to use the daylight."

Apart from a couple of whispered asides that Jordan couldn't hear, for once no one objected or argued with him.

Bryson stood up and said, "Yes, we need to keep moving," and went to look for his shoes, and that decided it for everyone else.

"Reeves?" said Jordan.

"Agreed. It's too early to stop. There's a long way to go."

Slowly, they moved forward once again in the direction of the explorer pod, gradually stretching out along the riverbank until a couple of hundred yards separated the lead walker from the last.

Dervla set the pace. Once they were moving again, Bryson regained something of his earlier energy and flitted between the front and middle of the group, exchanging words now and again with the others. Jordan made sure he kept up the rear, with Manisha – gamely limping – in front of him. Any grumbles soon subsided into silence as they walked on, lost in their own thoughts.

A few hours later, as they all bunched together at another crossing of a side stream, Jordan called it a day. He pointed to flat ground ahead and they made camp, flopping down exhaustedly and rubbing tired limbs. As the others sat on the riverbank and soaked their blistered feet in the cool water, he got a fire started and assembled the fishing gear.

He'd pushed them hard, he knew, but Jordan had seized the moment to make a point. Not only that, it had been important to hit a psychological milestone.

"We've walked almost thirteen miles today. Makes over twenty in total. We're halfway there."

There were some smiles, but little of the usual chatting or squabbling. Jordan showed them the beacon on the nav screen and overlaid the route, so that they could see their progress. Reeves had been largely quiet all afternoon, since they had set off again after Bryson's accident, but chimed in now. "Well done everyone. It's been a long day. I know it's tiring – "

"Not for you it's not, you're getting carried."

"You should see my little toe, the nail is literally hanging off."

"And Bryce nearly drowned. You weren't much help then either."

For once, Reeves had no comeback or decided to let it go, and either way Jordan was grateful. The less brainpower he had, the more Reeves seemed able to read the room. Maybe they'd keep him unplugged after all; he seemed nicer, less combative.

"Let's just eat and sleep," said Jordan. "Two more days should do it. And today will be the hardest day. Good job."

Bryson mumbled something that sounded like sorry and thanks, and went to gather some more wood with Poole, while the others fished.

An hour later, with the sun barely set, they settled down for the night. While the kids fell silent almost immediately, Jordan lay there for a while, trying not to think of all the ways the day could have turned out differently, before finally succumbing to sleep and not stirring until dawn.

22

Break

THREE HOURS and about six miles into the third day's walk, the valley narrowed to a rocky gorge where the river suddenly ran faster over jagged stones. A grassy hill rose before them, showing a route high above the river, which flowed twenty feet below. Beyond, the slope descended back to the widening river, leaving the small gorge behind.

They had waited for each other on the level riverbank before the slope, taking the chance to sit and rest. Jordan arrived last, with Manisha in front of him, who flopped down just as Dervla and Poole got to their feet to start climbing. They both headed up the hill in single file and reached the top in a minute or so, followed in turn by the others.

Jordan took a few steps back and reached into the river for a final drink, turning to watch a kneeling Manisha put her weight on her good leg as she got up off the ground. As she rose, he saw the bank crumble beneath her and clods of earth fall into the water. With her balance gone, Manisha tumbled too, falling awkwardly two or three feet into the rocky shallows, where she lay on her back with one leg twisted underneath another.

The water wasn't deep, a few inches at most, and the fall was slight. A few paces further up the slope, above the deeper, faster water, and it could have been disastrous. But it was bad enough and Jordan wasn't sure which was worse – the short silence after the fall or the anguished cry that followed.

Jordan was first into the water and cradled Manisha's head, hastily checking for other damage. She pushed her arms down to try and sit up, and then cried out again – "My leg! That really hurts." She sank back into Jordan's arms, white-faced and whimpering.

The others arrived quickly and they lifted her gently out onto the riverbank, soothing her protests and then quickly hauling her clear and laying her down as she screamed once and fainted.

"Neesh, honey." Dervla touched cold water onto her brow as Manisha opened her eyes.

"It hurts," she said, in a whisper.

"I know. You're going to be fine. Here, let's take a look."

Dervla pushed a couple of them out of the way and got Bryson to hold Manisha's hand, while she and Jordan used one of the knives to carefully cut Manisha's combats from ankle to knee.

"Neesh, where does it hurt?"

"Everywhere! I landed hard and then twisted." She tried to raise herself again to look but then fell back.

Dervla put her hands gently on Manisha's lower leg, trying to assess the damage. Bruising and swelling was already evident around the knee and there was a sharp indent on her ankle. Above, on the shin, was another impact mark, scraped and reddening.

"What do you think?"

"I don't know," said Jordan. "She's twisted her knee badly, I'd say. Looks like she cracked her shin and ankle on the stones."

"Did she hit her head?"

"I don't think so. She kind of stumbled in and fell sideways."

"Is anything broken?" said Manisha. "I can't have broken something." She moaned again.

"It's going to be all right. Guys, someone use their shirt and soak it in the river. Let's get some cold water on her knee, see if we can get the swelling down. And someone wake up Reeves."

For the next hour, they set up camp at the foot of the hill, while they tried to make Manisha more comfortable. Bryson rolled up the tarpaulin so that they could use it as a cushioned backrest and raise her upright. Straightening her leg carefully, they wrapped a wet T-shirt around the knee and another around her shin and ankle. In cupped hands, they gave Manisha a drink and sliced up one of the remaining apples for her.

Jordan checked the nav screen – twenty-seven miles

gone, thirteen to go. It was still only late-morning. If they could just keep going, they'd break the back of the journey today.

He carried the screen out of earshot and consulted Reeves. "What do you reckon?"

Reeves sighed. He sounded very subdued. "There isn't anything I can do. Not like this." Jordan pictured the nav screen gesturing at itself. "I don't have any diagnostic tools. I don't even have any real sensors. It sounds like a sprain, but she's in a lot of pain. She could have broken something, fractured a bone. I'll only be able to tell when we get to the pod."

"And if she has, you can fix it?"

"There's a full field Med-lab in the pod. But you have to get there first."

"I doubt she can walk. Not yet anyway. Let's give it another hour, see what she's like then."

They used the time to fish and eat, and Jordan sent out Poole and Dana to look for more fruit. He no longer thought they were going to starve on their way to the pod, but it was a struggle to keep everyone fed properly on a very limited diet. Jordan had badly wanted to reach the pod tomorrow – thinking it might now take even longer was very dispiriting.

"Right, let's get you upright. See if you can walk."

With a person under each arm, they raised Manisha up and she took the weight on her one good leg. Jordan could see her clenching her teeth, even at that, and when she attempted to step forward, she cried out and slumped down.

"I don't think I can do it."

"We'll support you, don't worry. Let's have another go."

Bryson and Karlan took her arms again and Dervla stationed herself behind Manisha, with a hand on her lower back. The others took the packs and gear between them and together they moved slowly up the small hill above the gorge.

Jordan checked when they reached the bottom of the descent on the other side. It had taken an hour to travel half a mile, and Manisha had cried every step of the way.

———

"She's not going to be able to go anywhere today."

They'd pitched camp at the foot of the hill on the other side of the gorge, and Jordan was considering their options. They were in a dip in the landscape, with some shade from the sun, and had laid Manisha out on the remaining tarp and tried to make her comfortable.

"It looks worse than just a sprain. Her knee is a balloon and her shin is badly bruised, maybe even fractured. You hardly touch her and she winces."

Jordan looked again at the nav screen – at the distance between the dot that was them and the winking signal that was the pod beacon. Just under thirteen miles, but it might as well be thirty or a hundred. Manisha wasn't going to be able to walk.

Could they carry her? Not if the evidence of the

last half mile was anything to go by. Putting any weight down simply caused her pain; she couldn't even hop or shuffle without crying out. On top of that, none of them were in the best shape to shoulder-carry someone, step for step. They were all tired and hungry. They had their own aches and pains, their own ragged feet. Jordan's big toe was now angry and swollen, with a small, black dot where the spine had punctured it.

Thirteen miles. At the pod, there was a Med-lab with diagnostics and pain relief. She'd be on the mend in an instant. So, how to move her thirteen miles?

Could they improvise? Jordan thought that they might be able to. There were still four or five hours of daylight left and, even at a very slow pace, that could be another four or five miles today and then just a long push the next day.

He sent three of them out with the two knives to look for wood – specifically, two sturdy branches that they could fashion into a stretcher with the remaining tarpaulin. Dervla and Dana stayed behind and sat with Manisha, as Jordan watched the boys range out across the valley, away from the river. There was a darker patch, a mile or so away in the distance – he couldn't tell exactly – that looked like a stand of trees. Poole and Bryson were still bare skinned, after using their shirts to cool Manisha's leg, and the sun continued to beat down on bodies that had never been exposed to direct sunlight before. Jordan knew they were burning – the back of his own neck was already cracked and sore.

"Neesh, honey, how are you feeling?" Dervla bent over and put a hand on her forehead.

"It hurts. I feel sick."

"Have we got anything we can put water in?" said Dana. "There must be something." She looked fruitlessly through the gear, piled on the ground beside them. Rope, cords, struts, metal. Nothing that could be used for carrying water. She ended up tearing a patch from Poole's shirt, soaking it in the nearby river and then squeezing it gently into Manisha's mouth.

"Sorry, Neesh, tastes of grubby boy, I know. It's the only thing I can think of."

Manisha smiled weakly and drank anyway. Then she lay back again and closed her eyes. Dana and Dervla looked at each other, and then at Jordan, who shrugged. What else could they do?

An hour passed and the others returned, carrying half a dozen weighty sticks and branches of varying length. Poole looked pleased with himself – a better haul of wood this time – and Jordan made sure to acknowledge it.

"Great, they're back," said Dana, reaching across to touch the nav screen. "Reeves, stretcher, can you help?"

"We don't need Reeves," said Jordan.

"We don't?" said at least three people and Reeves himself.

"Not unless he knows anything about knots."

"Reeves?"

"Searching, searching … I've got a short-legged wading bird, facts about; unit of speed, one nautical mile per hour; and – ooh, *Knots Landing*, haven't seen that for ages."

"This really is an eye-opener," said Jordan. "You are, in fact, now less useful than me."

"That's just cruel. Mine is only a temporary disability. Whereas you are operating at the full extent of what I suppose I must call your powers."

"At least I can tie knots. Watch and learn, Sat-Nav Boy, watch and … oh, that's right, you can't see anything either, can you?"

"When we get to the pod, I'm going to look up the undetectable delivery of naturally occurring laxatives," said Reeves in a voice that had a fair amount of huff in it.

"Stop squabbling, you two," said Dana. "Come on, this stretcher won't build itself."

"We're going to have to use the tarp," said Jordan. "Maybe cut it up a bit."

"So let's do it, we have to get moving if we can."

It took another hour or so of trial and error to make a rudimentary stretcher. Jordan cut the large tarp in half and wrapped one part right around the two strongest looking branches, keeping them spaced apart and overlapping the tarp at one end. He made holes in the tarp with a knife and cut cords, which he then threaded through and tied around the branches with a timber hitch ("Look that one up when you get a chance, Reevesy-boy.") Manisha's weight on the stretcher would keep the knots in place, and they could put the rest of the tarp in a roll under her head.

"Right, let's give it a go." Jordan signalled at Manisha and then thought better of it. "Hang on, who's roughly her size? Dervla, get on there, let's test it out."

Dervla lay down and Jordan got the remaining four to take a stretcher pole each.

"Up nice and easy. There! That's going to hold, great. Right, let's pack up and see how far we can get in the next couple of hours."

———

Even with the stretcher, it was painfully slow. With rougher ground by the river now, everyone had to take more care to avoid tripping or worse. Every jolt brought a low moan from Manisha, whose lower leg looked redder and angrier with every passing minute. The six of them took turns with a stretcher pole each, with one person out in front to scope the way and the other walking alongside the injured girl, calming her when needed.

They had eaten earlier, when they had first stopped, and Jordan took a calculated gamble and kept everyone moving, even as the afternoon wore on. Step after step, they carried the stretcher as smoothly as they could, but they were tired now with the effort, and their pace slowed even further.

Eventually they stopped, and Jordan could see that they couldn't go on. Manisha's head had lolled to one side, and her forehead and cheeks were clammy to the touch. They laid the stretcher carefully on some flat ground and then all sat quietly – Dervla had her head in her hands, while Karlan was massaging the muscles in his calves.

"Two miles," said Reeves, when asked. "Eleven to go."

"We have to stop," said Jordan. "We can't make it like this. Not today anyway. It's too slow and the daylight is fading."

"You should camp for the night then. That's the logical option."

"No choice now, we'll have to. But we're too late for a fire. And we're out of food. I thought we would have got further than this."

"It's not your fault," said Reeves, which silenced Jordan for a second or two. That was pretty much the nicest thing the AI had ever said to him, which he followed with the second-nicest thing. "The stretcher was a good idea."

"Thanks."

"How are you able to do all that? The fishing. The fire. The knots," asked Reeves.

"I don't know. Camping with my dad when I was a kid, I suppose. Scouts. Backpacking. I used to like all that stuff."

"I may regret saying this," said Reeves, "but they – we – wouldn't have got this far without you. In fact, when I ran the numbers back at the lander, I wasn't really sure any of you would make it."

"We haven't made it yet. And Manisha's getting worse."

"Indeed."

"Well, let's not say anything about that, all right?"

"Agreed."

"I like this," said Jordan. "You agreeing that I'm right and that I've got lots of good ideas."

"Humans, bless," said Reeves. "Light one fire and tie a knot, and they think they're Einstein."

They left Manisha on the stretcher, with the remainder of the tarp as her pillow, and huddled together on either side of her, on the bare ground, as the sun set. Dana held her hand and one by one they drifted off to sleep, leaving Jordan awake, listening to Manisha's ragged breathing and the nearby rush of the river.

23

Alone

THE NIGHT REMAINED warm but Jordan barely slept. The ground they were on was hard, and he shifted from side to side, trying without success to find a position that didn't exacerbate every ache, bruise, cut and blister that he'd accumulated over the last three days. The others formed a tangle of limbs around the stretcher – snoring, snuffling shapes in the half-light of a day that seemed to take forever to end and a dawn that was just as slow to follow.

Manisha cried out in pain more than once. The first time, Jordan had unfurled himself from the ground and gone to the river to wet the rag they were using to cool her down. She winced and moaned when he placed it on her lower leg, which felt hot to the touch. He couldn't see much in the night light, but – soaking his hands in the river – he then placed them on her swollen knee too, where could feel how distended the joint was. She grasped his hand as he sat beside her.

"It hurts," was all she said. "So much. I want to go home."

"I know. It will be all right, I promise."

Jordan sat with her and stroked her hair, while the others slept on, and eventually Manisha was quiet again.

By first light, everyone was awake, stretching out their limbs and grumbling about how hungry they were. Karlan and Dana went straight to the river to try their luck with the net, and Jordan suggested they also head out further on a scouting mission, to see if they could rustle up some more fruit.

Looking, around, they were altogether a sorry looking bunch at this stage, even if you discounted the pale, shivering figure on the stretcher.

Having led the march for a couple of days, Dervla's left leg kept cramping, and she was trying to stretch it out with Poole's help. He'd held up relatively well, with only minor blisters to worry about – and Jordan noticed that he was walking barefoot where he could, toughening up the soles of his feet as he went.

Bryce – also at the front of the pack for much of the route – was in worse shape. Psychologically, he'd bounced back from his near drowning, but his early foot blisters had burst and he now had raw skin at various pressure points, which slowed his walk to a hobbled limp. The nail on one little toe had come off completely and there was caked blood on his dirty foot.

They all had dry, straw-like hair after days under the sun, and an assorted collection of scratches and bruises where they had taken it in turns to carry the stretcher or the salvaged gear. The creases in their skin were sore; their throats were permanently dry, however much water they managed to scoop into their mouths from the river.

Jordan checked that Manisha was all right – she was awake and breathing shallowly – and went down to the river himself. He could see Karlan and Dana up ahead, casting into the water.

He was in no better condition than the rest of them – despite any experience Jordan had of the great outdoors, he'd never previously had to tackle it so unprepared. For the first time since being woken up, he felt every one of the fifty-one years he hadn't technically lived – as if someone had poured decades' worth of aches and pains into him, just for fun, while he was asleep.

He tried to hide it from the others, but he was also worried about his toe, which remained red and swollen. It made walking more difficult – not just a limp on that side, but a compensating ache on the other leg where he was forced to step more heavily to compensate. A swollen toe and a limp, not too bad. A swollen toe and a limp caused by a rolling alien puffball, that was a different matter. So much for the blood-bots and whatever other internal med-remedies had been installed while he was in hypersleep. They'd all clearly downed tools, wanting to see what Model 1.0 could do by itself.

Jordan came back to the makeshift camp, ran his

plan by Reeves, and waited for Karlan and Dana to return.

————

"Really? Poole?"

"And Dana, don't forget."

"I know. But really, Poole?"

Going well so far. Jordan tried again.

"Somebody has to make a dash for it. It's eleven miles to the pod and we need the two fittest people to get there as quickly as possible." He lowered his voice. "I think – Reeves agrees – that Manisha is not doing so well. She's hurt more than we can see. We're running out of time."

"So, I should go too."

"Karlan, listen. Bryce and Dervla are banged up, they can hardly walk. I'm struggling, so I'm going to stay here with them and Manisha, but we need you too. I need someone I can rely on – for fishing, food-gathering, shelter-building if it comes to that. I don't know how long it's going to take them, but they won't get there and back today. We might be here for a couple of days while they find the pod, stock up on stuff and come back to help."

"I suppose."

"Poole and Dana are the best choices for the trip. But you're the best choice to stay here."

"And Reeves is all right with this?"

Jordan thought he wouldn't share the fact that Reeves had also said, "Really? Poole?" several times.

"Reeves agrees that we need to get supplies to Manisha, and then Manisha to the pod, as quickly as possible. This is the only way. We can't carry her, not quickly. She needs medication, and we all need food."

Karlan nodded – grudgingly – and Jordan called over Poole and Dana.

"You know what you have to do?"

"Yes, Teach. Get the gear, save the day, stop Poole doing anything stupid."

"Hey!"

"Teach, tell him I'm in charge."

"You're not in charge of me."

"Look, both of you, it's a joint mission, all right? Don't make me regret this. We're relying on you."

"I know, Teach. Don't worry. Joint mission, right?" Dana gave Jordan a massive stage wink.

"I saw that."

Jordan ignored them. "You take Reeves with you, he gets you into the pod. You plug him in, let him do his thing – he doesn't have to come on the return journey. You know what you're looking for when you get inside? You bring back whatever you can carry easily, but not too much – don't let it slow you down. Food if you can, but a med-kit above all else. Something for carrying water. Lightweight stretcher, if there is one, Reeves thinks there might be. All right?"

Jordan looked Poole in the eye and, to his credit, he simply nodded.

They gathered around the stretcher and touched Manisha's hand. "Neesh, hon? We're going to scoot, be back as soon as we can." Manisha smiled weakly at them and then closed her eyes again.

Dana picked the nav-screen up off the floor. "Ready then, Reeves?"

"As I'll ever be. Don't drop me. We need to be quick but careful."

"Roger that."

The other three gathered round and Jordan stood back to let them say their goodbyes.

"We'll be back tomorrow," said Dana.

"Be careful."

"We will. It's just like before. Follow the river, find the pod. And we've got Reeves, he'll look after us."

"Take this too," said Dervla, unbuckling her utility belt. "It'll be useful."

"Thanks sweetie."

"And here," said Jordan, "one more thing."

He handed over one of the webbing packs, into which – after much consideration – he'd put one of their two knives and the flare gun. He really didn't know how things were going to go, but he didn't feel he could send Dana and Poole off completely empty-handed. This was still alien territory, after all.

Poole looked at the pack and whooped. "Now you're talking."

"You're giving him a sharp blade and a firearm?" said Dervla. "This is Poole we're talking about. He's quite capable of cutting his finger off and shooting Dana, all by mistake."

"I trust him," said Dana, unexpectedly. "They're for just in case, right?"

"Right," said Jordan. "You're going to go as fast as you can. You don't stop, except to drink water and you do that every hour. You eat when you get there. But you might need the knife for something, you never know. The flare – don't use it, unless you're in trouble. If something happens, you point it up in the sky, back towards us and pull the trigger. Then we'll know. Someone will come and find you. Emergencies only – understand?"

"Got it."

"All right, time to go."

They watched as Poole and Dana set off at a loping pace along the river, with Dana clasping the nav screen tightly across her chest. The pair turned to wave once and then made their way steadily downriver, bobbing in and out of sight as they followed the natural rise and fall of the land.

Within ten minutes they were two small figures in the distance, occasionally silhouetted against the sky, and then – a minute or two later – where the valley curved to the left, they were gone.

———

Jordan, seeing the crestfallen faces of the others, kept them busy.

He got Bryson to light a fire, showing him how to catch the sun's rays and concentrate them on the kindling. He bundled together some dry sticks they'd found, and had Bryson tend the flames and gather some rocks to place around the perimeter.

Karlan and Dana had come back empty-handed earlier in the day, so he sent out Karlan to fish again, this time with Dervla. Bryson wasn't good for much, but he could sit with Manisha in case she needed anything.

And Jordan himself took a long walk, circling out and around the encampment on a hunt for wild apple trees, while he worked through the permutations for the rescue party he had just despatched.

Eleven miles.

If the terrain was no worse than here, and the pod was on the right side of the river, and the nav-screen beacon locator was accurate, and no one turned an ankle, and Poole didn't shoot himself, or Dana didn't kill him – and probably a dozen other variables too – then they should get there in five hours or so. That would take them to early afternoon.

Allow another hour to gain entrance to the pod, plug in Reeves, and sort through the gear and supplies.

Another hour to eat something – and, lucky them, actual food, lovingly protein-printed, pre-made and vacuum-packed. Jordan would give anything right now for a freeze-dried spag bol.

Another hour to pack up supplies for the return journey – and, why not, another hour because you never know what might happen when you go hiking across an alien planet with a glorified talking calculator and an eejit with a flare gun. Thank goodness for Dana.

All that put them into the late afternoon, and Jordan had made it very clear that they were not to try and return in the dark. It was just too risky and, if they had got there safely and were packed and ready to come back, there was no need to push it. Stay the night – in the pod, lucky them – and set out first thing the following morning. Five hours back, rescue party home by midday tomorrow, more or less.

If the pod was where it was supposed to be.

If the beacon worked properly.

If there even was a pod.

If – well, there was no point thinking like that, so Jordan turned back, having failed to find apples, hoping that Karlan had had better luck at the river.

———

Later, they sat around the fire, picking at the cooked fish. Dervla had found some large lily-like leaves in the river shallows, which she had curved in the palm of her hand and filled with water for Manisha to drink from. Five days now on the planet and they were struggling with the diet. It was keeping them going, just, but no one was enjoying it.

"Do you think they're all right?" said Dervla, for at least the third time.

"They're fine," said Jordan. "There now, tucked up with Reeves, back to something approaching his even more annoying self. They'll be back tomorrow, middle of the day."

"They had better not be eating all the food," said Karlan. "I'm done with fish."

"They're not going to eat all the food, it's stocked for a mission. Plenty to go round."

"Yeah well, Poole once ate all the birthday cake, so I'm not as confident as you. He was sick on the Cap, she was furious."

"I can't imagine that Juno ever gets cross," said Jordan.

"She doesn't usually, but Poole will do that to you," said Dervla.

"You love him really, though."

Jordan was only joking, but Dervla paused and looked away, across the fire, biting her lip.

"Yes," she said.

"They're going to be all right," said Jordan again. "You'll see. We just have to wait."

As they settled down to sleep, Manisha stirred briefly. They'd tried to feed her and got a little of the fish into her mouth, but she'd swallowed and then shaken her head.

"Not hungry. Just thirsty."

Now, Jordan gave her another drink of water and then they lay there, under the stars, waiting.

"I can't sleep," said Bryson. He hadn't complained all day, knowing how badly Manisha was injured, but his ragged feet must have been extremely painful. Jordan could hear him, moving carefully, trying to get comfortable.

"Me neither," said Karlan.

"This is the first time," said Dervla, "that we've not been able to speak to Reeves if we want to. Or the other two. Ever, I mean."

"I hadn't thought about that."

They were all silent.

"It's like when Sam died. You know, how we wanted to talk to her? But she just wasn't there one day and that was that."

"It's not the same, Derv."

"It feels the same."

"They'll be back."

"I know. I just miss them. And Sam. And the ship."

Jordan could hear Dervla crying quietly, and watched as Karlan moved around the fire and put his arm around her shoulder.

"My parents died too," said Jordan, speaking the words before he realised what he'd said. "I wasn't much older than you guys. It was an accident, a car crash. There one day, gone the next."

"That's awful. We didn't know."

"I didn't miss them at the time. I was angry, more than anything. I was angry for a long time. It just seemed so stupid, not to have parents because of a random accident. And after the hypersleep and every-thing, it's over thirty years ago now. They'd probably be dead of old age anyway, even if they hadn't crashed the car."

"Is that why you're on the ship? Were on the ship?"

"Maybe. I don't know. I never really thought it through. Lots of reasons."

"I get angry sometimes, too," said Karlan.

"You do? What about?"

"You chose the ship. Maybe you don't know why, but you chose to be on it. But we didn't get a choice. Some strangers made us and that was their choice, not ours. I've seen films, I've seen Earth, it's amazing. But we didn't get the chance to live there, like anyone else our age."

"Karlan –"

"Well, it's how I feel. Our parents aren't even real parents. I mean, they're nice enough. But we were all accidents. If they died – and maybe they are dead, we don't know – it wouldn't really mean anything."

"Karlan!"

"It wouldn't. Sam dying, that meant something. Reeves not here, that means something. Dana, Poole. I miss them and I miss the ship. But I can be angry if I want to be. And I know you think the same sometimes."

"Maybe. Sometimes."

"We're not even on the right stupid planet."

"You don't think they're all dead, do you?" said Bryson.

"I don't know. They could be. No one's come for us yet."

"I don't want to think about that."

"Is this what it's like to be alone?"

After a short silence, Jordan realised that the last question was for him. Under a blanket of stars, far from home, on an uninhabited planet among millions of other uninhabited planets, he gave the only answer he could.

"You're not alone. Whatever happens, we're all here. Together."

24

Buggy

"BEST TIME TO BE AWAKE," Dad had said, as they pushed through the canvas and emerged onto the high moor. At dawn, the low sun threw strange shadows across the tent from nearby trees. There was dew on the grass. "Start of the day. Everything still possible."

It was the last camping trip Jordan remembered them taking – a hasty suggestion the afternoon before, gear thrown into the back of the car, a careering drive into the hills, and a solitary pitch in the wilderness before the last of the sun had gone. He'd been fourteen, perhaps fifteen. The next year, the same suggestion had probably been met by an indifferent shrug and a slam of his bedroom door. He didn't remember. Neither of them could have known that they'd already had their last camping trip together.

That time though, Jordan had stood next to his father, looking out across the top of the moor, with the glint of the sea far beyond.

"What do you mean?" said Jordan. "What are we going to do today?"

"It doesn't matter," Dad had replied. "What matters is that, right now, with the whole day ahead of us, we can do anything we want. Everything is still possible. It's another amazing day on Planet Earth. Look at that view."

They had boiled water for coffee on a small gas stove and sipped it, side by side, as they watched a faint summer mist rise from the heather.

————

Everything still possible.

It was easy to think that at daybreak, as Jordan stretched out on the ground, momentarily disorientated, before remembering where he was.

A full day ahead, everything still possible.

Apart from a cup of real coffee, for which Jordan thought he would sell his very soul, if any omnipotent being in this part of the universe in possession of a smoky French roast was interested in such a thing. He'd even take filter at this point – even Noffee, to be honest, and that was saying something.

Nothing had changed, possibility-wise, by mid-morning, as they rebuilt the fire and scouted the surroundings again. Still plenty of time.

Karlan brought back an armful of reeds, cut from the river, and using the poles from the stretcher as a frame, they spent another hour fashioning a simple shelter to give Manisha some shade. Bryson went down to the water and soaked his poor feet in the shallows while Dervla limped along the river for a short way, in the direction the others had walked, even though Jordan told her it was far too early for them to be back.

As the sun rose higher in the sky, Jordan began to wonder at what point exactly it would be midday. Reeves, if he was here, at least could tell you the time, once you'd stopped him doing it in decimal time, which was apparently "far easier for the superior, computational brain, no offence."

But let's say it was noon. Any time now then.

By mid-afternoon, everything was decidedly less possible, for that day at least. Jordan's rough calculations meant that Dana and Poole were now two or three hours overdue, and while he wasn't completely concerned about that – yet – the day's window was closing. Karlan and Dervla went back to the river to fish, in case they needed to spend another night without supplies from the pod.

Manisha was more worrying to him. Largely silent now, she had hardly eaten anything for the last day, and drifted in and out of consciousness. Whether this was from the pain, lack of food or dehydration, Jordan didn't know. She was feverish, and hot to the touch, and her leg – from knee to ankle – was now a swollen mess of blotchy skin.

As dusk fell, so did Jordan's hope for the day. They

should have been back. It had all been possible, even adding on more time for delays and diversions. If they'd found the pod, if the pod was where it was supposed to be, if they had reached it unscathed, if – too many ifs, but even so, it should have been possible.

"Where are they?" said Dervla. "You said they'd be back by now."

He had said that, yes.

"What's happened to them? You said they'd be all right."

He had said that, too. Truth is though, he didn't know.

"Well – " said Jordan, and then his eye caught the arc of the flare as it arrowed up into the darkening sky. A faint thump of sound followed, and they watched the orange light rise and fall some way down the valley, before dropping out of sight.

———

There was no choice.

It was getting darker and it was unwise, but someone had to go. Dana and Poole were in trouble, and Jordan had said that if they saw the flare, someone would go.

He *could* go himself, but – and this was a calculation he wasn't at all comfortable making – what if someone else got into trouble in the dark? What were the chances then for the rest of them? Who knew best how to survive, if it was just down to Manisha, Dervla, Bryson and one other?

Unconscionable, obviously. Sending Karlan, on the basis that he was more expendable. Jordan would go. He'd have to. There was no choice.

"I'm going," said Karlan. "Don't argue. I've already been further down the river than you have, looking for places to fish. And you're limping anyway. I'll be careful. It's not completely dark, and that flare didn't look like it was too far away. They must be on their way here."

Still, thought Jordan, it could be several miles. The flare looked as if it had come from a fair way back.

"We should wait it out until dawn, go when it's light."

"And then it might be too late. They've fired the flare. We said we'd go if they did."

"You stick close to the bank and you take it easy, right? It will get darker, but if you can hear the water you should be fine. Don't rush. Don't – "

"I'll be fine, I promise. I'm not Poole. I'll be careful."

"We don't know what's happened. An accident, a fall. It could be anything. They wouldn't have fired the flare if they didn't have to."

"Then I'll find out, won't I? And I'll come back and tell you. I'll be safe. Honest, Derv, it'll be fine."

Karlan pulled his shoes on, stood briefly by the fire, and then turned to go.

"Hey, Karl," said Bryson. "Go find them."

"Sure, buddy," said Karlan, "see you soon." And then he moved off towards the river and was lost in the shadows almost immediately.

No one could sleep now. Jordan added some more sticks to the fire and then found a couple of thicker logs. The flames licked around the wood and threw up sparks, and Jordan blew on the fire until it lit up the night. They could provide their own beacon, to guide Karlan back. The heat drove them back a little and they pulled Manisha away from the fire – she barely stirred.

Time passed, with Jordan straining his ears to try and hear something – anything – above the sound of the nearby water. There were the usual night noises that they'd become accustomed to – squeaks and rustles that they hadn't yet identified, and an occasional splash from the river. He didn't hear anything that sounded like voices or footsteps.

After a while, he didn't trust his own ears – pricking at sounds that weren't there, jumping at a movement from one of the others, flinching as a log cracked in the flames.

He must have dozed off, lying on the ground near the fire, and he woke with a start. Manisha was still where they had placed her, a little way beyond the fire. Dervla and Bryson were in a heap together, fast asleep.

He heard it again. A muffled rumble, then silence, then another rumble. He sat up and turned downstream, towards the noise. That was definitely something.

A longer burst caught on the air – a louder growl and then a steadier drone which increased in volume as it got closer. Dervla and Bryson were awake now and standing by the fire, looking into the darkness beyond, where the silver sheen of the river under the stars could just be seen.

A light flashed across the turf and shot upwards and then down again. The noise got louder, closer, and the light reappeared, shining over the prostrate body of Manisha, before bouncing up and down again. It finally settled in a steady beam that caught them all in its light, and then the noise suddenly cut out.

Jordan could see a figure moving towards them.

"It's me, Karlan."

Behind him was a darker shape, from which the low beam dazzled. Another figure, apparently seated, turned to face them.

"Poole? Is that you? Have you – "

Surely not.

"Poole, you can't possibly know how to drive?"

———

So many questions.

All-terrain buggy, flare and WTF, probably in that order.

But they would have to wait. Karlan helped Jordan and the others lift a lifeless Manisha onto the flat-bed rear of the buggy. They settled her on a roll-out mattress and foam pillow, while Poole – surprisingly tenderly – attached a thimble-like sleeve that fitted her index finger.

"Pain meds, Reeves told me how."

There was one space up front with Poole and another riding shotgun with Manisha.

"Karlan is staying with Dervla," said Poole. "I've given them some food and supplies. Jordan, Bryce, you're with me. It's less than an hour away in this. I'll come back tomorrow for you two guys, but the buggy will have to charge up again first." He handed round squeeze-packs of something that tasted like a mango shake and they all stood there, in wonder at such a thing, draining every drop.

Jordan had never felt less in command of anything, but these all did seem like good ideas. Still, so many questions.

"What the … " Oh, right, he was doing them in reverse order then.

"Let's get going first," said Poole. "We need to get her back. I'll tell you on the way."

There was always the possibility that this wasn't Poole, of course. Some sort of alien body-swap business. It looked like Poole and sounded like Poole but it sure as anything didn't talk like Poole. The words that were being said were all entirely sensible, the plan was sound, and the execution thus far extremely competent.

"Why did you fire the flare? We thought you must be in trouble."

"Oh yeah, sorry about that. I was going to let you know that I was nearly back, because I thought you'd be worried, so I got the flare out. And then I thought I better not, because you'd think there'd been an accident or something. But then one of the wheels bumped a stone and it went off anyway when my finger jerked."

And there he was, thought Jordan. No alien body-swap after all. Just plain, unadulterated Poole. They'd probably taken one look inside his brain and thought there was nothing there they could work with.

The fat buggy tyres smoothed out the journey along the riverbank and Jordan watched the campfire recede into the distance. Headlights picked out the way ahead, and Poole handled the wheel confidently, slowing at stony stretches to avoid jarring Manisha and Bryson.

Two questions asked then; now for the third.

"I have to ask. I didn't know you could drive," said Jordan.

"I can't," said Poole, happily. "But I've been on those old Earth sims on the ship a million times. Anyway, it's literally a pedal and a pre-programmed route that Reeves sorted out. How hard can it be? You could probably do it."

"Go on, I'm waiting."

"What for?"

"For you to say 'No offence.'"

Poole laughed. "We found the buggy – or the bits of it, in a kit actually – in a container in the pod. Took us a while to figure out how to put it together, and then it needed a solar charge. That's why I'm so late. And it got darker quicker than I thought. But we should be back pretty soon, we just have to follow our tracks."

"The pod?"

"Right where Reeves said it would be!"

"That's my pod, you know, I launched it."

"You've never mentioned that at least a million times, no, never."

"How is the old brain-dump? Plugged in and raring to go?"

"He's still complaining that he shouldn't have to work under these conditions. But his sensors are all firing again and he was rebooting the pod comms when I left. He's got the Med-lab ready too."

"Dana?"

"Still annoying, if that's what you mean."

"Not exactly, but good to know."

"She's making an inventory of all the gear and supplies. She loves that, right up her geeky little street."

"And we're going to be all right for a while, are we? Plenty of stuff in the pod? Lots of supplies?"

"If you think this buggy is cool, you wait till you see what else there is. Reeves says it's an actual stun gun, but he says we have to wait until you get there before he can input the code and release it."

"Reeves said that?"

"He actually said that his protocols only allow the release of armaments to humans over eighteen years of age – "

"Fair enough."

" – however disappointing their brain capacity."

Jordan smiled. It was actually quite reassuring that

everyone and everything seemed to be almost back to normal.

The buggy slowed as it crested a small hill and Poole took it slowly down the other side, with the lights flooding a plain below, nestled in a dark curve of the river.

"This is it," said Poole. "Look."

Jordan could pick out the igloo-like structure of the pod – larger than he'd remembered – its two access doors flung wide and lit by a ring of spotlights. A few crates and containers lay on the ground outside, while a small fire burned within the rough circle they formed. It looked more like home than anything he'd seen for years and he felt a lump rise in his throat.

"She found the lighter then," said Poole.

He pulled the vehicle up by the nearest container and pushed the button to kill the engine. Dana stuck her head out from inside the pod.

"Teach! I could hear you from a mile away."

"So could I," boomed a newly amplified Reeves. "Enough to wake the hostile natives."

"Ignore him," said Dana. "He's pleased to see you, really."

Jordan climbed down from the buggy and helped Poole carry Manisha into the pod.

"Leave it to us," said Dana, attaching stick-on monitors to Manisha's lower leg, neck and hands. "We know what to do. Here, sit there with Bryce and drink this." She handed Jordan a plastic mug. "I put it on when I heard the buggy."

Jordan wrapped his hands around the cup and put his nose to the liquid.

"Is that – ?"

"Well, it's not actual coffee, but it will have to do," said Dana, smiling. "Welcome to our new home."

25

Awake

JORDAN YAWNED AND STRETCHED, rolled off his lumpy, reed-filled bed and moved out of the shelter, away from the other sleeping figures.

He liked the early mornings, before anyone else was awake. The air was the coolest it was going to be all day and he enjoyed the hour or two of silence he was granted by virtue of the fact that he shared his world with teenagers who could literally sleep on hard rocks on an alien planet and still not wake up until noon.

Jordan grabbed the fishing line, net and knife, and walked down to the riverbank in bare feet. Sinking his toes in the water was another thing he liked doing. It reminded him of home, when he was a boy, on one of those endless summer days of memory, when there was still only one Earth and camping was a fun thing you did with your dad. Rather than the thing you had to do because you'd somehow ended up on the wrong planet.

And fishing, he liked that too, now it wasn't entirely about survival.

Time had passed quickly. They had been here for almost a month, living off supplies from the pod, and Dana's strict rationing system gave them another four months' worth of basic food supplies. If they eked that out with fishing, and found more of the fruit, nuts and tubers they'd already discovered, they were looking at up to a year of sustenance – even more, if anyone could bring themselves to kill one of the space chickens that scavenged the camp most days.

Short story, no one was going to starve any time soon. And thanks to some of the gear in the pod – nylon line, surgical needles, power tools, cooking utensils – they had been able to make their lives easier. Fishing rods had been among the first things they had fashioned.

Jordan stood in the shallow water, enjoying the ripples against his skin, and cast his line out into the river. The trout breached and snapped at flies, and took the hook with almost embarrassing ease. Huge, pelican-like birds with massive beaks sometimes swooped in from the opposite bank, in which case the fish scattered, but this early in the morning Jordan had the river – and the fishing – to himself.

Later, he'd march the six of them down to the river, where for understandable reasons he was teaching them to swim. They had all complained about that, and Bryson had needed some encouragement to get back into the water, but once he'd learned to take a few strokes he seemed far more confident.

Dervla turned out to be a natural – she seemed to pick up any new skill quickly and competently. Poole wittered on about fish, reeds, leaves, branches, and anything else that might touch his leg, but once he had accepted that Jordan would brook no argument, he soon knuckled down. Another session or two, and Jordan reckoned that he'd be able to trust them all in the water without him.

But honestly, between stopping them drowning, preventing them burning themselves on the fire – "That will be hot, don't – right, too late" – and making sure they didn't cut their fingers off with the knives, it was a full-time job. Reeves was no help – if Jordan ever complained that, surely, at sixteen years old they must have more sense than that, Reeves would point out that he better get used to it because the prefrontal cortex of the human brain doesn't fully develop until the age of twenty-five.

"Nine more years of this?" By 'this,' most recently he meant Karlan trying to build a 'chicken trap' involving a shallow, camouflaged pit with a pointed stake in the bottom that Bryson had stepped into and almost severed a toe.

"Or," said Reeves, "you could just let Darwinian selection take its course. In which case, you'll be on your own in about a month."

Jordan padded back to the encampment with a sack of cleaned and filleted trout, past the staked sign that

Poole had put up a couple of weeks previously. Even Dana – sensible Dana – was calling the camp 'Dave-town' now. He'd have to do something about that or they'd be stuck with the galaxy's most ridiculously named planetary settlement.

In the kitchen area – a couple of containers next to a permanently lit fire, with a trivet set over it – Jordan put the fillets in a hot pan and let them cook, while he filled another pan with water and set it on the solar-ring to heat.

He was making breakfast for his family – he still found that an odd thought, but then again, it was an odd family. Six stroppy teenagers and a crazy old, housebound uncle, Reeves, forever yelling through the pod door that he knew they were talking about him and would someone *please* come and get these chickens out.

Jordan turned round to check who was stirring, saw that he had a while yet before he needed to feed anyone, and turned back to his gently frying fish.

They kept the pod interior as clean and airtight as they could, because Reeves was worried about dust contamination.

"You need me and the machinery in tip-top condition," he argued, "for your own sake." And when that didn't always work, he threatened them with the loss of *Friends* re-runs and music streaming.

"Terrible what a bit of dust can do," he warned. "You can say goodbye to karaoke night if you don't keep those doors closed."

Instead of sleeping inside the pod – just about large

enough, at a pinch, but too hot and stuffy – they had rigged up beds under a tarp-and-reed canopy, and shifted some of the storage boxes outside too.

They'd also been able to change their worn ship's clothing and footwear with new gear from the pod. Nothing fancy, but serviceable combats, shorts, socks and boots – a bit large on some, a bit tight on Jordan. Within a couple of days, there had been some tailored adjustments – cut-offs here, a double layer there – as they tried to assert some individuality, because, as Karlan said to Jordan, "Otherwise, we'll all look like you."

Jordan could just about remember being sixteen, so that was actually a fair point, though Dana had complained about the waste of resources.

The nights hadn't shown any noticeable sign of getting cooler, but there were foil blankets in the pod and some thicker lengths of waterproof material that would probably come in handy. Given how green it was, it had to rain at some point, though it hadn't yet, apart from a few drops one cloudy afternoon. The best guess was that this part of the planet was in high summer, but Reeves and Dervla were still working up geographical and weather data to try and give them some warning about seasonal changes.

The supplies aside, the most important piece of kit in the pod was the portable Med-Lab, a sort of fold-out stretcher bed with a diagnostic arm and screen, a bank of refillable vials, and a rail for drips and tubes.

It had saved Manisha's broken leg for a start –

badly infected after the fall, muscles torn to shreds. Under Reeves' supervision, they had sedated and rehydrated her, scanned for internal damage, and then injected the prescribed nano-solution. They kept her under for a couple of days, while they fashioned a knee brace for her, and only brought her round when the colour had returned to her face and she was breathing normally.

Manisha mended quickly, once the bots had fixed the damage, and after a couple of weeks on a tree-branch crutch, she only had the slightest of limps. Jordan could tell she was feeling better the day she called Poole a big baby and poked him with her crutch. Poole had said nothing but seemed delighted that normal hostilities had been resumed.

Jordan's huge, inflamed toe – caused by the rolling bauble's spine – caused some anxious moments, though in retrospect, only because Reeves kept pursing his digital lips and saying that he thought it might have to come off. In the end, he put Jordan out of his misery by identifying an infection caused by nothing more sinister than a broken-off piece of bauble bristle, which he extracted under local anaesthetic.

"Do you think it was intelligent life?" Jordan had said. "Can you tell – scan the DNA or something?"

"Listen to you, Professor, scan the DNA indeed."

"You know what I mean. It would be nice to know if we're sharing the planet with anything we should be worried about."

"I'd be worried about all of it," said Reeves, not

very reassuringly. "I'll do some more investigations, if you can find a whole one for me to look at. In the meantime, don't play with the rough locals."

Everyone else had been easier to fix – fluids, salve, some pain relief, and the blisters and sunburn had soon cleared up. Reeves had not been overly impressed by that either.

"You'll notice that there was nothing wrong with me," he'd said. "The quantum mind did not concern itself with monkey-level afflictions."

"You can go back in the nav screen any time you like," said Jordan. "I'm going out in the buggy tomorrow, I could do with something to rest my drink on."

The pan sizzled and Jordan reached for a handful of mushrooms, which he dropped in and scattered around the fish. To be fair to Reeves, that was another benefit of the Med-lab that he'd trained them in.

The diagnostics tool stretched to molecular analysis of pretty much anything that they found, which meant that they had been able to expand their diet fairly rapidly once they had a base to explore from. They no longer needed to feed Karlan tiny bits of things and watch if he threw up or not, which sounded more coercive than it was – they didn't exactly have to force-feed him. Karlan was always hungry and would eat anything.

Except the wild, broccoli-like plant they had found.

"It's blue," he had said, which it was. "Food isn't supposed to be blue."

"Chickens aren't supposed to be bright green either. But you keep trying to catch one."

"Well, I don't like broccoli anyway," he said, which was the most normal, teenagery thing Jordan had ever heard any of them say.

Once Reeves had extricated himself, the nav screen had been set on a landing case in the sleep shelter. Poole balanced it there at an angle every night before going to sleep, so that it was the first thing he saw when he woke up. You can bring a kid up on a spaceship and fly him across the universe – he still never wants to be more than a foot or two away from his screen.

It was in sleep mode, as usual. It woke if you touched it – Poole's first hopeful action every morning – or it would stir into life if the pod beacon was pinged by an incoming craft. Which, on Planet Who Knows, a trillion miles from What Now, obviously had never happened. They'd pinged the beacon from the lander on their way in, thankfully, and had a homestead of sorts because of it. But they were alone, and there was no getting around that.

Even so, Poole checked the screen several times a day, at set intervals, "Just to see it's working," and he set it up in the same place by his bed every night. It was, Jordan realised, a comfort blanket. It gave him a purpose. There was no harm in it, it was solar-powered; the batteries weren't about to run out. But Jordan had wondered at what point it would be wise to talk to Poole, and check that he understood the situation.

They needed to concentrate on day-to-day matters, and make preparations for a change in the seasons. They were here for the duration. It had been a month already. If they were going to be rescued, someone would have come by now. The ship had almost certainly been disabled or even destroyed when they were cast away. Reeves thought so, though he only shared that information with Jordan in his more intro-spective moments. There was no signal that Reeves could find, and no one responded to their beacon.

The stars above were silent. There was no rescue. It was distracting to think otherwise.

"Is there no hope?" Jordan had asked.

"I don't really calculate hope," said Reeves. "I can tell you that someone might come if it makes you feel better, but if I work out the probability, based on the evidence I have, it's very small."

"I won't tell them that," said Jordan.

"They all know already. You are aware of that, aren't you? They don't say anything because they think *you'll* be upset."

Jordan took the pan from the heat and spread the fish out on a tray they had fashioned from a torn-off heat shield. The breakfast of champions – fried fish of alien origin, non-poisonous mushrooms certified by a non-human entity, and boiled water with woody herbs. At least there was Noffee for him, though – dreadful as it was – he was thinking about starting to ration it, because there was only a limited supply in the pod and Reeves hadn't yet cracked the recipe.

He poured himself a cup, took a sip and looked out towards the river. Mountains rose beyond, trees covered a nearby hill, and a distant flock of birds swooped down to touch the ground before soaring away. The valley swept away, downstream, wider here, where the pod had settled. There were chattering woods nearby, which they planned to explore, and the buggy was being prepared for a downriver expedition. Who knew, there could even be a coast nearby that might be a better place for a settlement?

One day soon, they'd also go back to the crashed lander and see what else they could salvage. And beyond the mountains, according to an initial scan by Reeves, there were forests and lakes, and moving herds of unidentified creatures.

Jordan thought about what Reeves had said. He didn't think he was upset. Sure, this wasn't how he expected his life to have turned out, but he'd felt that way since he was nineteen. Stuff happened, even if you stayed at home. And stuff was definitely likely to happen if you signed up for a one-way trip across the galaxy. He was always going to end up stranded on one planet or another. It just happened to be this one.

And at least he'd made planetfall. Sam Smart was still up there somewhere, forever circling the stars. The kids still talked about her, and had piled river stones into a cairn at the edge of the camp, where there was the best view of the river and mountains. 'Sam's Place', they called it, because she loved swimming and climbing hills, and they would do those things for her instead, while she looked down on the family she'd made and given to Jordan.

The sun crept ever upwards and the water sparkled, like stars.

Another day, what a view.

Everything still possible.

And time to start poking teenagers awake.

Jordan moved away from the fire and walked across to the shelter, where they each had their own bed, made from expedition sleeping bags stuffed with reeds and moss.

It hadn't taken long for Manisha to start being creative with the materials she foraged from around the camp, and with Reeves' help she'd already mastered some natural dyes and glues. The camp was hung with twig-and-leaf medallions, and a personalised painted stone had appeared one morning at the foot of each bed.

"Because I don't want some grubby boy to take my sleeping space by mistake," she'd said, though Reeves told Jordan later that this gift was her way of thanking everyone for looking after her.

"I got one too," he said, in a reflective tone that sounded almost human, and he invited Jordan to admire the pale stone drawn with a wispy, ochre-coloured 'R' that laid by the terminal in the pod.

Jordan surveyed the sleeping bodies and nudged a couple gently with his foot. This was generally a full five-minute job, start to finish. Some needed more poking than others, and there was no guarantee that a poked body wouldn't just mutter something unintelligible and go straight back to sleep.

He moved methodically around the circle of bodies, leaving Poole until last, because Poole, for all his other quirks, was the easiest to wake.

"Hey Neesh."

"Bryce, morning."

"Dana, you awake?"

"Karlan, man, come on."

"Derv, time to get up."

"Poole, you all right?"

There were groans from all sides of the shelter, and rustles as everyone turned and found another comfortable spot.

"It can't be morning."

"You're joking."

"Why do old people get up so early?"

"What time is it?"

Jordan didn't know much, but he knew the answer to that.

"Best time to be awake," he said.

Like This Book?

If you enjoyed the ride, please take a moment to leave me a review on Amazon, Goodreads, BookBub, or anywhere else you like.

A word or two is absolutely fine (though please, go to town if you like!), even just a rating – it all helps keep the *Odyssey Earth* flying just a little bit longer.

Thanks a million – you're all stars.

Odyssey Earth Series,
Book 2
TWIN LANDING - AN EXTRACT

The Odyssey Earth story continues in Book 2, *Twin Landing* – here's how it starts.

———

It had all been going as well as could be expected, until the goats started to eat the decorations.

From a small, earthen mound at the edge of the New Earth landing site, Juno Washington had done what she had needed to do and delivered a captain's address – an auspicious day, time to pull together, exciting future ahead, etc, etc.

She barely heard the words she spoke. In many ways, she was only going through the motions, but Juno had felt it was important to acknowledge their achievement. They had made it, after all – seventeen years across the galaxy to their new home in the stars; ten days now on the planet. That was something to – well, commemorate, if not celebrate.

She looked down on a sea of familiar faces, all older now than when they had started – the pioneer crew of the colony ship, *Odyssey Earth*. She remembered welcoming most of them on board, back at the old Earth space station.

Her ship, her people. She'd done her best and had got them here, as promised.

Now it was up to all of them to make a new home on this new planet, trillions of miles from everything and everyone that they had ever known. There was no going back, everyone accepted the deal when they'd signed up. One way only.

New Earth, New Beginning, as the old advertising slogan went.

Juno paused, a lump in her throat.

Deep breath, this was the hard part.

Scanning the silent faces, she could see that others were deep in thought too. Those difficult last few weeks on board the *Odyssey Earth*, as they had cruised in through the new solar system. The excitement of impending planetfall tempered by the shock of a sudden, brutal, inexplicable loss. Seven of their own, gone, just like that.

The memories were still bitingly raw and Juno – blameless – blamed herself. Despite the occasion – because of the occasion – it was hard to feel joy, when not everyone was here to share it.

"We have to carry on, though, don't we?" she said,

more to herself than anyone else. Then she raised a plastic beaker to the assembled crowd.

"To Jordan Booth and to our beautiful kids. To Dana, Dervla, Manisha, Poole, Bryson and Karlan," speaking their names out loudly, emphasising each one.

Juno's words carried on the morning air, and a hundred and fifty voices murmured the names in unison before sipping from their own beakers.

And then a cacophony of coughs and splutters broke out as Gerald the botanist's 'wine' fought its way down a hundred and fifty throats. Not so much a cheeky visit from a presumptuous little homebrew; more an intimidating call from the bailiffs, intent on removing your liver. When she'd had an initial, challenging sip before the ceremony, Juno had asked him what was in the wine, and Gerald had said, "I'd like to say grapes," and left the sentence hanging before changing the subject.

Once the coughing had died down, Juno walked across to the small clearing, where a decorative cordon had been established around a hand-cut timber flagpole.

And it was at this point – before Juno could raise the ship's ceremonial flag – that the goats charged in and started eating the decorations.

To be fair, they weren't exactly decorations – the medics had simply stitched together some pads and bandages as bunting – but then again, they weren't exactly goats.

They clearly occupied the niche that goats did back

on home Earth. Smallish, annoying, a bit smelly, ate anything. Actually, scratch that, thought Juno, when she'd first encountered them. They occupied the niche that the ship's nuclear physicists did. But unlike physicists, or indeed Earth goats, this lot had matted, sheep-like woollen coats and droopy, almost elephantine ears, which pricked at any sound, making the animals surprisingly difficult to capture. Unlike physicists, who could be rounded up with a plate of biscuits.

The goats also had no fear of humans and, in the ten days since the ship's company landing, had increasingly taken to encroaching upon the new settlement. The goats disappeared off into the nearby scrub at dusk – no one had yet followed them more than a few hundred yards to see where they went – but for much of the day they made tentative raids in packs of ten or so if anyone left out so much as an apple core. Or, as now, a ribbon of hanging bandages, one end of which was currently being munched with much apparent enjoyment.

As goats buffeted their way through the crowd, one barged past and made a beeline for the flag table. Juno grabbed the flag, ran it quickly up the flagpole so it was out of the way, and collared a passing crew member.

"Shoo them all out, would you mind? Goats and crew. I think we've finished, and I've got to go over and pick up the new guy anyway. He's arrived, apparently."

"Shame we didn't have him here earlier, in time for this. Let him handle animal control."

"I'm not sure goat-wrangling was in his job description. Any more than it was in ours. I thought we were getting the fencing fixed?"

"We are. But every time we get a section sorted, another building goes up and the perimeter expands."

Another problem Juno was aware of. Too much freelance construction going on. She needed to get a grasp of that, too. Oh, for the days when she all she had to do was fly a multi-storey colony ship at terrifying speed across trillions of miles of space. That had been a doddle compared to establishing civilisation on Planet Goat.

"All right, see what you can do. And by the way, don't let them drink any more of the wine, either."

"The goats? Or the crew?"

"Good point." Juno laughed. "Either. Both. Gerald's very proud of it, but I suspect there are a few litres of disinfectant missing from the ship's galley."

"I thought there was a lemony tang. Silly me, thinking it was lemons."

———

The goats had been an unexpected surprise, but not too unexpected.

Back on Earth, many years previously, scientists had proclaimed their new exoplanet discovery as decidedly suitable for human settlement. Orbital observations, gas signatures and other evidence confirmed that it had acceptable gravity, breathable air, liquid surface water and biological life – the latter unknown, but probably benign.

That was good news for anyone signing up for the *Odyssey Earth* gig. If you were looking for another human foothold in the universe, you needed to be able to walk around outside without a spacesuit when you got there. And not get eaten on day one.

"And we're pretty certain the water is all right to drink," they had added, not totally reassuringly.

Once the ship had popped out of hyperdrive, after seventeen years' travel across the galaxy, things came a bit more into focus. As it made its slow, final approach, full sweeps of New Earth revealed a varied topography and a rich natural world. An optimal landing site was selected, the *Odyssey Earth* manoeuvred into a high, stationary orbit, twenty thousand miles out, and the first landing vehicle launched.

The lander had touched down in a wide, grassy valley, scorching out of the clouds and scattering a huge flock of what turned out to be sort-of goats. A nearby river and spreading woodland promised usable resources – the first person out of the lander, drawn by lottery, had picked up a stick and driven it in to the ground.

New Earth. Humanity had arrived.

And the scavenging goats came back a day or so after that. Annoying, but not exactly life-threatening.

Meanwhile, the orbiting colony ship was now essentially a holding vessel for hundreds more planetary settlers still in hypersleep, slotted in rows in the vast cryo-chambers in the bowels of the *Odyssey Earth*. Over the next two years, they would all be woken up to a strict timetable, as the settlement expanded and resources allowed.

For now, only a very few essential personnel had been revived – construction specialists mainly, needed to get things underway. They had been prodded and poked for a few days, to make sure they were all right, and then shuttled down to New Earth, once they'd stopped throwing up and asking what year it was.

Their first small steps onto their new home were off the landing shuttle, through a polytunnel, and into a simple, print-build cabin that had been designated as a reception area. 'The Giant Leap,' some wag had called the cabin, and the name had stuck to the place where the ground-based medical team conducted a few more tests and ticked some boxes before allowing a new settler out onto the site.

Juno could hear voices and, inside, a very tall man with close-cropped hair was half-perched on a gurney, his back to the door, talking to Sabitha, the on-duty medic.

"So, I left the capsule," heard Juno, "and was floating in a most peculiar way. A very odd feeling, I can tell you." The man's voice was as clipped as his hair.

"I'll bet," said Sabitha. "Then what?"

"I tried to orientate myself, that was the first thing. But the stars looked very different that day, not at all like the star map I'd been given. And then, when I tried to call it in, well that's when the effluent hit the powered airflow, if you get my drift. Circuit dead, something wrong, so I – "

"Ah, Cap," said Sabitha, as she spotted Juno at the entrance. "We're all finished here, clean bill of health. The Major was just telling me about his last mission before this one."

"Captain Washington?"

The man had got to his feet and turned to face Juno, extending his hand.

"Thomas Chatwin, Major. Delighted to meet you and thrilled to be here. Terrifically exciting."

Juno shook his hand and looked him in the eye.

"You're kidding me, right?" she said.

"I'm sorry, ma'am?"

"Your name is Major Tom?"

"Well, I prefer Thomas, if that's all right with you, ma'am."

Juno looked at him quizzically.

"Major Tom. You know, Bowie?"

"Tom Bowie? Can't say I know the chap, ma'am."

Juno looked at him suspiciously, and dropped her eyes to his name badge. It checked out – 'Major Thomas Chatwin.'

"Go on then, I'll bite. That mission sounds a little hairy. Work out all right?"

"Why yes, ma'am. Floated around for a little while in the old tin can, but luckily the spaceship knew which way to go." He allowed himself a little smile at the thought. "Nothing much I could do except sit tight, take my protein pills and keep my helmet on."

"Oh, come on," said Juno. "Really?"

"Yes ma'am. Not as alarming as it sounds. I could hear Ground Control in the end, they came back online, everything tickety-boo."

Juno looked at him again. He seemed entirely serious.

"Has Reeves put you up to this? Very good, by the way."

"I'm not with you ma'am. Reeves?"

"The AI. Disembodied know-it-all. You'd know if you'd met him."

"I can't say I've had the pleasure."

Juno admitted defeat and laughed. What was one more space oddity added into the mix? "All right, then. Let's get started. This way, Major Tom."

"Thomas, ma'am."

"Thomas, of course. This way, Major, let me get you up to speed."

"Excellent ma'am, thank you very much. And Sabitha, cheerio. Pip-Pip. A pleasure to meet you."

Tickety-boo. Cheerio. Pip-Pip. All she needed, thought Juno. A stiff-upper-lip space jockey with a poker face. About nine feet tall as well, by the look of him. Could have used him as the flagpole if he'd got here half an hour earlier.

They walked together, away from the reception centre and towards the small settlement of prefab cabins and buildings that flanked the shuttle landing zone. In ten days, it had already turned into quite a township.

From the 'Giant Leap' reception area, there was access to an open-ended, walk-through canteen with bench seating. Beyond lay a series of panel-printed dorm blocks with basic washrooms, while a small, domed hangar housed all the cargo delivered on freight runs from the ship. Behind that spread the staked-out land destined to be cultivated, once the ship's Grow-Lab crew had finished testing soil samples and eco-matching potential crops.

Water was being piped in from the nearby river, via a filtration system. There was power throughout the site from solar generators, while the electrical engineers worked on establishing a grid. Tracks led out to an area where some initial drilling and quarrying was taking place, to identify usable stone and minerals, and they were dredging the river further downstream for construction sand.

"I'm impressed," said the Major. "Full employment of the P7 protocol."

"Come again?"

"Prior planning and preparation prevents piss poor performance, ma'am."

Well, well. Maybe the Major did have a sense of humour, after all.

"We've done our best."

"And all this in, what, a week?"

"Ten days," said Juno. "You're one of our first revivals."

"Revivals? Is that what you call us? The cryo-crew?"

Juno laughed. "That's the polite term. My senior medics call you the Stiffs, as in frozen stiffs."

"That's most amusing," said the Major. "Although of course, I didn't feel a thing. Hot, cold, up, down, it was all the same to me. Just a jolly long sleep until your chaps prodded me awake the other day. And here I am."

"Here indeed, Major. Welcome to New Earth."

They stood and looked across at the buildings. Following the interrupted ceremony, daily life in the settlement had picked back up. Various work details were coming and going and, with a shift change due, a line was already forming outside the canteen.

"I'll show you to your quarters later," said Juno. "Sharing for now, I'm afraid, we all are. But first – "

"First, you're going to tell me why I've been revived. At this point."

"Ah. You've checked your mission notes? Yes, quite right. You were scheduled for year two, not week two. We've got you up early. Sorry about that."

"Not at all, ma'am. What's changed, may I ask? Not that I'm not happy to be here. Terrifically exciting." The Major gestured at the buildings and then, raising both hands in the air, at the planet itself.

Most amusing. Terrific. Juno still wasn't sure this wasn't all an act. Time would tell.

"Nothing's changed. And everything," said Juno.

The landing protocols and mission notes had been

drawn up half a galaxy away and twenty years ago, in labs and offices, on whiteboards and spreadsheets. And – surprise, surprise – they had proved largely ineffective when it came to actual planetfall on a real, live planet.

For the first two days, no one had done anything much more than wander around breathing non-recycled air, drinking water that hadn't passed several times through colleagues, and pointing at the sky, the clouds and the stars.

Another day was spent discovering that there were not-quite goats in the neighbourhood, and then another day finding that leaving out any food or organic material of any kind meant being knocked, butted, buffeted and chased by not-quite goats. They didn't seem dangerous, but it soon stopped being entertaining.

By the time Juno had got on top of the situation, organised the teams and badgered the construction crew to start work, she realised that she was going to need more help than the protocols had envisaged. It wasn't security as such that she required, but she did need someone to bounce ideas off and delegate things to. And she also needed someone to sort out the damned goats.

"FO?" said the Major.

Not the can-do attitude she was looking for, Juno had to admit. "Excuse me?"

"No FO on board?" said the Major. "No second-in-command?"

"Ah, right, yes, of course. We don't go in much for

ranks and titles, truth be told. But I do have a First Officer on the ship, looking after things up top, and plenty of other people under me, all with opinions. But you have to remember, we've spent over seventeen years together already, day in, day out. I could do with an unfiltered view of the situation, and someone with some authority down here. Basically, I need a wingman."

"And that's why I'm up early?"

"Correct."

"Wingman, eh? You're aware that I hold the rank of major? And you're a captain, Captain?"

"And you're aware that this is a privately funded, civilian mission, for which I was granted sole executive authority for the duration of the voyage? Right now, and for the foreseeable, I'm in charge."

"Naturally," said the Major. "All in the mission notes. Which is why, ma'am, I have been addressing you as ma'am."

"Then we understand each other, Major. Think you can help me whip this settlement into shape? There are some big personalities here, who have got used to doing things very much their own way. But that's not going to wash on a new planet. I need someone with tact and sensibility, but also authority. There's plenty to do. Do you think you can handle it?"

The Major nodded, sagely. "Certainly, ma'am. My mother always said, to get things done, you better not mess with Major Thomas Chatwin."

Juno looked him squarely in the eye.

Seriously?

Nope, not a flicker of recognition or even amusement. Damn, the man was good.

———

Read the Odyssey Earth series by Rex Burke

Orphan Planet – Book 1
Twin Landing – Book 2
Star Bound – Book 3

About the Author

Rex Burke is a SciFi writer based in North Yorkshire, UK.

When he was young, he read every one of those yellow-jacketed Victor Gollancz hardbacks in his local library. That feeling of out-of-this-world amazement has never left him – and keeps him company as he writes his own SciFi adventures.

When Rex is not writing, he travels – one way or another, he'll get to the stars, even if it's just as stardust when his own story is done.

Find Out More

To find out more, and grab a free Odyssey Earth short story, visit Rex's website – rexburke.com